The Husband

THE HUSBAND

DARREN O'SULLIVAN

This edition published in 2024 by Joffe Books, London
www.joffebooks.com

First published in Great Britain as an original
audiobook by Audible in 2021 as *The Rain*
under the pseudonym B. B. Thomas

Cover art by Imogen Buchanan

ISBN: 978-1-83526-903-9

Never pain to tell thy love
Love that never told can be;
For the gentle wind does move
Silently, invisibly.

I told my love, I told my love,
I told her all my heart,
Trembling, cold, in ghastly fears –
Ah, she doth depart.

From *'Never Pain to Tell Thy Love'* by William Blake

JUNE 15TH 2019

Emma

I'm scared, more than scared, but it's time to confess who I am, and what I'm capable of. It's time to tell him everything, share with him all of the secrets I've kept, all the demons I hold. Because I can't do it anymore. I can't pretend to be one thing when my heart is telling me to be something else. I hope when I have shared it all, and he knows my true nature, he doesn't hate me. I hope when I've shared it all he isn't angry. I hope he understands it from where I am; I hope he lets me go. I hope he realises I'd be happier with someone else. I deserve to be happier with someone else. But I've seen what he can do, I know the darkness he has inside. When he knows the truth, all of it, I know, if I'm not careful, if I don't keep my wits about me, he'll likely kill me.

But then again, Em, you deserve it, right? You deserve whatever is coming your way.

PART 1:
US

CHAPTER ONE

June 18th 2019
Just another Tuesday

Rob

Shutting the front door with the back of my foot, I was glad to be home. It was a little after three a.m. I'd finished work an hour before but, needing to calm, had taken my time walking home, the twenty-minute brisk stroll stretching out to an hour as I listened to the warm wind whip across the fen, and the sounds of the animals that held onto the night. I was home a full three hours earlier than I should have been. The walk back from work was stifling, the air thick and hot, even at this time of night. I felt muggy, dirty; before I got into bed, I needed to shower. Tomorrow was going to be scorching hot again. The tenth unbearable day without any respite. Just relentless, ground-cracking heat that, if at the seaside or abroad would be pleasant — but here, working, and with no expanse of water in sight besides a reservoir out back, was closer to Dante's inferno than anything nice. Even the wind that constantly blows across the fen felt like a hairdryer. I couldn't wait for the weather to break: some rain, a cloud, anything to provide shelter from the heat.

Taking off my shoes, I waited to hear movement coming from upstairs, but nothing. Em and Sophie were both sound asleep. As I made my way into the kitchen, closing the door behind me before throwing on the light, in case it disturbed Em, I noticed that the kitchen hadn't been cleaned. Even after our argument, before I left for work. One of many we'd had recently. It was always about the same things: Em didn't seem to care anymore that our house was a mess; she didn't seem to care that I was trying to make it less so. The argument the night before was perhaps our worst; I said things I didn't mean, I'm sure she did too, and I know our neighbours would have heard, as did Sophie, who was startled awake and began to cry. Our row stopped abruptly when we both realised what we'd done — we had scared our baby. But we didn't resolve our differences as we should have. Did we ever these days?

Last night's dinner plates were strewn all over the side. On the floor in front of the washing machine was a pile of laundry she promised she'd put on, and on the corner of the dining table, the place where we eat, was a folded-up dirty nappy that wouldn't fit in the overflowing bin. I started to clean up noisily, pissed off that our row, that waking Sophie, that knowing our neighbours would have heard us, changed nothing. There was no point waking her up; it would only have caused another row. I didn't have the energy for it. Taking a deep breath, in through my nose, out through my mouth, the faint outline of talcum powder and Bepanthen washed in, and it soothed me just enough to try and see the world from another perspective, rather than my own tired one. Em isn't the tidiest person; she needed to budge a little, but I knew I needed to budge too. We all have our faults. I needed to reaffirm to her that she was a good mum, and that's what mattered. So what if the house was a tip most of the time? Being a parent was hard. And as far as faults go, Em's were mild — a mess could be cleaned. I resented doing it all the time, but it could be worse.

3

Since becoming a parent, Em is messier than ever, but I had developed an overprotectiveness of Sophie that was bordering on detrimental. I imagined worst-case scenarios all the time. If Sophie cried in the night, I would want to bolt to her, assuming she'd trapped her arm in her cot bed or fallen unwell, and if she coughed, my first thought was she was choking on something. It wasn't healthy. And if I was honest and had to pick between my wife's mess and my constant state of worry, the mess would win every time. Em was messy on the outside; I was messy on the inside. Realising this, I calmed down and tidied up. It didn't take long, and by the time I'd finished I wasn't annoyed anymore. Besides, I didn't fantasise about coming home and being pissed off because of something as stupid as an untidy kitchen.

Tonight's shift ending early was a treat. One I fully intended on using. I was owed some time back and my boss, Harry — a kind bloke who was born, lived and would likely die in this small town — told me I could claim them this week, a few hours shaved off the next four nights. Perfect. The relentless heat was keeping customers away, and less stock sold meant there was less to put back on the shelf. He said it was that, but really I think Harry noticed how I was when I came to work, the row with Em still lingering.

Like I said, Harry is a good bloke.

Finishing early meant I could climb into bed and hug Em, who would likely stir, ask if I was OK, and drift back into a deep sleep. We would have a rare moment, just the two of us, curled into one another. All forgiven, all forgotten, for an hour or so before Sophie woke for her pre-dawn feed.

I made myself a cold drink of water and sipped as I looked out of the kitchen window. The night skies here, you didn't get them in London, despite it only being eighty-odd miles away. There was no light pollution, no tall buildings and busy roads. No late-night takeaways, bars and clubs. Just endless, unbroken land and skies. And the blackest of nights. If the moon was new, the stars came alive like I'd never seen them before. Stepping outside, I drank my water and looked up at the heavens — so vast, so terrifyingly vast. The messy kitchen, our argument, fuelled by sleep deprivation and the relentless heat, meant very little up there. Our problems didn't matter. I was learning to love this place in the arse-end of nowhere.

But I hadn't. Not to start with.

Above me, Sophie began to cry out, and looking at the time, I saw it was only twenty-five past three. Just when we thought we'd figured out a routine of a regular four-thirty feed, it seemed it had changed. There would be no closeness with Em today. One day, maybe.

Whenever Sophie cried I could feel my muscles twitching, panic setting in. Injury, choking, the usual horror story played out in my head. Really, she was just hungry, and as she was breastfeeding there wasn't a lot I could do to settle her. Em had tried expressing, and Sophie would take a bottle in the daytime, but at night, she wanted her mummy to feed her. Needing the comfort of being in her mother's arms. Feeling her warmth, listening to her heartbeat. Just like she did in the womb. I could do some things for my daughter, but I couldn't ever do that. Sophie continued to cry, and I knew at any moment I would hear Em's light footsteps and soothing voice. *Any second now*, I thought, making my way towards the bottom of the stairs to say hello as Em passed into our baby's room. Sophie had only been in there for a week; it still felt weird not having her in with us. Placing my foot on the bottom step, I waited for Em to bluster past, saying 'Don't worry, I'm up'.

But Sophie continued to cry, and no steps came. I held off for as long as possible before bounding up the stairs, two at a time and into my daughter's bedroom. Picking her up, I began to soothe her the best I could, and carried her towards our room. I assumed I'd find Em stirring, or even so asleep she hadn't heard Sophie, which would be totally understandable given how little sleep she gets.

'Em?' I called out quietly, expecting the mound of crum-pled blankets to move, and her to sit bolt upright, wondering what had happened. But the covers didn't stir. I approached and, as I got closer, I could see something was wrong with what I was looking at. The mound wasn't big enough to have my wife under it. I pulled the covers back; the bed was empty.

'Em?' I called out, turning to step onto the landing and look into the bathroom, thinking maybe she had nipped to the loo and that was why she hadn't responded, but the door was open, the light off. Walking into the box room, Sophie still crying in my arms, I shielded her eyes and flicked on the dimmer light.

She wasn't there.

I began to panic. As fast as I dared, I went downstairs, calling Em's name. Sophie cried louder as her needs had not been met and, as I tried to calm her, I began turning on all the lights. I searched every room, even the kitchen where I had just been, for any sign of her.

But there wasn't; Em was gone. Em had vanished.

* * *

April 19th 2016

Emma

I haven't kept a diary for a long time, not since I was a kid, but something has happened recently, something unusual, which has pulled me to write it down. Kinda like when you need to take a photo in an exact moment, knowing your recollection won't do it justice. So, here I am. But this isn't a diary, not really, not like I used to keep between the ages of nine and thirteen. I'm not going to pour my heart into this as I did when I was young, documenting all the unnecessary things: he said, she did. I'm not going to doodle in the margins and draw hearts with my initials and the initials of the boy I like in it. I'm not going to force myself to say something every day, and likely repeat myself over and over. No, this is not going to be a chore, this is for those moments when I'm bursting to tell someone something and know I cannot. While the outer Em — the Em the world sees and smiles at and talks to and drinks with — is busy doing her thing, the inner Em will speak, and say the things that remain unsaid.

Hello, inner Em, it's been a while.

I need to start with reminding myself: I don't think this is a love story. It might be, it could be one day, but it isn't yet. This is an action flick. The bad guys are everywhere, toting machine guns and shouting at one another, probably in a German accent like in Dad's favourite film, *Die Hard*. The bad guys are the shitty friends, the lecherous men who only see my boobs and ass and have no idea what my interests, hates, fears and dreams are. The bad guys are wearing designer clothes and drinking expensive drinks in expensive bars. The bad guys are everywhere, yet somehow, I have managed to save myself.

Like I said, this isn't a love story.

But it does start with a boy.

Let me paint a picture, for my future self. The story doesn't start here, but last winter. It's cold, not snowing cold with white powder covering treetops and roofs, nothing so romantic. The cold is a damp rain coming in sideways, making my efforts to shape my hair useless. It's a grey cold: wet Tarmac and hunched shoulders. Wet leaves, slippery under foot. It almost stopped me going out, but it didn't, and by the time Jen — my new best friend in the big city — and I arrive at the bar, I look like a drowned rat.

Jen and I get a drink, maybe a prosecco or a Southern Comfort — I don't remember, there are many drinks that night — and we chat like two friends who've known each other for years, though really it's been just a few weeks. When you move somewhere new and find someone in the same situation, bonds are forged quickly.

I dance, drink, drink some more, the music loud, the room jumping; I'm pressed against several strangers. Some innocently, others less so — and then, at the bar, ordering my umpteenth tipple, I bump into him. The boy.

At first, I don't give him a look. I have a type; we all do right? And this boy, he doesn't fit mine. No tattoos, no physique that tells me he would never love a woman as much as he loves himself. No self-assured swagger or witty one-liners to try his luck. He's a bit doughy, a bit plain. He apologises for bumping into me, even though I'm pretty sure it was the other way around. And he smiles at me. One of those smiles that is unapologetic; real. And perhaps because I'm pissed, perhaps because Steve, the on-and-off-and-on-again ex who I moved to the big city to escape, is so serious all of the time, I smile back.

In this diary, Em, the only rule is you have to be honest. Easy enough, right? No one will read this, just you — and even if someone does, it won't be until you're old and grey and being moved into an old people's home or mortuary, so whatever you say here won't matter anyway. It will either be unimportant or something to laugh about. So I'll say it as it is. What I'm going to say next, I'll likely call myself a narcissist for it — but hey, if I can't tell the truth here . . .

As I smile back at the doughy boy, I wait for him to introduce himself, offer to buy me a drink, something that usually happens. But he simply apologises again, tells me to have a good night, and turns away to continue talking with his friend. And, if I'm honest, I'm a little put out by this. I'm not an egomaniac (well, up until writing this I didn't think so, anyway) but an ego rub wouldn't have gone amiss. Steve, my on-and-off ex, had messaged, saying he was thinking of me. And it stirred up all of those feelings I didn't want to feel anymore. I wanted to bury them in an exchange with a total stranger.

And yes, I'm also aware of how pitiful that sounds.

Jen and I finish up and leave before the bar starts to kick out, before desperate people looking to get laid are magnetically drawn to us, and make our way back along the South Bank towards the Underground and our respective flats, two stops away from each other. I thought that would be it, but of course it wasn't, otherwise there would be no point keeping this diary, would there?

Now spring is here, the nights have drawn out, and, grabbing a quick drink after work today in a pub close to my office, I saw him. Same smile, same kindness I felt before, but was too drunk to process. And when he saw me, I knew he recognised me too.

I made the first move, not drawn by lust, more curiosity. I bought him a drink, he thanked me, and we talked. No touching when we made each other laugh, no eyes drawn to lips, wanting to work out how to kiss them, just talking. I'm not used to that. He works in marketing — I could have guessed — but unlike those I've met before who work in marketing and find it drab, dull, lifeless, he seems to like it, and I seem to like him more because of it. He's lived in London his whole life, but likes to travel — Canada's at the top of his list. He said he likes the space, the trees. I told him about my holidays to Ibiza and Majorca– he hasn't been to either, and I felt embarrassed for not being cultured. Embarrassed? I know, right?

He shared a little about his past, and I shared a little (although much, much less) about mine. A drink became a second, which then became a meal. Nothing fancy, battered fish for him, a salad for me. I don't know why I bought a salad.

He let me eat some of his chips.

We didn't kiss, we didn't go back to his or mine to have sex (I would have said yes, too). Instead, we've exchanged numbers, agreed it would be nice — not fun, but nice — to meet up again, and we said goodbye.

As far as a love story goes, this one starts pretty tame. But like I said: maybe, Em, this isn't a love story. You've had your fair share of those, a lot of which are with the same person. Maybe, Em, maybe this is something better?

CHAPTER TWO

One hour missing

Rob

At first, I didn't ring the police. I assumed at any moment Em would arrive from somewhere and scoop Sophie from my arms to feed her. Apologising for nipping out for a cigarette (I knew she still had one from time to time). But after checking the house again, and trying to ring her mobile several times, getting only voicemail, I began to panic. Sitting on the sofa, calming Sophie while staring at the front door like a dog waiting for its owner, I knew I needed help. Something was wrong, something was terribly wrong. I rang the police to report her missing, and as the duty officer spoke with me, I struggled to hear most of the questions as Sophie was growing more and more distressed, emulating my feelings. I knew I needed to get milk in her, I should have done so straight away when I realised Em was gone, but I didn't, assuming she would come in at any moment. Taking Sophie into the kitchen, I cracked open the seal on an Aptamil formula and poured it into her bottle. At first, Sophie was reluctant. It was still dark which, in her eyes, meant she should be drawing straight from her mother, and she hadn't had formula before, which no doubt tasted different. But with some soothing, some patience, she began to feed.

The police arrived within an hour. I wanted them to be quicker, to respond in a way I needed them to; with urgency, importance. But when asked on the phone if there was any sign of anything untoward, I answered no. Nothing was out of place, nothing disturbed. As far as I could tell, Em had simply walked out of the house. But that was the problem: Em wouldn't just leave, not without saying, not leaving Sophie on her own for I didn't know how long. Sophie could have been there, by herself, all night. And when I thought of that, Sophie alone, I felt sick. I saw two police officers climb out of the car, and before they could knock on the door I opened it, Sophie, fed and settled, asleep in my arms.

'Mr Clarke?' A female officer asked.

'Yes, please come in,' I rushed, fumbling myself out of their way to allow them to cross the threshold.

'Thank you. I'm PC Cahill, this is PC Sinclair,' she said, gesturing to the officer beside her, a tall man with a hard stare. 'You've reported a missing person?'

'Yes, my wife, Em, Emma.'

'May I sit down?' she inquired, and I apologised, showing them into the living room where she perched on the sofa. I sat down in the armchair opposite. The other PC stood in the doorway.

'Mr Clarke. Would you mind if my colleague had a look around?'

'Why?'

'Just to get a sense of what might have happened.'

'I see. No, not at all,' I replied, looking from PC Cahill to the tall policeman whose name I'd forgotten.

'I'll take my shoes off,' the tall officer said before leaving the doorway in the direction of the stairs. A few moments later, I heard his heavy footsteps ascend.

11

'How old is she?' PC Cahill asked, looking at Sophie in my arms.

'Ummm, six months,' I replied. She wasn't, she was five months. I didn't know why I told her otherwise.

'She looks very content in your arms,' PC Cahill continued. 'Tell me about Emma.'

'Ummm, I don't know, she's Sophie's mum, she doesn't work, we moved up from London a few months ago — no, more than a few, Sophie wasn't quite born, sorry, I don't know why I said . . .'

'It's OK Mr Clarke, take a breath.'

I nodded, did as I was told and continued. 'She's originally from here. Her family live nearby. Sorry, I don't know what to say.'

'You're doing fine.' She smiled. 'Has Emma ever left before?'

'No.'

'Popped out to see family, a friend?'

'No — I mean, yes, she has friends, she sees her parents once a week or so, but she wouldn't leave in the middle of the night. She wouldn't leave Sophie.'

'How did you discover she was gone?'

'I came home early from work.'

'What time?'

'I finished about 2 a.m.'

'So, around two?'

'Yes. No, I mean, I finished at two. I got home around three.'

'I see,' she said. 'Anyone corroborate this?'

'That I left at two, sure, my boss, Harry. I saw him as I clocked out.'

'What were you doing between the hours of two and three?'

'I walked home. I took my time.'

'Can anyone confirm that?'

'What? No, I was on my own.'

'Then, when you got home around three . . .'

12

'I got myself a drink. A glass of water, not booze or anything,' I said, shifting, wiping my one free hand on my leg. Feeling like, because I was speaking with the police, I had done something wrong. I could feel my breathing become sharp; a sweat broke out on my forehead.

'Sophie started to cry, wanting a feed and I thought Em was getting up — Sophie breastfeeds — but she didn't, and so I came upstairs, and saw she was gone.'

'What time was this?'

'Half past three, maybe.'

'Rob — can I call you Rob?'

'Sure.'

'Rob, this next question might be difficult.'

'OK.'

'How was Emma before you went to work last night? Was there any sign of her being upset?'

I hesitated. She was upset, so was I. But that didn't have anything to do with this. It couldn't. Em and I argued often, tonight wasn't anything new. It was our business; something we could fix on our own.

'I don't think so.'

'Anything at all, it might help us know where she's gone.'

I thought about the moment I left for work. She was at the dining table, a small glass of wine in her hand. She'd told me she wouldn't have any more; one small glass wouldn't hurt Sophie. She didn't look at me when she spoke. She was still reeling from our disagreement, as was I. She said she was OK, but was she?

'She seemed fine; I think,' I said. It was just a row. Nothing more. We were used to them now. She and I were no different after it than after any other row.

'And recently, say in the last month, how has she been?'

I wracked my brain, tried to remember anything, but every single aspect of our lives, besides Sophie, seemed hazed out of my memory. Had Em been OK? Had we argued more than usual? Did we speak to each other in the same way we used to before Sophie? But then, through the fog, came a memory of

13

about a week ago, when I'd seen her staring at her mobile. I'd thought she was watching something on YouTube or Facebook, but as I drew level the screen was blank. I asked her about it; she said she was miles away. Daydreaming. I took her at face value, but now the memory seemed sad. And then I remembered the smoking. She'd given it up for years, but recently I could smell it on her, masked by perfume, but still there.

'She might be down, a little, I guess?'

'Why do you think she is down?'

'I don't know. I . . . Maybe she was tired, Sophie is breast-feeding at night, she was a little flat, maybe.'

'Was?'

'Is. I meant is.'

'Being a mother is tough,' PC Cahill added, considering me.

'Yes, it is. But she's really good at it.'

'So, her leaving, it's not something she would usually do?'

'No, no, not at all. You don't think she's done some-thing? Do you? Oh God, you don't think . . .'

'I'm not thinking anything at the moment Mr Clarke, just trying to understand what's happened here.'

'I see. Sorry.' I took a breath, tried to calm myself down. 'This is a little overwhelming. I don't understand why she would just leave.'

The other police officer came back downstairs, leant in the doorway and shook his head to suggest he couldn't find anything out of place.

'Mr Clarke. You didn't happen to find a note or anything?'

'A note?'

'Left to you, by Emma, perhaps explaining where she is?'

'No, nothing.'

She nodded. 'You said she sees her parents once a week. What about your parents, is Emma close to them?'

'No, my parents passed away.'

'I'm sorry.'

'It was a long time ago.'

14

'And her parents, you said they live nearby?'

'Yes, her mum and dad live only about five miles away, near Ramsey Forty Foot.'

'Can you tell me their names?

'John and Frances Murphy.'

'Have you called them?'

'No, I . . .'

'Perhaps you should have. She might be there.'

'Yes, sorry, I don't know why I didn't think of that.'

PC Cahill looked at the tall officer and then jotted their names down in her notepad. 'Is there anyone else she's close to?'

'No. I don't think so.'

'Mr Clarke.' The tall officer, Simons or Sullivan, chipped in. 'The house, is it always this untidy?'

'It's a little untidy.'

'But is it this untidy?'

'Are you judging me for my house being a mess?' I said, on the defence.

'No, not at all, I just want to get a sense of whether she left quickly. There are lots of clothes on the floor upstairs. It suggests she might have packed in a hurry.'

'Packed? What, like a suitcase?'

'Have you noticed if any of her possessions are missing?'

'I don't know.'

'Have you checked?'

'Checked?'

'For anything missing?'

'No, No. I rang you.'

'I see,' the tall officer said, eyeing me.

'Shall we look now?' Cahill said, standing up. I did too, and with Sophie still asleep in my arms, I walked around the house, followed closely by the officers like I'd done something wrong and needed escorting. Upstairs, Cahill asked if we had suitcases, and when I said we had three, she asked me to check for them. All were there. Cahill and Sinclair exchanged a look, but I didn't know what it meant. Then I noticed that her old

15

rucksack, which was usually on the floor of her wardrobe was missing, and when I told them, they exchanged another look. Her drawers were full of her clothes, at least I think so. We had piles beside the bed, some on the floor of the wardrobe, some on airers in the box room at the back of the house.

'Anything else missing? Besides the rucksack?' Cahill asked.

'Maybe, I don't know.'

'You don't know?'

'Em has a lot of stuff.'

In the bathroom I couldn't tell what, if any, toiletries were missing, and when I told Cahill, a third look was exchanged between her and the other officer.

'We tend to bulk buy, it's more cost effective.'

'I hear that,' Cahill said, 'these things aren't cheap.'

On the back of the door there should have been two bathrobes, mine and Em's, but only mine was there.

Back downstairs, I noticed a pair of her shoes were missing, her running trainers. I told Cahill who wrote it down.

'So, as far as you can tell, she only took a bathrobe, a rucksack and trainers.'

'A bathrobe, in this heat?' the tall officer added, raising an eyebrow.

'It's not a dressing gown type of bathrobe, it's a little silk thing she throws over her nightwear. I got it for our anniversary.'

'And when was that?'

'Our anniversary, a couple of weeks ago.'

And yet another look I didn't understand.

After that the tall officer left, walking through the lounge into the kitchen. Sophie stirred in my arms and I gently bobbed her back to sleep.

'What does it mean, just a bag, some shoes and a robe?' I asked.

Cahill ignored my question.

'Did Em get out and about?' she asked.

'No, not really. I've tried to get her to go to baby groups, you know, Music Bugs, that sort of thing, but she's never been keen.' I don't know why I felt so defensive. I hoped it didn't show.

'Do you know why?'

'I guess, Em has been a little not herself lately,' I replied, feeling a crushing guilt press down on me. Should I have noticed more?

'Could you elaborate?'

At first I couldn't, but then the things I should have paid more attention to came back to me. I thought of the few times I'd caught her crying. She offered excuses: hormones, tiredness. She said on a few occasions she was crying because Sophie was too perfect. I didn't ask again. I should have seen the need to do more. But then there were the other times when Emma was happy and laughing and saying how wonderful life was. The rest I'd thought was natural after having a baby, the usual ups and downs.

'She doesn't want to do much, I guess.'

'Much as in . . .'

'Go out for dinners, explore. Go to parks or the cinema.'

'It's tough with a little one.'

'It is. Her parents offer to babysit all the time. I assumed she wasn't ready to let go but . . .'

'But?'

'But now I see, Em might be struggling with something.'

'Any idea as to what?'

'Oh God, do you think she was maybe post-natal?' I said, my attention turning to Sophie as she stretched and yawned in my arms.

'We have to consider it, some mums struggle and feel ashamed to say so. Knowing is half the battle. I'm sure, when we find her, things will be all right,' Cahill said, offering a sympathetic smile.

I nodded, unable to hold PC Cahill's eye as I felt so ashamed. Sophie began to grizzle. 'I need to change her, do you mind?'

'No, not at all Mr Clarke, do what you need to do.'

I rolled out a changing mat. As I changed Sophie's nappy, I was grateful for the distraction. Had Emma been struggling, and I hadn't noticed?

Stephens or Smart called for Cahill from the kitchen and she left me to finish changing Sophie. When I'd buttoned up her Babygro, I joined them. The tall man was in the garden, by the back fence behind our peach tree.

I stepped out with Cahill, and as we approached I looked at where he was pointing the torch. A piece of cream fabric was caught in a snag in the wood.

'That's Em's bathrobe,' I said.

'Are you sure?' Cahill asked.

'Yes, I'm sure.'

'Look,' the other officer said, pointing to the floor. Despite the summer being fierce, the soil cracked and dead, beyond our garden was a small draining dyke for the farmers' fields that remain wet. Sometimes it was deep; in April it threatened to spill over into out garden, but now it was almost dry. The soil was peaty and tacky still, and on the other side of our fence, two footprints were embedded in it. She had climbed over the fence and walked away. I looked up to where she had walked and, despite the sun beginning to rise, I couldn't see anything. She had climbed over and walked into the vast, black nothing that stretched for miles behind our house. My wife had put on her robe and trainers, grabbed a bag and maybe a few of her things. She left her daughter alone in the house, climbed the fence and disappeared into a field, and I didn't have any idea why.

* * *

July 5th 2016

Emma

I thought when I started this I would write in my diary weekly, updating my exploits and adventures. Truth is, I'm working bloody hard, and when the day is done I'm too tired do anything other than eat, drink and sleep. I say that, but I'm not so exhausted by Friday that I stay in and catch up on some well-earned rest. I've been out, spending what little money I have with a few friends I've made. Jen included, although I feel myself drifting from her. She tries too hard; she's always chasing the next good time. She reminds me of the me that I'm trying to leave behind. Maybe, just maybe, I'm growing up?

Last week, we got to a bar by 9 p.m. and by 10.30 she'd ditched me for a one-nighter with a tall man; strong arms, tattoos. How funny it feels to have the shoe on the other foot. I could have written about that, perhaps I should have. How it felt, what I realised about myself. But I didn't. The moment will become a faded one, joining the stack of other moments that are colour-damaged and curled at the corners.

But I'm writing it in now.

The normal work, eat, play, sleep, isn't so normal anymore. I've got some things I need to catch up on. Some moments that I want to be in Technicolor when I look back. I'll spare you, future self, the boring details and get to the point. Life shifted; life started to become something different — whole, perhaps — when Rob Clarke messaged.

After two weeks of nothing, I thought he wasn't bothered. And if I'm honest (as I said I would be in this book) I was a little pissed off. As far as I was concerned, I'd lost interest in the doughy boy who wasn't my type anyway; I was out. But his message, it wasn't what I expected. I was waiting for him to tell me he'd been snowed under at work, or he meant to message but . . . yadda yadda yadda. Same old bullshit. But he didn't. He told me he was intimidated, that I was out of his league; he told me he'd taken two weeks to pluck up the courage and he'd wanted to text me twenty minutes after getting home from our accidental date.

Accidental date, I like that.

I made him wait until the next day before I replied. When I did, I pressed him on why he'd messaged now and he responded instantly, telling me he didn't want to look back and wonder what would have happened if he'd been a little bit braver.

And just like that I was back in, and I'd agreed to meet for a second date, our first non-accidental one. Same pub, same table, same time.

We drank and laughed and shared — I shared more with him than I thought would be possible. Obviously not all, not those deepest, darkest things I hang onto. I didn't want a grey cloud to blow over something that could be bright.

At the end of the first non-accidental date, we kissed.

Hang onto that moment for as long as possible Em, it was a good one.

It wasn't the fervent trying-to-get-into-my-pants kiss, the kind that missed the point of kissing by trying to get ahead. Forge on, plant seed. It was one that was wholly in the moment. Hands where they should be, not grabbing at anything, but both gently on my cheeks, in the moment too. I wasn't expecting it; my usual type were all passion, all lust, and I didn't have high hopes for the mild-mannered, polite, doughy boy from London who, if I'm honest, didn't turn me on like those who had come (pun intended) before. And yet I was wrong, I was so very, very wrong. I wanted him badly. And he made me wait until accidental date number three.

These past few months have been something out of a film. These past few months, I have felt — happy.

Hang onto that too, Em.

Here's what I know about Rob Clarke. It will change, maybe for the worse, hopefully for the better.

He is kind. He listens. He is tender. He is surprisingly good in bed. He doesn't question my past, he doesn't want to know about exes, he only thinks forward. And when we're out he holds open doors, he gets along with my friends — he tries, I mean, really tries. And they like him. But not as much as me. I like how he loves to swim and is scared of earthworms. That's kinda cute. I like how he loves to sit in bed stroking my hair while he reads to me. Books that are his favourite, which I've never taken the time to look at. I like how a Sunday morning has become not about nursing a horrendous hangover, but something gentler. I like that he enjoys old movies, Hitchcock and such.

I like how I miss my old life, and Steve, less and less each day.

I used to think Rob Clarke wasn't my type, but maybe he had been all along, and everyone before was the mistake. A fun mistake, but still a mistake.

I don't wanna jinx it, but this thing with him, whatever it will become, it feels real. Scary and real.

Maybe, Em, maybe this is a love story after all?

CHAPTER THREE

June 19th 2019
One day missing

Rob

PC Cahill and Sinclair (he retold me his name when I called him Smith) stayed for another hour, asking more questions about her mental health, about us as a couple. I told them we were OK, solid, as normal as everyone else. Again, I didn't tell them about the row we had before I went to work, and I didn't know why. Perhaps saying so would also say I was the one who drove her away. That I had pushed her into leaving our baby. Cahill told me the next steps. They would do a door-to-door, ask neighbours, get her picture out there, see if anyone comes forward with information, see if she comes back. And when I asked what I could do, she told me nothing. Stay home, keep my mobile on loud, wait for Em to come home.

'Don't jump to any conclusions, Rob,' Cahill said. But how could I not? I still didn't understand. Sure, Em and I had our challenges, what couple with a newborn didn't? But to up and leave in the middle of the night, walk out of the back door, climb the fence and disappear? To leave Sophie alone to fend for herself? It didn't make any sense, and yet that was how it was. That was what she did. She needed help, she wasn't in her right mind. I couldn't sit and do nothing. I needed to find my wife.

'Where have you gone, Em?'

With Sophie in my arms, another nappy changed, her bottle given, I stepped into the garden. The sun was barely up and already I could feel the heat on my skin. I scanned the floor for any sign: a clue as to why she left. Nothing. If you didn't know, it was just another day. Nothing sinister, nothing lurking in the shadows. From the outside, I was stood in a small garden, beside a medium-sized peach tree, and beyond the fence sat a huge field, one of the countless, endless fields that made up our small patch of earth. In the far distance, white wind turbines shimmered in the heat. Between them and me, nothing. I put my hand on the fence where Em's bathrobe had snagged and looked out beyond.

Where have you gone, Em? Where have you gone?

My phone started to ring from the kitchen and I dashed back towards the house to grab it. My heart beginning to pound, stirring a butterfly in my stomach, hoping it was Em saying she needed some space, but wanted to come home. In the short time it took me to get across my lawn, I played out the entire conversation in my head.

Rob, it's me.

Em? Are you OK?

Yes, I'm fine. Rob, I'm so sorry. Come get me, come get me, I want to come home.

Yes, yes, I'm coming for you.

Rob, I'm so sorry, I'm so, so sorry.

Emma, don't be, I'm here, tell me where you are . . .

Reaching the phone my stomach dropped at seeing the caller ID. It was Em's mum, Frances. As I answered, I couldn't hide my disappointment.

'Hello, Frances.'

23

'Robbie, the police have just called. What's happening?'

'Frances, I wanted to call you.'

'Why didn't you? The police were shocked you hadn't.'

'I'm sorry, it's . . . I'm struggling to process this.'

'Don't go anywhere, we're coming over.'

'No, Fran—'

She hung up before I could tell her it wasn't a good idea, that Sophie was unsettled, that I was unsettled. Ten minutes later, Frances and John were knocking on my door, and as I opened they blustered in, and the suddenness, the panic, made Sophie start to cry.

'Robbie, what's happened, where is she?'

'Frances, I need you to calm down,' I said, picking up Sophie, bobbing her gently.

'Calm down? My daughter is missing!'

'Fran,' said John, placing a hand on her shoulder, his voice deep and soothing. She turned into him and burst into tears.

'You should have called us,' she said, between sobs.

'I'm sorry. I should have. I hoped she would come back, say she went for a walk, say she needed some air, I don't know.'

'OK.' John stepped in, his voice neutral. 'Start at the beginning, tell us what you know, and then we'll all do what needs to be done to find her.'

By the time I'd explained to Frances and John what I knew — Sophie crying, Em not in bed, her bathrobe, backpack and trainers missing, the robe snagged on the fence — Frances had calmed down enough to listen.

'She needs our help,' Frances said, her sobbing under control, but still lingering close to the surface, ready to spill.

'I just don't understand. I don't understand why she left like this.' I said.

'Rob, did you and Em talk about how she was feeling?'

'No, not really. We were just, you know, getting on with it,' I replied nonchalantly, again refusing to take the opportunity to say out loud that we argued fairly often.

24

'She didn't tell you how she was feeling?'

'No,' I replied, looking from Frances to John, as they exchanged a knowing glance. 'What aren't you telling me, John?'

'Em didn't tell you?'

'Tell me what, John — no, she didn't say anything. What is it?'

John swallowed, cleared his throat and looked to Frances who gave him a nod, the tears spilling once more.

'Em is down.'

'What do you mean she's down?'

'She is . . .' He trailed off, unable to find the words.

'Depressed.' Frances stepped in. 'Em is suffering with depression.'

'No,' I said, shaking my head. 'Nope, I'd know if she was.'

'She told us,' John said quietly.

'When?'

'About a week ago, at her last visit to ours. We know our daughter, we could see she was down, and when we asked she just told us.'

'She said she was depressed?'

'Yes.'

'She specifically used those words?'

'Yes, Rob, she did.'

I opened my mouth to say something, but the reality was setting in. My wife was suffering with depression, and I didn't know. My wife was suffering with depression, and I hadn't helped her.

'Did she, did she say what was causing it?'

'No,' John said. 'But it's something she's struggled with her whole life.'

I nodded, unable to speak, unable to understand why I didn't know this about my wife. I looked at Sophie in my arms, who was now settled and staring up at me.

'We have to find her,' I said, eventually.

'Yes, we do.'

I didn't always see eye to eye with the Murphy's. They came from a long line of farmers, which meant two things in this part of the world. One, they were mistrusting of outsiders and two, they had money. Old money. The fact that I was a kid from London who grew up on a council estate meant I didn't fit. Not in their eyes. I had seen some of Em's exes and understood why. They were usually groomed, of wealth themselves and had a status I didn't think would suit me. But despite being beneath them in so many ways, what was clear, and we all understood, was that I loved Em fiercely. I suspected it was something they weren't used to for their daughter, but I've never asked. Frances had a way of patronising me and John kept his distance — 'a farmer's way', Em called it. We didn't see eye to eye, but now that didn't matter. We didn't need to be eye to eye, we needed to be eyes out, looking over the fen, trying to work out where Em had gone.

As John and I sat at the dining table working out our first step, Frances sat quietly with Sophie in the living room. She looked defeated, the saddest I'd ever seen her. People do funny things in a crisis: some stand up, march on, find a way through, and some crumble. Frances was the latter. I would have been, too, if it wasn't for John.

John pulled out a map of the Fens and flicked to page forty-one, which had our town on it. We found the lane, the cluster of houses, and pinpointed the house Em and I lived in.

'Ok, Robbie, where did you say she climbed over the fence?'

I pointed into the back garden and at the spot where Em's robe had snagged. He pointed down on the map and followed the line.

'If she went west, like you think...'

'I don't know what I think.'

'There's nothing for four miles.'

I looked down at the map and focused on the line John had drawn. Four miles of nothing. Four miles of flat, endless fields, only broken by the reservoir out behind our house and the shimmering turbines a mile or so beyond that. As my mind started to drift to horrors, akin to the horrors I see in my mind every time Sophie coughs in the night, John tapped me on the shoulder, snapping me back.

'We need to get Em's face out there. This is a small town, people know people. As soon as one of our own is missing, we'll get help. Have you got a picture? We can get it run off at the print shop in town.'

'Yes, sure.'

I scrolled through my camera roll; hundreds and hundreds of pictures of Sophie. Eventually I found one of me and Em, cheek to cheek, smiling for the camera. It was from a few months before Sophie was born. Had it really been that long since I took a picture with my wife? Cropping myself out of the shot as best I could, I showed John.

'She really has the prettiest smile,' he said.

'She does.'

Feeling motivated, John and I headed for town. Frances opted to stay with Sophie. I wasn't keen; I wanted to keep an eye on my daughter at all times now. But dragging a baby around town, plastering pictures of her mother's face everywhere, it wasn't fair on her. The sun was too hot, the air thick and cloying. Besides, what if Em came home while we were out?

Giving Frances a list of instructions — when Sophie needed her bottle, when she needed her nap, her favourite toys to play with — John and I left, climbed into his car and headed for town. As we pulled out of the lane we lived on (a beat-up old road with weeds thriving in the cracks that cut through a small cluster of houses, nine in total, all, including ours, needing a facelift) I saw the tall police officer, Sinclair, on the doorstep of one of the neighbours. The older couple in their seventies who never smiled when I said hello. Because the road was a dead end past our house, both Sinclair and the man turned to look. I waved to Sinclair, I don't know why; he didn't return it. Nor did the man beside him, they both just watched as we drove away.

I didn't think anyone would care about Em leaving in the night, but I was wrong. By the time John and I had made three hundred photocopies of Em's picture, with the heading Have You Seen Emma Clarke? and my mobile number, and started to tape them up in town, people knew. Some nodded sympathetically, some eyed me suspiciously, although I had no idea why. One older man asked if the pretty woman was my wife. I said she was.

'Well, I hope you find her.' he said, taking a copy of her picture and walking away, a line of sweat down the middle of his faded grey shirt.

John and I put Em's picture on community noticeboards in coffee shops, and laid them on the desks in the Post Office, and every newsagent I went into put one in the window. In one café the lady who ran it gave me a cup of coffee on the house, and I smiled as I left. Sometimes the smallest act of kindness goes a long way.

Two hours and one sweat-soaked T-shirt later, Em's face was everywhere in town and, with nothing else to do, we headed back. Sophie was down for her nap when we arrived, and Frances said the police had popped round and would come back later. She had also rung the hospitals, but no sign of Em.

The hospitals, why hadn't I thought to ring them myself?

I hoped that people would call within an hour of the posters going up in town, but one became three, that became five, and still no one had called in to say they'd seen her or knew where she was. John suggested he and Frances went home as Em might go back there, and I agreed. Besides, the three of us sat anxiously waiting was rubbing off on Sophie, who started to know something was wrong. She went down for her second nap at four, and once she was sound asleep, her grandparents kissed her on the forehead and said goodbye.

Waving them off, I watched until they got to the bottom of the lane, turned left, and drove away. No sooner had they gone, a police car turned in and, knowing they were coming for me, I stayed on my doorstep.

'Mr Clarke, seems like you're waiting for us,' Sinclair said as he got out of the car. There was something about him I didn't like — maybe because he clearly didn't like me for some reason. Cahill got out from the driver's side; she didn't share the same obvious dislike.

'Rob, can we come in?'

'Of course.'

'Note how he didn't ask if we'd found Em?' Sinclair said quietly, but I heard.

Once in the living room, I offered them a drink. Both declined.

'Where is your daughter?' Cahill asked.

'Asleep in her cot. So, have you found Em?' I asked, deliberately directing the question to Sinclair.

'No.'

'I've been putting up pictures in town, we've called the hospitals, no one has seen her. I don't know what else to do?'

'Rob, we want to talk about before you left for work the night Em disappeared.'

'What do you want to know?' I asked, my heart skipping a beat.

'Neighbours have said they heard a row about 7 p.m.?'

I knew the neighbours heard us, and I knew they would say so when the police knocked on their doors. I should have been prepared, but I wasn't. My heart started to pound, and my mouth dried out. I looked for a drink, a glass of water, but couldn't see one.

'Mr Clarke? Is what the neighbours are saying true?'

I cleared my throat, 'Yes, yes, Em and I had a disagreement.'

'What about?'

'You know, the usual, the house is a mess, we are both so tired.'

'Why didn't you tell us this, Mr Clarke?' Sinclair asked. I didn't like the way he looked at me, like I was prey.

'I don't know, it didn't seem important.'

'You have an argument with your wife the night she disappears, and you didn't think it was important?'

I didn't reply. If I did, I'd be condemning myself as a suspect, but my silence condemned me also. I should have just said when they first came round. Now it was too late, anything that came from my mouth would only make it worse.

'Rob, mind if we take another look around?'

'Why?'

'Just in case we missed something. You are within your rights to say no.'

'No, it's fine, anything that helps get my wife back.'

Sinclair slapped on a pair of white gloves and began to move through to the kitchen. Cahill smiled at me, a smile that was more of a question, before following. I trailed at the back, not knowing if I should.

Cahill and Sinclair looked over the whole house and the back garden once more and, finding nothing that would help, Sinclair went out to his car.

'Why is it I feel like a suspect here?' I asked Cahill, when I was sure Sinclair was out of hearing distance.

'We have to rule out all possibilities.'

'I wouldn't hurt my wife.'

'Rob, not telling us about your row, it raises eyebrows.'

'Sorry, I just don't know what to do or how to be. This is too much for me.'

She nodded, and I believed it was a nod of understanding. 'Rob, if there is anything else you need to tell us — if you and Em were in a bad way, if she was in a bad way — we need to know. There might be something in it that helps us find her. Do you understand?'

'Yes, yes, I do.'

'And is there?'

'I can't think of anything else.'

'Ok, well, sit tight, and if you do think of anything, ring me. I'll be in touch soon.'

Cahill left, and once the door was closed, I moved into the living room and peered at her and Sinclair who were talking in their car. Sinclair looked up and, panicking, I shot away from the window, hoping he didn't see me.

***

March 18th 2017

Emma

Oh Em, what have you done? What have you fucking done? You know you get bored; you know you change your jobs often, friends periodically. Christ, you've not lived in the same place for more than two years in your whole adult life, bouncing from rented flat to rented flat. Some solo living, some house shares. Your window for all things is six months. Six months in a flat, job, friendship, and you're itching for something else. You did it before, when you were in a long-term relationship, you cheated for years before you broke up. But then you meet this guy, your doughy guy, and all of a sudden, you don't want to move, you quite like your job and Jen, the new friend in the big city, is actually now a real friend. Meeting Rob has helped you do all of that. To feel settled, calm. And still, you've managed to fuck it up.

God, I hope this doesn't come back to haunt me.

There is no question I am now in love with Rob Clarke; the question is why I won't let myself embrace it. I spend most of my week in his flat, I call him on the nights I'm not staying. He has even met my 'charming' parents. Which is something I never thought I'd say again after the colossal nightmare that was the last time they met a partner of mine. That story is for another time. Actually, that story is for never again.

If I'm honest with myself, and that's kinda the point of this diary, I wasn't expecting it to go well. Rob isn't someone my parents would approve of. He's not local, he doesn't come from wealth, he's a few years younger (Mum insists I'm better off with an older, wiser man) and he isn't the poster-boy image they want to show off when they meet with their snotty friends.

'My daughter is dating a handsome man, oh, yes, I suspect he's modelled before. Our grandkids are going to be beautiful.'

So, when I brought a younger, normal-level-of-attractive Londoner from a council estate, I was expecting the disappointed conversations, my parents trying to embarrass him, make him feel not worthy. And to their credit, as we sat at their dining table, a Sunday roast spread in front of us (Rob being very complimentary of Mum's cooking) they tried. Mum started with the whole 'what does your family do', like everyone's family is as fucked up as ours with incestuous claims over the business. Rob's mum didn't work, she raised four kids, his dad worked for a paint company, mixing chemicals to create the latex needed to keep the paint on the walls, until he died when Rob was eleven. Rob spoke of his parents with pride, and when Mum turned her nose up, he didn't seem to notice. Of course, after prodding about his background, she moved on to the next most important thing, his education. Rob doesn't have a degree. As she literally rolled her eyes I was about to jump in and defend him, but he didn't need it.

'My mum fell ill. I left college and took a job to help around the house.'

'Oh, I'm so sorry. Is she OK now?' Dad asked.

'She passed away a few years ago.'

Dad nodded and, just like that, one of my parents seemed to approve. Not that I wanted their approval.

I've written all this, and still I've not said what I've done. As wonderful as it is to feel like I have real friends, as wonderful as it was to have Rob meet Mum and Dad and survive, it doesn't change the fact that I fucked up in the biggest way possible and I hope, for my sake, that when I re-read this what I did is dealt with, and not another one of my dirty little secrets.

I could blame him, but that would be a lie. No, as much as I would love to say Steve messaged me first and I was swept up into my past, the truth is, last week, home, bored, I messaged. I still don't know why. Curiosity, perhaps? Could it even have been kindness? Regardless, it was wrong. I let myself get swept up in a text conversation about the fun we used to have, and before I knew it I was on my way out. Just a drink, for old times' sake, right? My on-off-on-off ex who I'd known for years, shared so much with. I even told him about Rob. How we met, why he was different. I spoke of our first date, the first time we kissed. I know, speaking to an ex about these things should have felt weird. But, strangely, it felt cathartic. I think speaking to Steve was part of my closure on what we once were. It felt like a confessional, telling my ex about my new lover. But it also felt right. We had shared so much, why not this too? We were two chaotic souls drawn together into a chaotic relationship that had remained secret all these years. Speaking to him about loving someone else, it felt like the ending of one part of my life and the beginning of something new. And I realised that was why I'd messaged first, in a strange way. I needed his blessing.

One quiet drink with Steve became two, and we moved on to how we met, my old life and my new life merging together through a cloud of booze and the noise of other people's conversations. Two drinks became three, that became four, that became some powder off of a pub toilet seat, again for old times' sake.

And then a few hazy hours later, I'm hanging, coming down, in his bed. I tried to leave without waking him but he stirred, and as our eyes met, the guilt I felt was compounded. I said sorry. To him, for Rob, and to myself, before leaving.

I am like a broken record, snagging in the same place, doomed to stay in this fucking loop unless I force myself to stop, lift the needle and place it down anew. And I know why I don't: the record, the song, it's familiar, safe. I know it well, it knows me better, but I don't like the song anymore, I've heard it too many times.

Fuck, Em. Fuck.

CHAPTER FOUR

June 20th 2019
Two days missing

Rob

Em's disappearance uprooted my sense of safety, and I didn't want to be more than a few feet from Sophie's cot. So I sat on her floor and dozed. I barely slept. Despite the need for it, I didn't want to close my eyes, because when I did, horrors came. Visions of Em running away, crying, wanting to hurt herself. Visions of me not being good enough, visions of her hating our daughter. They would snap me awake, my heart racing. I paced, drank coffee — copious amount of coffee — and took care of what I could. I started by asking my boss if I could take this time off as annual leave. And at no point did I let Sophie out of my sight for more than a minute. I told my boss I needed to be at home, explained what had happened, and that I couldn't afford to not be paid. He agreed to allow me to take my remaining annual leave now. It was only a few days, but a few days was better than none. Feeling like I'd won a small victory I started to search in earnest, both in my memory and in my home, for something that might tell me why my wife upped and left in the middle of the night. I emptied her drawers, pulled her clothes from the wardrobe. I looked under the bed, pulling out old bank statements and letters. There was no secret debt, no strange correspondence. Nothing. I looked under the sofas, on the kitchen pinboard; I checked the cupboards, under the sink, bathroom cabinets, I even checked the fridge and freezer, and again, nothing. I couldn't see anything that would help, I couldn't see anything missing. As far as I could tell, Em left without taking anything more than the bag, her robe and a pair of trainers. No clues, no explanation. She'd just disappeared. Intentionally vanished with only the clothes on her back.

Exhausted by turning the house upside down, I found myself staring out of Sophie's bedroom window. I kept looking at the point where I knew two footprints sat in the peat. The point where Em landed before she walked away from her home, and her sleeping daughter. For a moment I thought I saw someone moving in the fen, close to the reservoir, but it was my tired eyes playing tricks. I knew it was wishful thinking. But I let myself go there, I let myself imagine it was Em, walking back through the field, waving at me when she was close enough for me to see her face, and by the time she was at the fence I'd be downstairs, opening the back door to the garden.

Em?

Rob, I'm so sorry.

It's OK, everything's going to be OK.

I would leap over the fence, pull her close, kiss her as we both cried, before helping her back into the garden, and she would run upstairs, pick up Sophie and we would both cry all over again.

Of course, it didn't happen — it wouldn't happen — but one element of my fantasy was true. I was crying.

Knowing I'd not rest at all away from Sophie, I lay on her floor, listened to her gentle breathing. I rang Em's mobile: the dial tone sounded four times and clicked into voicemail.

'Hi, its Emma, sorry I can't get to the phone, leave your name and I'll ring you back.'

I missed her voice.

My final thought, before I slipped into brief oblivion on Sophie's floor, was of a number. One hundred and eighty thousand. I'd done some research; that was the number of people who disappeared in the UK each year. One hundred and eighty thousand.

I did the maths. That equalled one person every ninety seconds. I couldn't shake the thought: our lovely, doting Em, my wife, Sophie's mummy, a stat, and in the time it took me to think that, another person had gone missing somewhere.

I was only asleep an hour or so, two tops, when Sophie woke me up crying. Groggy, I carried her downstairs, where I changed and fed her. There was no point trying to settle her again, she was awake, and she was missing her mummy too. Not knowing what to do, I decided to go out. The sun was barely up, the day wasn't relentlessly hot yet, and Sophie hadn't been outside since the day her mummy left. Loading Sophie into her buggy, I grabbed my wallet and headed out. Part of me felt guilty for not staying at home in case Em came back, but I had my phone — if she came back while I was out, she'd surely call me. As I stepped out into the early morning, I was surprised to see the man who lived opposite was up and getting into his car. I smiled, wanting to look like someone who was coping. He nodded back, climbed behind the driver's seat and pulled away.

The walk to the town centre was uninspiring. From the end of the road, it was a straight line along a narrow path. The cluster of weather-beaten old houses, one of them ours, disappeared and on either side, fields stretched far into the distance. Beside the occasional car, I didn't hear anything but nature, and my daughter babbling. The early morning birds were singing in full voice.

I took my time walking into town; the twenty-minute quick walk took us just under forty. The repetition of placing one foot in front of the other and the endless landscape were mesmerising. Combined, they created a silence in my head that soothed, slowed, centred. It was the calmest I'd felt since I got home and discovered she was gone. And because I knew it would be short-lived, I held tight to it. Every time one of the many questions about Em came into my head, or I started reassessing the way I'd missed her being depressed, I took in the scenery, focusing on a field in the distance where I could see a farmer working, and pushed it to the back of my mind. The questions would come again, but the respite was nothing short of bliss.

That realisation was followed by a moment of crushing guilt. The feeling wasn't there for long, though, as my phone started to ring. I pulled it out of the change bag slung over the handlebars of the buggy and saw it was Frances. I answered, not able to say hello before she spoke.

'What have you told the papers?'

'What, nothing. Why?'

'John has just been called by one of his farmhands to say Emma is in the *Ramsey Informer*. What did you tell them, Rob?'

'Frances, calm down, I haven't spoken to anyone other than the police.'

'Well, they're saying horrible things, Rob, horrible. Where are you? Are you out?'

'Sophie and I have gone for a walk.'

'What? What if Emma comes home and no one is there?' she shrieked. 'I'm coming over.'

'But . . .'

'I'm coming over now.'

'Frances . . .'

She hung up before I could tell her to give me an hour. Turning around, I sighed heavily, feeling overcome with exhaustion, and began to trudge my way home. I should have looked online to see what was being said in the *Ramsey Informer*, but Sophie was grizzly now, wanting attention, and I carried her in one arm so she could see the world, and pushed the buggy with the other for the mile walk home. When I turned onto my lane, Frances and John were on my doorstep. They looked like they hadn't slept either.

'Robbie, why on earth did you go out? What if Emma came home?' Frances said, panic etched into the crow's feet around her eyes.

'I needed to take Sophie for a walk, she's having a hard time too.'

Frances opened her mouth to say something but stopped herself. Unlocking the front door, I cursed: the house was a tip from my frantic search in the night and I'd not tidied anything away. I apologised for it, and John tapped me on the shoulder twice before making his way to the kitchen to make a coffee. Frances looked at me, accusing me of something with her gaze, before taking Sophie from me. I frantically cleared space for her to sit down. She wasn't pleased, she never was, but as she gave Sophie a cuddle I could see Frances' tight lips soften into a smile. I sat in the chair opposite her and caught her eye.

'Sorry, I was looking for clues,' I said, gesturing to the mess.

'I'm sorry too, Robbie,' she said, the first time I had ever heard her say that word to anyone. 'I'm having—'

'I am too,' I said. 'Frances, I haven't spoken to the papers. I promise.'

She considered me for a moment, nodded and then turned her attention back to playing with Sophie on her lap. Knowing she needed her granddaughter's love, I left them to it and joined John in the kitchen.

'John, what the hell has the paper said?'

'They said Em has vanished, abandoning her baby; they said she's having a mental-health crisis, that she's high risk for self-harm.'

'What?'

'Yeah. They've dragged her through the mud a bit. Me and Frances too, dug up some old things that should have been left alone.'

'What sort of things?'

John shifted, paused. It was probably the heat. Probably. 'Just stuff about when she was young.' He continued, 'We look after our own here, and we don't forget things.'

'What sort of things, John?'

John didn't say anything, but pulled the paper out of his back pocket and dropped it on the table. Em's disappearance was on its front page. LOCAL WOMAN MISSING. I wondered, would they even print it at all in the *Metro*? I doubted it. Not with one every ninety seconds. I read some of the article. It spoke of Em being from here, leaving for a bigger city before coming home to raise her young. They had details of her leaving, the approximate time of day, they even knew she went over the back fence and into a field. How did they know that detail? A neighbour perhaps?

Then they spoke of her youth, how she was a little wild at times. Nothing I'd deem newsworthy, a few run-ins with the police, occasionally infrequent attendance at school. Kids' stuff. Kids' stuff — but still, unexpected from Em. I didn't know any of this. I didn't know Em had a side to her that would cause gossip. My Em, quiet, thoughtful, kind. But was she really? I'd always assumed my Em was happy, too. Despite wondering if I ever really knew my wife, I couldn't understand why Frances was so upset with the gossip, and not wondering how they knew details about her leaving.

'John, this is just kid stuff, it doesn't matter.'

'Of course it matters.'

'Why?'

'We have to protect—'

'Protect what?' I shouted. 'What is more important than finding Em?'

My outburst was unexpected, even for me, and opening the back door I walked outside. Despite the heat now creeping up, I needed to try and cool down. I wanted to scream, to cry, to hit something, but instead, I leant into the peach tree, and looked out over the endless heat-shimmering fields.

Where have you gone, Em? Why did you go?

I heard someone come into the garden but I didn't look, my eyes trained on the way she would have walked. John came and stood beside me. He handed me a cup of coffee and for a moment he looked too, no doubt imagining Em scrabbling through the thick corn crop, over the uneven ground, into the dark.

'John, I . . .'

'It's OK my boy, we're all under a lot of stress. I can't imagine what you're feeling, especially with Sophie too.'

'I'm coping, just, but I don't understand.'

'Me neither.'

'Where has she gone?'

'I wish I knew.'

'John, I didn't speak to the papers. I promise.'

'They seem to know a lot about what happened.'

'Yeah, I was thinking the same.'

'Well, someone has spoken to them.'

John and I returned our gaze to the stretch of land Em would have walked over. Then, silently, we made our way back to the house. Looking and longing wasn't going to find my wife.

I'd hoped that once Frances had calmed down and believed that I didn't do anything to harm their name or reputation, things would settle. John and I would ring around local businesses, Cahill would call for an update — but that wasn't to be. Within an hour of John and Frances arriving at my doorstep, the reporters came. Wanting statements, asking questions. At first, I tried to oblige.

Em is thirty, five feet five. About sixty-five kilos, I'm not sure what that is in stones. Fair hair, green eyes. Yes, she is a doting mother, no, she wasn't appearing to be living through a crisis. Yes, our marriage was strong. Yes, yes, I miss her terribly.

And then I was asked a question that made me understand I shouldn't be speaking to them.

No, I had nothing to do with my wife's disappearance.

CHAPTER FIVE

Rob

The Murphy's stayed most of the day. John helped me tidy, Frances entertained Sophie, and after they left, Sophie and I spent the afternoon playing, reading and watching her favourite, Mr Tumble, on TV. I made dinner for us both. Different dishes, same mealtime, and as the night took hold I readied my girl for bed, keeping to the routine Em and I had worked so hard to achieve. As I held her in my arms, giving her a night-time bottle, I looked out from my bedroom window into the street and the houses opposite me. Number five, the house with all the kids, was busy. Lights on in every room, two stressed-out parents downstairs trying to watch *Gogglebox* as little ones ran around. I didn't know their names, or any of my neighbours' names. It wasn't the sort of place where you introduced yourself to those who lived closest, but then, was anywhere? Next door to the madhouse was the old couple, who had eyed me with suspicion since the day we moved in, and I'd tried to say hello as I unloaded box after box. At number seven the house was dark, but their car was on the drive.

After her bottle, Sophie settled, and by 7.30 p.m. she was sound asleep. Downstairs, I searched Em's Facebook. She'd not posted in months, but that wasn't uncommon: she wasn't a regular poster, more of a timeline watcher. I looked on Google Maps on my phone, bringing up the satellite image of our house and panning out, tracing the direction we knew she left in, trying to see where she might have gone. But all there was, was endless flat nothing. My head felt heavy and thick from looking. So I stopped and let the silence of the house creep in. When Sophie was awake, when the sun was up, I had a small sense of purpose; I was either caring for her, or actively trying to find my wife. But now I felt lost. I felt alone, the hours too long, and too quiet as I waited for Sophie to wake and need me. I turned on the TV; flicked through the endless Sky channels. People were either happy, which made me ache in the pit of my stomach, or they weren't, which only made me feel worse. I almost settled on a documentary channel, but in it an African Wild Dog cub was abandoned, for being too small to keep up with the pack. I knew it would die, it was just nature's cruel way, and I couldn't watch it happen. I turned it off and stared at the blank screen for a while. Working out what to do with myself. In the absence of the TV, the silence found its voice and began to press around me, intimidating me. I stood up, stretched, groaning as my muscles pulled to that line between pleasure and pain and as my moan dwindled, the silence crept back.

What to do, what to do?

I could read but felt too tired; I could listen to music, but somehow enjoying music whilst my wife was missing felt wrong. Ensuring the baby monitor was in my pocket, I got up and walked into the kitchen, counting the steps I took as I did.

Seventeen.

When I was young, struggling to care for Mum and work full-time, I found counting calmed me. I'd not counted like that since then.

I left the light off as I made myself a drink, my eye drawn to the peach tree. It often reminded me of when I was young,

42

of endless summers and sleepovers with my grandparents in the weeks after my dad died. Despite him passing on, life was good, simpler, a purer time. I didn't worry about things other than what was right in front of me. There was no past, no looking hopelessly into the future, just the now, and the now was enough. I could almost hear my granddad talking to me, sharing a joke or telling me everything would be all right when I grazed my knee. And, for the first time in a very long time, I missed him. It wasn't enough just looking at the tree, I wanted to be closer, I needed to touch the rough bark and listen to the wind rustling through its leaves. I opened the back door, stepped into the garden and walked towards it. The night was almost perfect, cooler than it had been recently and clear; the breeze was calm, whispering. The stars were out in all their glory. On the baby monitor, Sophie moved, and I held it up to my ear to make sure she was OK. After a moment, her heavy breathing returned. I looked up to her bedroom window, all was quiet, all was still, all was as it should be.

Well, not quite.

Looking back at the night sky, the stars were misaligned, their natural order interrupted. They had shifted off their points, despite me not knowing where they should truly sit. Even the heavens seemed affected by what was happening. And then, even though I knew I shouldn't, even though I knew it would only cause me pain, I took out my mobile, checking for something, anything from Em. I rang her number. I knew it would click to voicemail, but I still held onto hope she would answer, say she needed me, ask me to save her.

Sometimes, when I daydreamed, she was close by, sometimes she was back in London. And the reasons varied: she'd had an accident, she went for a walk and got lost, she was going to leave forever, but had a change of heart. And I would save her.

Running the scenario in my head filled me with hope, for that brief moment after dialling and before it clicked into voicemail. I knew it would, I needed to hear her voice and it broke my heart.

A light caught my eye, far off in the fen, close to where I knew the reservoir was. The light roamed the ground, occasionally flicking up and pointing in the direction of the houses. For a split second, I thought it just might be Em. I walked towards the back fence, the same spot Em climbed over, and thought about doing so myself, but a dog barked from somewhere nearby, one of the neighbours' I think, and the person out back with the torch turned it my way. Fearing I'd be seen, I backed off and hid behind the peach tree.

Jesus, Rob. Sort it out.

When the light passed, I moved back into the house, closing and locking the door behind me. Even though I hadn't done anything wrong, even though being in my own back garden of an evening was totally acceptable, I slid down the door, hiding under the glass. And the silence of the house took its cue and pressed on me. Punctuating it, a clock ticking, the house clicking and clanking as it moved. Sophie breathing. Placing the baby monitor on my lap, I went into my phone's photo album, needing something to push away the silence. I didn't need to scroll, as the last thing taken was a video of Em and Sophie at a baby music play session the library put on. It had taken a lot to get Em out that day, I remember her reluctance, until I said it would be good for Sophie, for all of us. And when we were out Em was on edge, she couldn't focus, she kept looking around — for what, I didn't know. Retrospectively, it was social anxiety, and I didn't pick up on it.

I tapped the play button on the video and turned the volume down as Em sang 'The wheels on the bus go round and round'. Sophie giggled, they both giggled, but Em looked sad. I could see it now.

'Smile, Em.'

She looked at the camera. 'You're not videoing this?'

'Of course.'

'Rob!'

'This is just for us, for when we're old and grey. Isn't that right, Sophie? Mummy will love this video one day.'

Sophie cooed and I repeated the question, my voice high and melodic, making her coo again.

'See, she agrees with me.'

Em rolled her eyes, then sang the next line directly into the camera. 'The people on the bus go up and down, up and down, up and down.'

'The voice of an angel,' I said, and the video stopped. The final frame was Em staring at the camera. Her eyes heavy, her smile forced. The people on the bus go up and down, but Em was just down.

Tapping the video, the date stamp appeared at the top. It was from three days ago, the morning of the day Em disappeared, and yet it looked and felt and sounded just like any other morning. Swiping, I looked at photos taken in the week leading up to her disappearing. Smiling, happy, playing with Sophie. Changing Sophie, kissing Sophie. Love spilling out of every picture. But in some Em also looked tired, she looked sad. How was it I didn't notice until now? One picture stood out. It was of Em pushing Sophie on a swing; Sophie was smiling, the image slightly blurred. Em was smiling too, but it looked forced, and she wasn't looking at Sophie in the swing, but at something behind where I was taking the picture from.

What were you thinking, Em? What was going on in your head?

It didn't make sense. None of it. Em never once said she wasn't fine, she never once sounded like something was troubling her. But Em is good at keeping things close to her chest, better than I could possibly have thought, because, of course, it couldn't have been fine, could it? She'd told her parents she was depressed. And now she was gone.

I scrolled back past the hundreds of pictures of Sophie, past the picture I cropped for John, to the night of our engagement party. March 16th, 2018. Like all things us, when we decided to do something, it happened quickly. We moved in together late 2017, mid-March the next year, we were engaged. That May, after we found out we were having a baby, we married. Eloping to do so. And when we decided to move, in less than a month we were in the van driving up the A1.

In the picture from our engagement party, Em and I were in a bar close to our old flat in Clapham. Em is giving the camera a thumbs up, her other hand pointing towards the T-shirt I'm wearing, grinning like an idiot. I, however, am less impressed. People have things they hate, irrational things that aren't worth so much attention. Mine is T-shirts with slogans. So when Em insisted I wore her engagement gift to me, a top that said 'Owned by Em' and a stupid arrow point- ing to the left, where she stood, I was proud, because of what it stated, and appalled in equal measure. The top was a hit with strangers who, discovering we were going to be married, gave Em and I the worst hangover we'd ever experienced the following morning.

What I would give for that again.

Unable to look at the picture anymore, I locked my phone, and in the low light my reflection in the glass looked haunted, like the ghost I was becoming without my wife.

Double checking all the doors were locked, I headed upstairs, into Sophie's room. She lay sound asleep, her arms above her head without a care in the world. It made me want to cry all over again. Grabbing a blanket, I lay on the floor beside her cot and listened to her gentle breathing until I fell asleep.

***

December 9th 2017

Emma

It's funny, every time I write in this journal, before I've put down a single word, I read what I've said before and I tell myself I need to write in it more. I guess flicking back through the pages, reading my thoughts, hearing my own voice, is therapeutic. I mean, I won't write in it more, I know me, best intentions and all that. But as you can see, future Em, you're writing in it now. And here's why . . . ready . . . you sure?

You've taken the plunge. You have moved in with Rob. The fairy tale lives on, despite several cataclysmic fuck-ups.

He shared my bed, most of my heart, it was right that the next step is to share a postcode. I did it to break the cycle, to lift the needle. To change the track. I couldn't keep doing it to Rob, loving him while sleeping with my ex. I couldn't do it to me anymore. So I met with Steve, one last time, and told him I was moving forward, moving on. He didn't take it as I thought he would. I expected him to cry, or beg, but he simply smiled, telling me it was OK, and that he would be there when I realised I was making a mistake. I tried to argue that the only mistake I had made was coming back. That he and I, together, were a broken entity. And I had learnt that through being with Rob. I wanted him to understand, agree, but he just smiled knowingly.

'You'll come back to me, Emma, because that's what you do, you come back, over and over. It's who you are, it's who you'll always be.'

I hated that, despite not wanting to think it, a part of me knew he was right.

But still I left. I'm tired of being that woman. I still had my doubts about what I was doing, still unsure if I could really live without Steve, but in that moment I knew it was time to walk away.

For good this time.

Rob and I picked the wrong day to move me into his flat: the first of the autumn storms had blown in, the rain was relentless and the wind blew fallen leaves that slapped onto my legs and felt like slugs. As we loaded, I couldn't help but worry. Was the storm a metaphor for what I was doing? Was the universe or God telling me to stop? The storm is coming, it will blow your house down.

Shut up Em, that's the big bad wolf.

Saying goodbye to a chapter of my life I didn't think would ever end was harder than I thought it would be. As I handed in the keys to my landlord James, who also lived there, I wasn't just saying goodbye to him, or my little room overlooking the train lines. I was saying goodbye to being alone. To not having to be accountable, to living in the moment. But still, it felt like a small sacrifice to make. Rob was giddy with excitement. He didn't show it to my face, but I could see it in his eyes, and it made me feel giddy too.

With my life squeezed into nine boxes, two suitcases and a scattering of bin bags, we drove to his, barely able to speak. He was as nervous as I was and, once we were in, the door closed behind us, Rob handed me a set of keys. My keys. He put them in my palm, wrapped my hand around them and kissed me on the back of the hand. And I knew then I hadn't made a mistake. Not this time.

Em, you've finally got something right.

They say living with someone is tough, and I don't want to jinx it (I've said that before, haven't I? When did I become superstitious?) but I've been here for nearly two months now in Rob's flat, our flat, and it's easy. Without the need for discussion, if one cooks, the other cleans up, if one hoovers, the other is changing the bedding; there's a synchronicity between us, a dance, and we are both the choreographers. We decorated our Christmas tree last night, our small, fake little perfect fucking tree. With the lights and ornaments, listening to old Christmas songs as we decorated. After, we curled up on the sofa, watched *It's a Wonderful Life* on the TV. Rob knows most of the lines. I've only seen it once, when I was very little, sat on Nana's knee. It makes me miss her. I should try and see her before Christmas.

Who are you kidding Em, of course you won't.

After the movie, Rob and I had sex right there on the sofa and fell asleep, under the glow of a hundred small Christmas lights.

God, I've become someone sickening, a walking fucking cliché.

Rob doesn't know, of course, about what I did. How could I tell him, it would only break his heart and knowing that would break mine. Steve has messaged a few times since; he rang once, our conversation short and awkward. I said Rob and I are now serious (we were before, but I try to kid myself that we weren't). I even told Steve that I love Rob, that I want a future with him. I'm going clean, I'm quitting the drug that is my old life of hand to mouth, moment to moment. I'm reaching for more. When I hung up, I was sure I'd not be called again.

Another goodbye, another step forward.

Go on, Em! If only the you from twelve months ago could see you now.

CHAPTER SIX

June 21st 2019
Three days missing

Rob

At 4.12 a.m. I was awake. Another night with barely a blink of sleep. Sophie was up too, the early morning feed. She used to go back to sleep after; content, belly full, dry nappy. But not now. Not since Em left. I took her downstairs, opened the back door and, making sure she was wrapped up in her blanket even though it was probably twenty degrees already, stepped into the garden. The wind blew steadily, southerly, warm, and I could hear the sound of crickets chirping away. Walking to the back fence, to the spot, I looked out over the fields. The same question as ever on my lips. *Where have you gone Em? Why did you go?*

Before I could stop myself, I'd swung my left leg over the three-foot fence and carefully climbed over, my feet landing close to where Em's footprints had been found. And with my baby in my arms, I walked. From the garden, the field looked impenetrable, but now I was in it I could see a small path, about as wide as my feet, if I was stood straight and they were together. Narrow enough not to be seen, but wide enough to follow. I walked, and quickly saw several other paths, scars in the field, heading in two more directions. I turned left, kept walking and after ten minutes, Sophie and I stood in the middle of the field, half a mile from our small cluster of houses, cast in the shadow of the ever-growing sun behind. Miles away from anything else in all other directions. A person could easily disappear here. But saying that, there was literally nowhere to disappear *to*.

To my left I heard a dog bark, the same dog from one of the neighbours' houses. Not wanting to be seen in the middle of a field holding a baby, I ducked down into the tall corn and ran back towards home. Climbing the fence I looked around, making sure I'd not been seen, then went inside.

By 9 a.m., Frances and John were back, and I'm ashamed to say, when Frances offered to take Sophie for an hour so I could clean myself up and grab a shower, I jumped at the chance. I spent half of that time standing under the hot water, letting it run through my hair, removing three days' worth of sweat and fear, and once I was out, in a clean pair of shorts and T-shirt, I felt rejuvenated for the day. I was going to find Em.

When I came back down, the living room was empty, and my heart skipped. Before panic could set in, I heard Frances and John in the kitchen. Following their voices, I became aware of another: PC Cahill. As I stepped in, Cahill was sat at the table, Frances and John opposite, Sophie on her nana's knee. Sinclair stood by the back door, arms crossed, staring at me. John, acting on cue, got up to make a cuppa. It was his way of showing he cared. It worked for me too.

'Hello, sorry, I was in the shower.'

'It's perfectly fine,' Cahill said, with half a smile. Sinclair wasn't smiling. Was I falling prey to the classic good cop bad cop? Or was there something more to it?

'John, Frances, you should have come and got me.'

'Rob, it's OK, we've only been here a few minutes.'

'What's happened? Have you found Em?'

'No, not yet.'

'Then why are you here?'

'Woah!' Sinclair said, standing upright from his leaning position.

'Sorry, sorry. I'm just . . .'

'It's OK, we understand,' Cahill said. 'Sit down, let me fill you in.'

I did as asked. Sinclair returned to his leaning position, arms still crossed, and I could feel his eyes on me, watching my every move.

'I'll start by telling you that as its been over 72 hours, Emma's disappearance is being taken over by Detective Inspector Keats.'

'Oh, will you not be helping anymore?'

'Yes, we are still on the case, it's just gone further up the chain, it's a good thing, more eyes looking, Keats's first job was setting up a hotline number for Em. It's being shared in town and on our Facebook page. The reach is good. Already people are ringing in with possible sightings; we're following each and every one up.'

'Good, that's good,' Frances said, Sophie wiggling, trying to get free. I took her, opened the fridge door and grabbed a bottle of baby milk. Warming the milk in a saucepan, Sophie then fed and settled in my arms.

'When will we speak to him or her?'

'Him, soon. DI Keats is following every lead. We have also released information to the press.'

'Yes, we've seen.' John said.

'I need to clarify — the details of Emma's youth, that's not us. I suspect they've spoken to old friends, boyfriends and the like. Sorry,' Cahill said, apologising to me for referencing Em's old lovers.

'It's OK. How did they find out details about her leaving at night, climbing over the fence . . . ?'

'I thought it came from you, but Mr Murphy has said you've not spoken to the press.'

'I haven't.'

'Then I suspect it's from a neighbour who watched us when we came over the first time,' Cahill continued. Sinclair shifted behind, his eyes still on me. 'I'm glad you haven't spoken to the press; it can get messy sometimes. But I've been told BBC *Look East* want to cover the story.'

'The BBC?' John said, handing me a coffee.

A young mother, disappears in the middle of the night, leaving her baby home alone. Its good TV, I thought. Or at least I think it was a thought. Cahill and Sinclair shared another look. Had I just said that out loud?

'We wanted to come and warn you first, about the BBC, and tell you, you don't have to go on TV if they ask. Our advice would be to hold off.'

'I want to find Em, if it helps . . .' I said. Frances nodded, agreeing.

'These things have the habit of turning a missing person's case into a circus. I don't want this to get muddy with speculation and hearsay.'

Hearsay in these parts was currency. I agreed, reluctantly.

'PC Cahill,' Frances said. 'I saw in the paper yesterday that Emma was at risk of hurting herself. You don't think . . . ?'

'It's hard to say. The people around this table know Emma better than anyone but, in my experience, we can't rule it out. If she was post-natal, as suggested, we need to find her fast, and get her the help she needs.'

'Well, you need to hurry up!' Frances said, her outburst startling Sophie, who started to cry. Giving Frances a look, I stood up, lifted my daughter from her grandmother's lap and walked into the living room to comfort her. Shortly after, Cahill and Sinclair left. Cahill told me to 'hang in there' as the officers got into their car and pulled away. Frances sat next to me on the sofa, stroked Sophie's hair as she slept in my arms.

'I didn't mean to shout.'

'It's OK.'

Reaching for her bag, Frances pulled out her mobile and I looked at her quizzically.

'If the BBC is interested, I say we call them.'

'But Cahill—'

'—Isn't Emma's family; we are. It might cause speculation, but it will also mean more people are talking about her, helping us find her. Robbie, let's find our girl. What do you say?'

I smiled. I had struggled to form a relationship with Frances, but we were unified in this. Nodding, Frances googled a number, and dialled.

CHAPTER SEVEN

Rob

Things happened quickly, and for the first time since I discovered Em was gone, I felt something like hope. Despite Cahill's advice, it felt right to speak to the local media. The more people who knew Em was missing, the more chance we'd find her, and help her. Frances took the lead, coordinating the task of going public on a much wider scale. She was efficient and focused, and John and I knew better than to interrupt. She needed the direction it gave. John made tea, I looked after Sophie and Frances organised the gathering press. By mid-afternoon, several local papers and online media outlets, as well as someone from the BBC, were on my front lawn; waiting, speculating. Likely fabricating, too. Em disappearing was my worst nightmare; for them, it made a good story. I knew that, and I didn't care that they were gathering like vultures, concerned only with ratings. If it helped bring Em back to me, to Sophie, it was worth it. But it didn't just bring the media, town folk had also made their way to us: some to help, some to be nosey, some wanting their fifteen minutes of fame. By the time the heat of the day had passed, Frances, John, Sophie and I were in the back garden, behind a lectern covered in an array of microphones. They said it would feel more personal if we were in the garden, and I didn't question it. We stood with the sun on our right-hand side. In front, and beyond the people now in my private patch of land, was the direction Em had gone. Despite it being after six, the sun still felt hot on the side of my face as I stood, shoulder to shoulder with Em's parents. When we were told they were ready, Frances stepped up and John joined her, his arm around her shoulder.

'I'm Frances Murphy, Emma Clarke's mother. Three nights ago, my daughter went missing. We don't know why, we don't know where she has gone. She left in the middle of the night, not taking any of her belongings with her; she climbed over the fence behind you all, and disappeared. She left her daughter, my grandchild, alone in the house. Emma is beautiful, kind, funny. She is a doting mother, a loving wife.'

Frances turned and looked at me, her eyes brimming. I nodded, encouraging her to continue.

'I want to thank everyone for helping so far — and Emma, if you are watching this, please, come home. You're not in trouble, you haven't done anything wrong. Come home and let us help you.'

A question shot out from the crowd; I couldn't see who asked.

'Are you saying Emma is unwell?'

'I . . .' Frances looked back at me again, and I nodded. It was OK to say she was struggling; finding her was more important than reputations. 'Yes, we think Emma is struggling with her mental health. She is at risk; she needs our help. Emma? It's OK, I know I've not always been the best mother when it comes to matters of the heart, but I am now. Come home, we miss you, your daughter misses you.'

It was too much for Frances and she started to cry into John who held her firm and guided her away from the cacophony of questions that followed. I gave Frances a hug and, with Sophie in my arms, stepped up to the microphones.

'I ummm.' I started, feeling lightheaded, sick. 'Em, come home, please come home.'

'Mr Clarke, why do you think your wife left?' A voice rang out from somewhere near the back of the crowd. I looked to find them and saw Cahill, Sinclair and a third man who I assumed was DI Keats standing at the back of the group. They didn't look pleased. I smiled to Cahill, thankful she was here. It showed she cared; her presence brought comfort. 'Mr Clarke, why did she leave?' the voice asked again.

'I don't know, I just need help to find her. To bring her home. Please, I just want her home, with me, with our baby. If anyone has any information about where Em is, please get in touch with the police.'

A reporter from near the back of the gathering, close to where Sinclair was stood, fired a question my way, one I was not prepared for. 'People are saying you did something to her. What do you say to that?'

'What?' I said. It was followed by a nervous laugh. The whole point of this circus was to find Em, not fuel nonsense fake news. 'No, no, of course I didn't.'

'Why are you laughing, Mr Clarke?'

'Because, ummm, I just want to find my wife,' I replied, but it was unlikely anyone heard as there was another explosion of questions and flashing bulbs, and as reporters tried to get closer for a better shot or voice note, the surge pushed down the lectern I was stood behind. One reporter came so close I worried Sophie would be crushed between our bodies. Frances looked at me, stunned, and began to cry once more, as did Sophie in my arms. I backed away from the lectern and, unsatisfied, the reporters began to press in more, pushing us backwards. I could hear them demanding for me to explain myself. They were so close, so loud, I could only focus on getting my baby out of the chaos, the stampede. A hand shot out and grabbed me and began to drag me back towards the house. Cameras were in my face, flashing bulbs blinding me, and as I was thrust into the kitchen, Frances and John following, I saw it was Cahill who had grabbed my arm. Once the door was closed, Frances slapped me across the face. 'What the hell are they saying, Robbie? Why would they say you did something?'

'Because people love gossip. She's left, that's all. The media are just being the media,' I said, my cheek stinging. 'We should have listened to Cahill.'

'Too right you should have,' Sinclair said as Cahill pulled Frances away. She spun into John who held her as she sobbed, her grief muffled in his shirt. He watched me over her head, the same question written all over his face. Sophie was distraught now, wailing in my arms. As Cahill went back out to calm the crowd and get them to leave my garden, I left the kitchen for the lounge and, sitting on the edge of the sofa, I calmed Sophie by singing and stroking her nose. Like I always had, faking to her that all was OK. It seemed to work. The door opened and John came in. Behind him, I saw Frances sat at a dining room chair with her head in her hands.

'Rob. Mind explaining what that was all about?'

I got to my feet, on the defence. 'I don't know, John, honestly, I don't.'

'Why would they say you've done something?'

'Because it sells papers? I didn't do anything, John.'

'I heard someone say that disappearances are usually connected with home life . . .'

He didn't finish his sentence, we both knew what he wanted to, and couldn't ask.

'John. This is me you're talking about. I love Em, I love her so much. I haven't done anything.'

I watched John soften, then he placed one of his wide hands on my shoulder. 'Of course, Kid, sorry, I lost my head for a bit. Tonight has been a complete shitshow.'

'Yeah,' I agreed, sitting down, feeling all of a sudden too exhausted to stand. 'But at least it will get people talking, and hopefully finding Em.'

'I hope you're right, Kid, I hope you're right.'

* * *

Emma

There's a saying, I'm paraphrasing now, but it's something like, 'On a long enough timeline, everyone's life expectancy reduces to zero.' I don't recall who said that, could be Shakespeare? Actually, when I think about it, I think it's from *Fight Club*. Regardless, the saying is true. Long enough time goes by, and we are all dead. We all know it, but we mostly choose to forget.

That line ran out for someone I loved.

My beautiful nana, the woman I turned to in my hour of need, the woman I used to go to as soon a school was done each day, just to tell her how it went. The woman I confided in when I was dumped by a boyfriend or failed an exam, is gone. It wasn't a shock: she was old, frail, suffering with dementia, but it doesn't make it any easier to bear. And it's made me realise, the last time I saw her was about two years ago. Just as she started to get unwell. After a lifetime of jabbering away to her, I didn't know how to speak anymore, I couldn't watch her forget things. I was scared. And now — now I wish I'd gone to see her at Christmas.

She didn't know about my life now, my boyfriend. And I'm ashamed of that.

We buried Nana on a wet Tuesday morning last week in that god-awful place between Christmas and New Year when days don't matter and everyone is fat, tired and fed up. In the same piece of land where my grandfather was buried twelve years before, up in the arse-end of nowhere, near where Mum and Dad live. A depressing bit of land that seems to suck the energy and life out of everything, and everyone around it.

I told Rob he didn't need to come. He hadn't met her and we both knew my parents weren't keen on him and would be fragile. It wasn't going to be a pleasant experience for any-one, but he told me he would go to the end of the world and back to be by my side. I could have argued the point, but he looked at me in a way that told me he really would travel to the end of the world. And when we got there, he hugged my parents, said he was sorry, and to my surprise, Dad asked if he would help bring her in, with him and four pallbearers. He probably asked out of necessity and Rob agreed, said he would be honoured. Rob, a man my family didn't approve of, carried my nana into church, because he knew how much she meant to me.

With what I have done. The mistakes I've made, how do I deserve someone like this? I've been such a shit person.

I was upset Nana had passed, but you know what really broke my heart? Nine people were there to say goodbye. Nine. Me, Rob, Mum, Dad. The vicar, and four people from the funeral service who helped carry her in. That was it. Eighty-six years on this earth and nine people came to say goodbye. One person for every nine and a half years she was alive.

She left me her necklace, the one she always wore, the one I'd always loved, and I don't deserve it. My nana, she was everything that was good in the world. Patient, kind, funny. Loyal. I hope part of her lives in the necklace and passes down her qualities. I hope I become someone better than I am.

Even now, writing this makes my heart ache, but it has made me think about life; what's really important. I'm in my late twenties now, and what have I got to show for it? What have I achieved? What is my legacy? I've questioned, if I were to die now, who would be at my funeral, who would mourn me?

CHAPTER EIGHT

June 22nd 2019
Four days missing

Rob

The night had been a rough one. The press didn't leave, but instead moved from the garden to the street out front, hoping to get something to follow up on the first news report. I'd watched it, the news, in the middle of the night when Sophie had woken for her night-time feed. At one point Em's picture filled the screen, the same one John and I had put up in town, and I felt relief that surely someone would come forward. However, the news didn't focus on her leaving, on her struggling, on her needing help. But on me and my press conference. I saw myself smile, I watched myself laugh nervously, and I knew how it looked. I knew what I'd think if I was on the outside looking in. After seeing it, I couldn't sleep. Instead, I moved nervously through my own home, expecting any moment that someone would come and take me away from my daughter. Thankfully, dawn broke, the sun rose and Sophie did too. We had a quiet morning together, playing, trying to be as normal as humanly possible. I dressed her in a cute, light blue Babygro with a giraffe on the front — Em's favourite — and gave her a bottle before winding her and laying her down for her mid-morning nap. And, for a while, I sat with her, singing quietly, her eyes on mine. I wondered how much she knew, how much she understood. I hoped none of it. I hoped her world was just about primal things: food, water, shelter, warmth, love. And I hoped it didn't matter to her future where those things came from. I hoped I was enough, for now at least. Thankfully, she settled before I could ask any more questions, and back in my room, our room, I grabbed the baby monitor from the bedside table. Outside, the small gathering of press and neighbours saw me by the window, and cameras raised to get a photo.

Vultures.

I made my way downstairs and waited for Frances and John to arrive. They were later than usual but, in the aftermath of the press gathering, I suspected they'd had a poor night's sleep too. Outside, people lingered. Waiting for more shocking revelations or statements. It hadn't been my intention to cause a storm the previous night, and I had no idea what to think next. But still, a thousand dark blue questions floated. And I needed answers. Waiting to be sure Sophie was asleep, I began to search the house. Hoping I'd find something that proved she was thinking of leaving, something I could show to the police, the media, and make them look where they should be looking — out there, not at me. Starting in the living room, I moved the sofa away from the wall, pulled off all the cushions, upended it, pushed my hand down the small cracks between the arm and base. I pulled out the drawers in the TV unit; quietly emptied the contents onto the floor. I don't know what I was looking for but I needed to look anyway. I needed something to tell me why my wife left, and where she'd gone. In the kitchen, I took everything out of the cupboards and stacked it all on the dining table. I pulled out the washing machine, the bin, the fridge freezer, despite knowing I'd not find anything there. I did it anyway, because in doing so I had some control. And, as expected, I found nothing.

By the time I heard a rolling wave of questions, indicating to me the Murphy's had arrived, it was too late to try and tidy enough to stop the raising of eyebrows. I stepped over upturned drawers, and around sofa cushions, and answered the door before they knocked. But it wasn't them, it was Cahill, and the man I had seen last night.

Oh God.

Behind them, bulbs flashed, capturing me peering from behind a half-closed door.

'Rob, can we come in?' Cahill asked.

I hesitated — it was only for a beat, but the man noticed. 'Yes, sorry yes,' I said, opening it wider so they could step across the threshold, and then I closed the door behind me.

'Sophie is asleep upstairs,' I said, hoping they would know to keep quiet, but I'm not sure they heard me. Both of them stared into the lounge in disbelief.

'I was trying to find anything that would help me understand why Em left,' I said, as way of defending the chaos. Knowing what it looked like. 'Maybe we should go into the kitchen?'

'Uh-huh,' said the man, considering me like I was an object, or a piece of art work on display.

Walking in, I moved crockery from the table to the side, so there was enough space to sit, and offered them both a drink. They declined. Sinclair wasn't with Cahill, and I was glad for it.

'Mr Clarke,' The man began. 'I am Detective Inspector Keats; I'm heading up the investigation into your wife's disappearance.'

I nodded and he continued.

'Wanna explain what your little stunt was about last night?'

'Stunt?!'

'My understanding is PC Cahill and PC Sinclair tried to warn you it would become a circus if you spoke out before we were ready. The hotline number has been ringing off the hook since.'

'Surely that's a good thing.'

'It would be, if it wasn't mostly time wasters. People claiming they've seen her in several places around the country. We've had three people talk of unexplained lights from the fields.'

'Well, are you following it up?'

'They claimed it was UFOs.'

'Look, I just want to find my wife.'

'Well, you haven't helped yourself.'

'What do you mean?'

'You don't read things online, do you?'

'I'm not sure if you've noticed, but I'm going out of my mind here worrying about my wife, as well as trying to look after a baby. So no, I haven't bloody well looked.'

'Mr Clarke—'

'So, get on with whatever you want to ask me, then get out and find my wife.'

'Rob, calm down,' Cahill said.

'Just, just find her, please.'

'We're trying. Believe me, we are. You need to help us.' Cahill said, and I believed her.

'I'd like to ask you some questions.' Keats said, taking over now Cahill had calmed me.

'Questions, sure, fire away,' I said, sounding more sarcastic than I intended.

'Hey, you need to calm down, Mr Clarke, and be cooperative'.'

'I *am* being cooperative!'

'You're also laughing when asked if you did something to your wife.'

He paused. 'There have been some pictures shared online, Rob. Pictures of you,' Cahill said quietly.

'What?'

'And some things have been said, not very kind things, trolls and the like. But the pictures raise eyebrows, and I just want you to help us make sense of what we're seeing.'

'Pictures? What pictures? I don't understand.'

Cahill pulled out her phone, unlocked it and handed it to me. As I took it, I caught Keats eye. He was watching my every move. Looking at the phone I saw a picture of me, a coffee in my hand, smiling, head turned up to the sun. I looked at peace, at ease. It took me a moment to realise it was taken when John and I were putting up the missing person posters in town.

'The café owner gave me a cup of coffee for free, I was grateful.'

'You sure?' Keats said. 'From here it looks like—'

'I can see what it looks like. Is there more?'

'One,' Cahill said, taking the phone back and scrolling along. When she handed it to me, I couldn't hide my shock. It was from when I climbed back into the garden from the field with Sophie in my arms.

'Wanna explain that one?' Keats asked.

'Sophie couldn't sleep, I was anxious, we went for a walk.'

'Into the field.'

'Yes, into the field.'

'The same field Em disappeared into.'

'Yes, the same field. I was trying to understand where she's gone.'

'Uh-huh,' Keats said.

'Is there something you want to ask me?'

'No, is there anything you want to tell me?' He replied.

Over the baby monitor, Sophie started to whinge. She was awake and wanted to be picked up.

'Rob,' continued Cahill, 'we are going to have more questions — your behaviour last night . . .'

'I was freaking out.'

'Well, it has made a lot of people point their fingers.'

'At me?'

'Should they be?'

'If I did something to her, why would I tell everyone? Why would I be trying to find her? My wife is ill, she needs our help. Why are we wasting time with this nonsense?'

'The night she disappeared — your neighbours have reported to PC Cahill that they heard a disagreement between you and Emma, can you tell me what you were arguing about?'

'I don't think I should talk to you without someone being present.'

'That answers that then,' Keats said, standing upright as if to leave.

'No, I just don't want things being taken out of context, that's all.'

'Uh-huh,' he said, for the third time.

Sophie's whinge became a cry, and I stood up to go and get her.

'My daughter needs me; you can show yourselves out.'

Not waiting for them to say anything else, I left the kitchen, went upstairs and picked up Sophie. I heard them talking as they left, and once the front door was closed, I held my daughter tight, and I cried.

Ten minutes after my cry, there was more noise outside and a knock at the door. Going into my bedroom, I looked out of the window, expecting to see the press on my doorstep trying to get a quote about Em's disappearance, or my innocence, but it wasn't them. They were there, but firing questions and taking photos of Frances and John.

'Rob?' John called out. 'Let us in.'

Downstairs, I opened the front door and Frances squeezed through, followed by John, who closed and locked it behind him.

'Bloody hell, they're like piranhas at a feeding frenzy.'

Frances would usually comment on John swearing in front of their granddaughter but she didn't; her mouth was agape as she stared into the living room. She didn't say anything, she didn't need to. As she took Sophie for a cuddle, I could see she was worried: about me, perhaps, but more likely she was worried for Sophie. Twice in a few days she'd come in and seen my house looking like it had been raided, and I knew what that must make me look like.

I expected her to want to talk about the state of the house, my dishevelled look, but it would have to wait. John and I were going out. The Murphy's had been busy. John knew the man who owned the field behind our house and he'd agreed we could search it. Word had got around, and people had come to help. Looking out of the living room window, I saw the crowd. I assumed they were all press as camera bulbs flashed again, but behind them, I saw lots more people without cameras, patiently waiting.

'What time are we doing this?' I asked, excited to be proactive, terrified by what that might mean.

'Now,' John replied, walking through to the kitchen. 'Frances will stay with Sophie.'

'John and I have been talking,' Frances said, bobbing Sophie in her arms.

'OK?'

'We think it might be a good idea if Sophie came to stay with us for a while.'

'What? No, Sophie stays with me.'

'You're going to be out all day, its cooler in our house and, well . . .' she looked around at the mess, the chaos.

'I need Sophie with me.'

'You need to sleep, you look terrible. Let us help? I brought up two children of my own — it was tough, but I can't imagine how much tougher this is. I just thought, under the circumstances, it would help you?'

'Do you and John think I can't parent my own child?'

'Rob. Come on, it's not that at all. You need a break,' John said quietly.

'I need Em back.'

'And we'll find her.'

'And I need my daughter.'

'And you have her. Look, you need some rest, how about she comes and stays with us for one night, she'll have a great time.'

I hated the idea of the house being completely empty — no wife, no daughter — but they were right. I was burnt out,

67

and Sophie would see it. I nodded, and John patted me on the shoulder.

'I'll go pack her bags,' I said, defeated.

Tears filmed my eyes the entire time I collected the clothes, nappies, bottles and toys into a small suitcase.

John and I helped Frances and Sophie to their car, warding off people trying to take photographs and ask us questions. And once they had pulled away, escaping the chaos, the noise, I knew Frances was right. Sophie didn't need this.

With my daughter gone and my responsibility for looking after her gone with it, I turned my attention to the back fields, where John's friends — old farmers and their families — were beginning to congregate.

'John, what if we find something . . .'

'I don't know, my boy, I don't know.'

I greeted each and every person who had come out: some returned the greeting with a warm smile, sympathetic, and some with a look of suspicion. I didn't care what they thought, or what their motivations were for being there. They were helping, so I thanked them anyway.

As we donned high-vis vests, John gave out simple instructions to the group.

'I don't profess to be an expert in this. So we'll keep it easy. Let's take our time, walk in a line, and if anyone spots something, call out and raise a hand, so we can see you. If you start on the left of the line, stay left, right, stay right, make it easy to find one another out there. And Derek,' John said, looking at the oldest member of the party, the owner of the land we were going to search, 'thank you for letting us do this. And to be clear. We know what's being said in the papers. None of it's true.'

They all looked to me, and I simply said that I didn't hurt my wife. That she just left. That she needed our help. It seemed to be enough for Derek, who nodded, saying he didn't know me, but trusted John.

We climbed the fence into the field and, keeping a line as best we could, as John said, we began to walk out into the vast nothingness. The corn was thick and tall, and within minutes I couldn't see most of the group, only the bending of corn ears as they pushed through. For hours we trudged, the sun melting our brains, searching for a clue to what happened, a clue I hoped we would and wouldn't find in equal measure. The ground, hot and uneven, made progress slow. We stumbled and sweated, and as the afternoon drew on, we began to wane. I heard a few talk about what they would give for a good downpour. I wished for one too.

There were around fifteen of us on the search, plus a few reporters, taking photos, asking who people were. At first I wanted them gone, but they were being respectful, learning about Em from people who knew her. I didn't mind. It all helped, and I listened in to stories of Em as a little girl. Stories of her as a teenager. The trouble she caused, the things she did. She was a rebel, a wild child who cared little for rules or consequence. I was seeing a side to her I didn't know. A side I didn't think existed. Em was none of those things now — but then again, the Em I knew wouldn't leave in the middle of the night without explanation. The Em I knew wouldn't abandon her daughter. And when people spoke, they looked at me with pity. Like they always knew she would do such a thing. I had to ask myself, who was the woman I married? Who was she really?

Over several hours, the fifteen of us managed to cover a patch of field that stretched two, maybe three miles, and found nothing. Coming back in, we veered off route to cover more land, John and I on the far left edge of the line. Less than half a mile from the house, we hit the bank of the reservoir. I climbed the slight mound, sat down at the top and had a drink of water. John sat beside me and, for a moment, we looked out towards the house.

'John, I gotta ask. The papers mentioned Em's past — is there something more than teenage mischief? Is there anything I should know?'

John didn't answer right away. Eventually, he shook his head.

'Em was a bit of a wild child. She struggled.'

I considered him. Maybe he didn't know everything about his daughter, in the same way I didn't know everything about my wife. But someone might, someone from this town, someone who knew Em when she was young. A friend, an ex, perhaps.

Back at the house, I made everyone who'd helped on the search a cold drink — water, juice, a few opting for a beer when offered. And after they left, I hugged John, told him I'd call later to say goodnight to Sophie, and went back into the chaos of my house.

The sun dipped below the horizon, the night took hold and with it the silence of being the only person in a home that should have housed three. I missed Em. And taking out my phone I called her mobile, just to hear her voice as the voicemail kicked in.

I called Frances, spoke to Sophie and said goodnight and, grabbing a beer, I sat in the back garden. I stared at that same bit of fence where Em climbed over, and I drank.

Someone knew something; someone knew where my wife was. I just had to find out who.

* * *

March 30th 2018

Emma

I'm such a fucking mess. Such a fucking, fucking mess. To the outside world looking in, this entry should be happy and positive. To the outside world, I am recently engaged to be married. My doughy boy got down on one knee and asked me to be his wife, and I said yes, without hesitation. Everything is on the up, right?

Rob proposed two weeks ago, and while he's stayed in a giddy, only-looking-forward state of mind, I've slipped back;

become reflective. In part, it's necessary to understand how life has unfolded, to put yourself in a position of perhaps being truly happy in future. And right now I'd love to be able to say I did just that: thought reflectively, had a private smile to bygone days.

But you didn't, did you, Em? You had to call your ex. You had to see him one last time. Perhaps to test yourself, have some final closure? Who knows; I certainly don't.

Why can't you just be fucking loyal?

Could it be that, subconsciously, I know I'm no good for Rob, as Steve once told me? That he deserves someone better; the person he thinks I am? Or am I just self-destructive? I told Rob I was meeting Jen for a celebratory drink. I used his proposal, our engagement, to sneak out and back to Steve. I intended to just chat, drink, explain I was now getting married, in the hope we would both let each other go. I intended to tell him I'd seen him around, that I didn't want him turning up at my workplace anymore. I was going to challenge him on being outside our flat. I was going to be firm. But it didn't happen that way. We barely spoke. It was, perhaps, a physical goodbye. Perhaps part of me was afraid of what I'd just committed to, and hoped to be caught, to force my hand, to make it all fall apart, just like my life tended to. Falling apart was what I knew, what I'd come to understand. Rob offered something else. Steve and I, we were always so sexually compatible . . . I hope I'm wrong and it was just a moment to say goodbye to that. I hope I don't go back again. I don't know what Rob would do if he ever found out — and, worse, I can't help but think that one day I'll do something stupid and mess it up for good. It's time to step up, Em, be a better person.

So, yay, I'm getting married.

CHAPTER NINE

June 23rd 2019
Five days missing

Rob

Waking on Sophie's floor, I got up and looked for her. Of course, she was at her grandparents', but it didn't stop the terror flooding in for that brief moment, half asleep, when I didn't recall. Her empty cot, my tired mind, it drew a conclusion that wasn't true. I was barely coping with the gut feeling that someone took Em; I'd die if someone took Sophie. I'd die painfully, like someone was pulling my heart out of my throat. I checked the time, 4.57 a.m. I almost called Frances to make sure everything was OK, but stopped myself. Panic checking wouldn't show I was coping, and I needed to cope. For my daughter. I stretched and looked out of the window. Dawn had arrived, the sky a magnificent pink. It was going to be hot again; too hot. In the distance I could make out a person, the same dog walker I'd seen a few times now. I watched them until they disappeared.

Knowing I wouldn't go back to sleep despite only grabbing a few hours, I went downstairs, made myself a coffee and began to tidy the house. I hoped in doing so I'd find some-thing I'd overlooked. But as the hours passed I found nothing. Needing company, I put the TV on and worked with it in the background and, at 8 a.m., I was shocked to hear my wife's name spoken by a reporter on the morning news.

'And what of thirty-year-old mother of one, Emma Clarke . . .'

Dropping the cushion I'd been replacing on the upright sofa, I scrambled to find the remote and turned it up.

'. . . police are still baffled as to where she has gone, but speculation is wrapped around the house where she lived, as investigators try to discover what really happened. We have been told there is a suspect in this investigation but, as yet, no arrests have been made. The question remains: where did doting mother, Emma Clarke, go?'

'There are no suspects, she had a mental-health crisis and fucking left me!' I screamed as I threw the remote at the TV, cracking the screen, distorting the morning news reporter's face. People would be watching this and the question would fuel speculation; more wild stories of something other than the truth. I needed to tell them otherwise, or else people wouldn't look for her, they'd continue to look at me instead. I ran upstairs, showered and dressed — I needed to be in town, talking to people, making them see what was true.

It took me thirty minutes to get into the town centre and, despite it only being just after nine, sweat stained my armpits.

I couldn't help but feel, as I walked in, that people were staring at me. I guess news rarely happened in a place like this, and a place like this was one where news travelled fast. I tried to smile at people: some returned a smile, some didn't.

It reminded me of what my dad said to me once, when the medication was strong and his filter for how he should talk to his little boy well numbed: opinions are like arseholes . . .

I decided to start at the coffee shop where the kind owner gave me a coffee on the first day Em was missing — it was only four days ago, but it felt a lot longer. As I stepped inside, she was one of those who smiled.

'Morning, can I grab a flat white please?'

'Of course.'

'I'm not sure if you remember me but . . .'

'I remember. You're the husband of that missing woman.'

'I am. Can I ask a question?'

'Of course,' she said again.

'Have you lived in the area for long?'

'All my life. I've had this place for, what, twenty years now? It wasn't a coffee shop back when I opened; they weren't as popular then, it was a greasy spoon, you know, all day fry ups.' she said, grinding coffee.

'Did you know Emma, as a kid?'

'I knew most of the kids from back then; a lot of them hung out here after school. But I didn't know her to speak to, only she was one of a group who popped in from time to time.'

'I see.'

'Sorry, I know that doesn't help.'

She finished making my coffee and handed it to me. I took out my bank card to pay, but she refused; it was on the house, again.

'Thank you. I'm trying to find people who knew Em — friends, boyfriends, that sort of thing.'

She nodded, grabbed a piece of paper and a pen, and wrote down a name and address. 'If anyone asks, I didn't give you this, OK?'

'Of course.' I looked at the name, Melanie Timpson. 'Who is she?'

'She and Emma were friends as kids. I know her address — well, her parents' address — they used to be regulars here.'

'But not now?'

'No, we lost touch a few years back. Melanie's mum died, her dad drifted away, as so many do. He is still there, though — if Melanie isn't, he might be able to tell you where she is.'

'Thank you.'

74

'Don't thank me yet, it might not help.'

'But it might. Someone has to know where my wife has gone. And Christ knows I need to do something.'

'Well, I hope Melanie can shed some light.'

'Me too.'

Outside I found a bench near a children's park, opened Google Maps and punched in the address: it was just a fifteen-minute walk away. By the time I'd finished my coffee I had worked out what I was going to say, and I left, my phone guiding me to Melanie Timpson's home.

The house was outside town, up a narrow, single-track lane with no footpath on either side. Very few cars passed, but those that did passed quickly, forcing me to walk in the long, dry grass. When I found the address, I hesitated: it was a hundred feet back from the lane, and isolated. Large iron gates covered the front drive, and beyond the gates sat several rusted old cars, covered in dead moss and long grass, and a battered caravan with several windows missing. The house beyond wasn't faring much better: paint-stripped window frames and a roof with several broken tiles, like teeth in an aged boxer. A willow tree swung in the breeze, tired from the relentless heat. Not finding a bell or intercom, I tried opening the gate. It was unlocked and as it swung, rust grinding on rust, it alerted a huge dog who charged from behind the old tree, barking. I grabbed the gate and closed it again, just in time. The dog, a beast of a Rottweiler, jumped into it, knocking me to the ground. Its teeth bared as it snarled, foam dripping from the corner of its mouth. Getting to my feet I backed away, hoping to God the gate didn't fall down, as it looked like it might. Behind me, a car beeped its horn. I hadn't heard it approaching and I jumped, turned, raised my hand in apology and stepped out of its way. The car, a beaten up old Jeep Cherokee, turned into the drive, and a man in his seventies climbed out.

'Shut up, Harry,' he said to the dog, his voice gruff like he'd smoked a thousand cigarettes. He wore a shirt, open but for one straining button mid-way down, showing his dark old skin, as thick as a rhino's. Matted grey chest hair. As he turned his attention to me, his breathing laboured, he looked at me like I was a piece of shit. Like he wanted to hit me just for being near his house. 'Who are you?' he said, reaching back into his Jeep. I thought he was going to pull out a bat or crowbar and I backed away, looking around and realising I was completely alone, besides him and his murderous dog. But he didn't grab anything to hurt me with, just a cigarette that he lit. 'Well, who are you? What do you want?'

'My name is Rob, Rob Clarke.' I paused a beat, waiting to see if my name caused a reaction, it didn't. 'Is Melanie around at all?'

'Why do you want to know?'

'She was friends with my wife. I wanted to ask her a few things about their friendship growing up.'

'Uh-huh.'

I couldn't help noticing the same distrust as there was with Sinclair, and more recently, Keats. It was just the way some were up here.

'Is she around?'

'She don't live here no more.'

'Is she close by?'

'Why do you wanna know about their friendship?'

'My wife, she's gone missing. You might have seen it on the news.'

'I don't watch the news.'

'I see. She disappeared five nights ago. I'm trying to find out why. Her name is Emma, she would have been Emma Murphy back then. Do you remember the name?'

Something flashed across his weather-beaten face; anger, perhaps.

'Yeah, I remember that name,' he said, taking a long drag on his cigarette.

'I'd really like to talk to Melanie about her.'

'Mel ain't here.'

'Could I ask where she is? It will really help.'

'You want help, you ain't getting it from me. That Emma of yours, she was a good-for-nothing shit who got my girl into a whole world of trouble. I ain't surprised she's gone, I hope she never comes back.'

'Mr Timpson, that's my wife you're—'

'I don't care if she's the Queen of England. I hope wherever she is, she's miserable for it.'

'But—'

'I suggest you go, before I open that gate and set Harry on you.'

'Mr Timpson, if Emma did something wrong, I need to know.'

'I ain't telling you again.'

The old man limped over to the gate and put his hand on the latch. He told his dog to stay and opened it. I took a step back.

'Walk away, before I tell him to A. T. T. A. C. K.'

He sounded out the letters so the dog wouldn't know what he was saying and, because he did that, I took the threat seriously. Raising my hands in defence, I backed away, turned and walked quickly down the lane, not daring to look over my shoulder until I was closer to the main road. Once I did, the old man and the car were gone.

CHAPTER TEN

The walk back was tough. Melanie's father's reaction to Em was one of hatred; loathing. Em did something to get his girl into trouble, and his reaction to hearing her name, his threat to set his dog on me . . . I needed to know what had happened, in case it helped me find my wife. Perhaps coming back here stirred up old things, perhaps she ran because she couldn't face what she did when she was young. Perhaps I wasn't a bad husband after all?

I found Melanie on Facebook. Her account was private so I added her as a friend, hoping she'd accept. I was so engrossed in trying to see something of hers online, searching Instagram and Twitter, that I nearly walked into a man approaching on the footpath. It wasn't until I reacted to avoid colliding with him that I realised it was PC Sinclair.

'Out for a morning walk?' he asked.

'Trying to find out anything that might help. Something I see you're not doing?'

'Yeah, I heard you were in town, bothering the locals.'

'Bothering them? What's your problem?'

'No problem, what's yours?'

'My wife is missing!'

'And instead of being at home you're out, getting coffee, harassing people at their homes.'

'What?'

'Mr Timpson called in just now, said you turned up, uninvited, tried to force him to give you details about his daughter's friendship with your wife.'

'Force him? He nearly set his dog on me.'

Sinclair smiled. 'Yeah, Harry's a mean old dog for sure. Why were you asking questions?'

'I'm trying to find out something that will help me find my wife.'

'Uh-huh,' he said.

I'd had just about enough of his snide comments and sideways looks.

'If you wanna ask me something, go ahead and ask.'

'No, not yet.'

'Well then, get out of my way.' I went to walk past him but he stepped across and forced his shoulder into mine, like a childhood bully in the school corridor.

'What's your problem, Sinclair?'

I tried to walk again, and again he shoved me. I wanted to shove him back, maybe even swing and knock that smirk off his face, but people were watching, and although he wasn't in uniform, everyone knew he was a police officer. So I bit my tongue, lowered my head and walked by and continued on my way home, my blood boiling hotter than the Tarmac melting under my feet. As I walked I replayed the conversation with Sinclair in my head, dozens of times. In my mind I responded differently. I was more articulate, braver; I told Sinclair I wasn't going to be bullied by him. I even imagined him trying to hit me, but I dodged and took him to the floor. His arm twisted behind his back. And I whispered for him to back down. He agreed, of course, as it was all in my mind.

I got home at a few minutes past twelve. Frances and John were on the drive. John climbed out first, and making sure it was all right, I opened the back door and scooped up my daughter. She smiled and grabbed my face, happy to see me, and all of that anger, all of that resentment, all of the uncertainty, just faded.

The Murphy's stayed with us for an hour or so, then left. They were organising a vigil for Em, right in the town centre, to draw everyone out, and then, with an army of people, we would search again. Frances talked of speeches, prayers, candles and hope. She'd created a Facebook event for it, stating it would be at nine tonight, at the tower clock in the middle of the High Street and hundreds had liked or commented on it. Lots of them sharing stories about my wonderful wife. Frances agreed she would take Sophie again so I could go out searching too. That gave me a few hours, just me and Sophie. Once John backed out the drive and the front door was shut, I set out all of Sophie's favourite toys in the living room: her stacking cups, her activity mat, her noisy, bangy toys. We read books, we crawled over the floor together, I blew raspberries on her tummy after changing her nappy. It felt like a good day, a normal day, and I half expected Em to come down the stairs at any moment.

You two. I can hear you laughing from the bedroom.

Just having fun.

I swear, sometimes I wonder how I had one baby, but ended up with two kids.

Well, if you can't beat them.

I couldn't agree more.

She'd smile and join us on the floor, playing, laughing — any moment now, any moment. I watched the stairs with one eye, expectantly, even though I knew Em walking down couldn't possibly happen.

At just after three Sophie went for her afternoon nap. The heat made her cranky, so I set up a fan in her room with a cold cloth over it, so it blew cool, moist air into the room. It did the trick, and within ten minutes she was sound asleep. Then the house felt too silent. The clock ticked louder than before; the house creaked ominously. To try and stave off the pressing feeling, I cleaned, put a load in the washing machine, and had a cup of coffee leant on the kitchen side, while scrolling through the nonsense on Facebook. I had joined the *Ramsey Informer* Facebook page, hoping something about Em being found would pop up. Nothing. But Frances' vigil page had come to life. The page had the same picture of Em, the one I had cropped myself out of, her smile beaming unapologetically. Frances had been busy: hundreds said they were attending, and she thanked each and every one of them individually. Some asked whether I was going to be there. I didn't know why that was important, but Frances answered that Emma's entire family would be there. I read some of the posts. Some were unkind, stating that disappearances didn't just happen, and nine times out of ten it was linked to someone from the home. But most were speaking of hope, of determination, and I couldn't help but feel that tonight would be positive. We could find her; I could feel it in my gut. Closing Facebook, I drank my coffee and found myself staring at the back fence again, the last place Em was known to be.

There was a knock at the front door, and the familiar leap in my chest. It might be Em, coming home, too ashamed to use her keys to let herself back in.

'Coming,' I said, trying to keep my voice level. If it was her, she would no doubt be fragile — I needed to be cool, calm, in control. I took a deep breath and opened the door.

'Mr Clarke,' said PC Cahill.

'Oh, hi,' I replied, unable to hide my disappointment, which was replaced quickly with a strange feeling deep in my gut, one that became the feeling of fear. Cahill and I had chatted a few times, we were on familiar terms. She called me Rob. The fact that she was now calling me Mr Clarke again said something was going on. Something new. Under her arm was a folder; my eye was drawn to it.

'What's happened?'

'May I come inside?'

'What's this about?'

'Rob, we need to chat.'

I nodded and stepped to one side so Cahill could come in. She closed the door behind her and waited for me to lead her to the lounge. 'No PC Sinclair today?'

'No, not today,' she replied, noting my anger.

'And what about Detective Keats.'

'No, Rob, it's just me.' she said, really focusing on holding my gaze. The intensity told me she was about to tell me something new.

'We've checked her phone records, her credit cards. Her bank account and Facebook account.'

'And?' I said, shifting nervously.

'Her bank account was accessed yesterday.'

'Yesterday? Why didn't someone tell me?'

'We were hoping to find her through the ATM's CCTV.'

'And did you?'

'Yes, we believe it was her.'

'Where was it?'

'Newhaven.'

'Newhaven? What the hell is she doing down there?' I asked, rhetorically. 'How much money did she take out?'

'Everything she could.'

'Are you sure it was her?'

PC Cahill reached into her folder and pulled out a print-off from the CCTV camera. There was no mistaking it — it was Em. Her head was down, looking at the keypad, but she was wearing a red dress I knew was hers. I hadn't noticed it was missing, but I was sure I'd not seen it in the searches since. Over her shoulder was her rucksack. There was no denying it. I couldn't see her face, but I was looking at my wife. Cahill tried to say something but I wasn't listening — I needed to know for sure it was her. I ran upstairs, two at a time, opened Em's wardrobe and looked inside. Swiping at her clothes I looked for the dress. It was usually tucked in a corner, so it didn't get creased when other things were hung and removed. It was gone. I pulled out all of her clothes and threw them on the bed — most things were there, but the red dress I loved was nowhere to be seen. I tried to process what else could be missing — perhaps some jeans. Some underwear and socks. I didn't like what it told me. I went through her favourite books on the shelf above our bed; a few were missing and I'd not noticed. Slowly, I left the bedroom and made my way back downstairs, unable to fully process what I was thinking or feeling. I didn't want to draw a conclusion — but really, what else was there? Em hadn't had a mental-health crisis around being a mother, or something from her past.

Em had planned to leave.

'Rob?' Cahill said coming up the stairs, stopping mid-way.

'It's her,' I said quietly, leaning against the wall, fearing I might fall when the realisation fully sunk in. 'What else do you know?' I asked, unable to look at her.

Cahill cleared her throat, indicating that whatever it was, it was bad, and I took a deep breath to prepare myself. 'We picked up an exchange through Facebook Messenger between her and a man called Steve Burton. Do you know anyone by that name?' Cahill continued sympathetically.

'No.'

'Are you sure?'

'Yes, I'm sure. I don't know anyone by that name. What did the conversation say?'

PC Cahill hesitated. 'It spoke of them running away together.'

'What?' I said, hoping I'd misheard.

'I'm so sorry, Rob.'

I didn't reply, but covered my mouth with my hands, rubbing the five-day-old stubble that was sharp on my palm.

'We also found proof of two tickets for a ferry across to Dieppe in France, in both their names.'

I didn't reply but took a deep, shaky breath and nodded.

'Rob, if anyone can . . .'

'Thank you, PC Cahill,' I said, lifting my head up high, pushing down all of my grief and anger and shame and rage. I

83

had worried for Em, pleaded to a God I didn't fucking believe in for her to be OK. I had forgiven her for leaving and willed my own soul to be strong enough to help her when she came back.

'There is a vigil, tonight for Em, I . . .' I stopped, choking on my own words.

'We can stop it if you like?'

'No, no, I'll do it,' I eventually said.

'Of course. Rob, I'm so sorry.'

I nodded and looked back from my bedroom doorway into Sophie's room. She was sound asleep still, oblivious to the truth that her mummy deserted her — not through mental health, not through struggle, but because she was lusting for someone else. Cahill offered her apologies again and headed for the front door. Telling me before leaving that if I needed anything, just to call her. I didn't bother following to show her out. Back in our — no, my — bedroom, I went to the bottom draw beside the bed. Em and I kept our passports right at the back. Moving old phone chargers, bookmarks and keys, I pulled out the envelope they sat in. Mine was there, Em's wasn't.

I was wrong. Nothing happened to Em. She just left. She *could* leave her daughter alone. She did. And despite knowing I couldn't stop loving Em, I would never forgive her for what she had done.

* * *

July 1st 2018

Emma

I've not written anything in this in a long time. After my last entry (which I've just read again and felt sick for it), I've focused on trying to do exactly what I said I would, be a better person. So, I've thrown myself into the idea. I like where it's taken me. I feel like I'm becoming someone new, someone

84

better. I don't message Steve anymore. I'm focused on Rob and me. It's tough, to feel like I can trust myself with him, and I still wobble from time to time, doubting I can see the transformation through in me. My track record isn't good, but does that mean it can't change? Become a woman who is settled, happy, secure? For the most part, I feel solid with Rob, but when I do wobble, usually late at night when he's sound asleep beside me, I think that I must leave him. Because, one day, I'll just fuck it up anyway. I nearly called it off, three times, but by morning, I couldn't. I love him and, despite the worry, I'm too selfish.

And I'm glad I didn't do anything stupid, because — and this is the point of this entry — Rob and I are having a baby. And knowing I have a life growing inside me changes everything. The old Em, she doesn't exist anymore.

Rob and I have been planning our wedding for a while now, aiming for late summer, but I needed to be his wife before we announced our pregnancy; before I started to show. I didn't want anyone to think we were marrying for that reason alone. I wanted to be someone who did something right for a change, so we ran away to Gretna Green and did it, him in a suit, me in a cream dress (there is NO WAY I could wear white). I was never one for a full-blown wedding, the church, flowers, organist — it's not me. I think Rob liked the idea of something traditional, but he wouldn't say. I hope he doesn't regret our decision.

Marrying Rob feels right and wrong at the same time. Right because I love him, I do. Wrong because I know who I am, deep inside, and I'm terrified I'll let him down. Let *them* down. Them. Not just one life to ruin, but two.

I guess some parts of me want to do things the right way. Go you, Em.

It's funny to think (well, maybe not funny, sad perhaps) that my last entry in this book was only a few months ago, a few short, short months. Since then I've nearly backed away, got married instead, and am now with child, (as poor Nana would say).

Writing that down terrifies me — there is now so much to lose.

Recently, when I'm lying awake at night, Rob, my husband asleep, carefree and content, I can feel our baby moving inside me. Not a kick, more like a roll, like something tiny is turning over. I shouldn't, I know, but I can't help but think of that old Sigourney Weaver film, *Alien*. It's horrific to think a tiny person might burst out of me like in that film, though I'd never say it out loud. Not even to Rob — does that count as another dirty secret? I don't know anymore.

I haven't thought too much about whether it's a boy or girl, I'm trying not to get ahead of myself. Mum had three miscarriages before I arrived. I don't want to get too attached. Despite Rob knowing my mum's history, he can't help himself. He's started a list of potential names, a column if it's a boy, and one if it's a girl, and when he thinks I'm asleep he speaks to it, tells it he's its daddy and he loves it. I swear, that man.

Although I'm not letting myself get carried away, not like Rob, I have caught myself thinking about whether or not our one-bed flat in Clapham is the right kind of place to raise a child. There's nothing wrong with it, but it's a far cry from the childhood I remember: space, clean air, a garden to play in. I wonder what Rob would say if I mentioned us moving — if, you know, all goes well, and the time comes?

I also keep thinking about moving for selfish reasons (again). Besides the fact that I could start my family somewhere safer, quieter, it would also remove me from the temptations I fall prey to every time. Namely, Steve. Who arrived at my work last week, out of the blue, and invited me for lunch. I said I was busy, I didn't want to see him, I didn't want to see him ever again. But he threatened to tell Rob about us, and left me no choice.

I'm going to be a mother — I need to find a way to leave that part of my life behind for good.

No more fuck-ups, Em, because you're in something much bigger now.

CHAPTER ELEVEN

Rob

Frances was true to her word, and her efforts meant that, as I approached the town centre still reeling from what I'd learnt, it was packed full of people, out to support us in our hour of need. Sophie was asleep in her buggy, and as I made my way through the throng, some patted me on the back, some nodded, some scowled. People were talking to me, but I couldn't process what was being said. All I could hear was Cahill's voice, telling me Em left with another man.

After Cahill had left, I rang Frances and tried to explain what had happened. But she was short with me, stressed, busy, and I couldn't find the words to say that Em had abandoned us all. She hung up before I could try. It left me no choice but to come out and tell everyone and stop a needless search. Besides, people were giving up their time to help a stranger; they needed the truth. There's that Bible quote, the truth will set you free. I'm not a religious man, but I hoped it was true. I hoped I could tell the truth to all these people, and Sophie and I would be free for it. Even if I don't understand what being free is anymore. Being free used to be about working hard to provide for my wife and daughter. Being free was coming home to a quiet house as both of the people I loved the most slept. Free is a cuddle in the morning and a kiss before falling asleep. Free is feeling safe in the knowledge that my life won't change much from one day to the next. All that is gone, but I had to hope I'd not be a prisoner for it.

By the time I reached Frances and John, who were stood on the raised steps under the town clock, a portable amp and microphone beside them, Sophie was awake again. The noise and bustle of people had stirred her. I lifted her out of her buggy and tried to drag it up the steps to join Frances and John. Frances stepped forward to take Sophie, but I said I wanted to hang onto her. I needed to. Em slipped through my arms; I couldn't cope if Sophie did too.

The town clock struck nine, and as it tolled, the crowds fell silent, a prayer for Em. Heads lowered, faces caught by a hundred candles, like a Christmas glow. It was moving, despite what I knew. People cared. Em mattered to them. Sophie stopped crying and I bobbed her, looking out at the sea of heads bowed down in prayer. I heard a cough from somewhere in the crowd, and looking towards it I came eye to eye with Sinclair; no uniform, off duty. He stared at me unblinking until Frances picked up the microphone and spoke.

'Thank you for coming this evening. Five days ago, our beloved daughter Emma disappeared. She took only her trainers, a few items in a bag and her dressing gown. She might be unwell, struggling to cope with being a new parent; there is no shame in that. We just don't know where she is. What we do know is that five days is too long to be left with these questions. I hope our prayers can be answered tonight, and we find Emma and bring her home.'

Frances stepped back, patted her eyes with a tissue and, in the crowd, people nodded their heads. Some wiped tears away from their eyes too, and I could see in them a determination. A readiness to find one of their own, whatever the cost. John looked at me, indicating I should say a few words. I wanted to tell them first, before the truth was known by all, but I couldn't wait. The crowds would soon go out looking for her — some were already twitching, checking torches, tightening rucksacks. They wanted to search, but it was a search that I knew would reveal nothing. Em did climb the fence and walk into the Fens, but she wasn't alone in doing so. She met with someone called Steve Burton, and they went away. Em was the one who did wrong, and I was feeling guilty for it. I took the microphone from Frances and held it up to my mouth, creating feedback.

'I want to start by saying thank you.' My voice echoed off the walls in the narrow town centre. 'These past few days have been the most difficult of our lives. Em's disappearance has been both terrifying and upsetting beyond words. And the fact so many of you have come out tonight, it brings me hope.'

A few people clapped from the back of the crowd, but I didn't look for them. I couldn't. 'But this evening I found out something I think you all need to know.' I lowered the microphone and turned to Frances and John. They looked to one another, concerned. Taking a deep breath, I lifted the microphone again.

'PC Cahill, who has been working on Em's disappeared since that first night discovered something today.'

The crowd waited silently for me to continue.

'And I want to say again, thank you for coming out, but we won't need to search for Em anymore.'

'Have the police found her? Is she OK?' A voice shot out.

'Nothing bad has happened to Em, she isn't having a mental-health crisis. She—'

My voice snagged. 'My wife just left.'

Tears filmed in my eyes, and as I blinked, one fell onto Sophie. 'Em decided she didn't want to have this life anymore. She has moved away, with someone else. She didn't want us. Thank you for . . .' I couldn't finish my sentence; my words snagged in my throat once more. Putting my head down, shielding Sophie, I pushed my way through the crowd, deflecting the many questions people had. Some were angry ones, demanding I told them more, but I couldn't, I just couldn't. Forgetting the buggy I walked quickly, managed to escape the crush of people, and got home as fast as I could. And once I was back, I gave Sophie her bottle, changed her bum, read her a story like I would any other day, and laid her in her cot for the night.

Once she was settled, I lay on her bedroom floor, and I cried until I'd shed a lifetime of tears.

PART 2:
ME

CHAPTER TWELVE

July 3rd 2019
Fifteen days missing

For the sake of my daughter, I don't look back.

But today it's impossible not to think about the life we once had because, six months ago, at seven minutes past seven in the morning, Sophie was born. Which means we were likely moving from delivery to theatre for the emergency C-section that was needed. Em had to sign forms, consenting to the Caesarean they were about to do. They threw numbers, like one in a hundred and fifty thousand chance that Em could be paralysed by the spinal block, one in a hundred chance that Sophie would suffer a laceration caused by the scalpel, but she didn't care, she was too tired after hour upon hour of pushing with no results. I remember how scared we both were, how I sat holding her hands as the needle went into her back, paralysing her from the waist down. How her hands shook when she was lowered onto the table and a screen was erected just below her chest. It happened so fast, recalling any of it in detail is difficult. Everything is fuzzy, right up to the moment when the most incredible sound I'd ever heard rang through the operating theatre. The sound of my daughter crying out. Until the day I die, I will never forget that moment. Every detail is crystal clear in a sea of foggy recollection. Sophie was whisked into another room and I felt torn — Em needed me, she was still around forty minutes from being fully stitched up, but Sophie — I needed to be with Sophie. I'd never felt a draw like it before; it was something bigger than me, bigger than anything I'd felt in my life. The love like a sonic boom in my chest.

'Go to her, don't let her out of your sight,' Em said, the spinal block making her shake so much her teeth chattered. I did as I was told and stepped into the adjoining room where Sophie had been laid on a small, warm table to be checked over. I tried to ask if she was OK, if my daughter was all right, but the words didn't form as I burst into tears. She was the most amazing thing I had ever seen. Her tiny hands, too perfect to be human, her little legs, curled under herself like she was still in the womb, filled my heart beyond capacity until I was drowning in the glow of her soul. Once she was given the all-clear, she was swaddled and placed in my arms. The responsibility almost felt too much as I walked back, slowly placing one foot down before I dared pick up the other, into the theatre to join Em. And then, I introduced her to our baby.

'Is she all right?' Em asked, tears flooding down her cheeks too.

'She's perfect. You did it, Em. You did it.'

Thinking of that morning hurt. It used to be something Em and I shared every now and then, our amazing story of how two became three. Unique and personal to us alone. I still didn't understand how a mother who loved so hard back then could just get up and leave. But I shook it off before the thought became yet another unanswerable question. For the sake of my mental health, I knew I had to accept what I couldn't change, like it says in the first part of the serenity prayer, I was also trying to be brave and change what I could.

But, I wasn't sure I could always tell the difference between the two.

Despite how hard it had been recently, how low I felt at times, we were together, the two of us, finding our own rhythm. I sometimes suspected that Sophie missed Em — a longing for something she couldn't quite understand. This time in six months, on her first birthday, Sophie wouldn't remember her at all. It was a sad realisation, but also necessary, for the sake of us both. In the days after I discovered the truth about my wife, I looked for Steve; I wanted to know more about the man who'd robbed me of my life. But it was like looking for a needle in a flaming haystack. I thought he'd be on Em's Facebook friends list. He wasn't. And yet they had spoken, the police had told me as much. It didn't make any sense. A few days of being able to do little else but try and work out how to find him left me scarred and I had to stop — again, for the sake of my daughter, for the sake of us both. The haystack had left me burnt.

A half birthday isn't something people usually celebrate, but I thought for our broken family it should be. Frances and John agreed. A celebration was what we all needed, Sophie too. I walked into the living room and showed Sophie a small pile of wrapped gifts for her, the paper bright and covered with pictures of glittery unicorns. I waited to see if she'd react and she did, her eyes lighting up at the sight of the bright corner of the otherwise neutral room. And even though I knew she didn't comprehend the context, I sang 'happy half birthday' to her as I placed her on the floor in front of her gifts. Once I'd finished singing, I clapped, and she clapped back.

'Happy half birthday my little girl,' I said, before opening the presents with Sophie. She had little interest in any of them and was much more concerned with the paper itself — I'd known it wouldn't be any other way. With it being just me and Sophie, I knew I could have not wrapped the presents at all, I could have just presented a new toy for Sophie to play with and she wouldn't know the difference. But somehow it mattered. It mattered a lot.

It didn't take long for us to unwrap Sophie's gifts since I couldn't afford to buy her many: three new books, a new dress, some bath toys and a baby piano she could sit at and bash until her heart was content, which I'd bought second-hand from Facebook marketplace. The grand sum of money spent on the most important person in my life: thirty-eight pounds. Thirty-eight measly pounds. It broke my heart. Not long ago, that would have been a light bite to eat and a few drinks. I took so much for granted. I wanted to give her more — I wanted there to be a mountain of gifts before her, expensive and stimulating — and when I imagined it, Em was there, because despite what she did, despite how angry I was at her for leaving with another man, for abandoning her daughter, I still loved my wife. But I had to wonder if she ever really loved me; loved us.

How long did it go on for, Em?

How long were you being unfaithful?

Did I really matter?

Once the gifts had been opened and all of the unicorn paper had been gummed, we had a birthday picnic breakfast, an old beach towel saving the carpet from the inevitable chaos of dropped yogurt, pieces of apple and Weetabix. Sophie made a mess; food was in her hair, all over her pyjamas and the towel probably had more on it than Sophie did in her belly. But it didn't matter, she was happy, today was her day. Every day was her day.

Cleaning up after breakfast, I took our bowls and my empty coffee cup into the kitchen, and through the back door I was sure I saw John in the garden, disappearing around the side of the house. It wasn't surprising, he often popped in via the back, his farmer's ways I guessed, and he and Frances were due any time. I walked to the back door and unlocked it.

'Morning, John,' I called out, expecting him to come around the corner, but he didn't. Confused, I stepped into the garden and peered around the side of the house. He wasn't there. I assumed it was my eyes playing tricks. I couldn't remember the last time I'd had a decent night's sleep — it was so bad I'd been at the doctors twice about it — but as I pulled the door to, I noticed a damp print on the ground, no doubt created by the dew on the grass that would all burn up within the hour. It looked sort of like the toes of a shoe just on the edge where the lawn connected to the patio.

'John, are you out here?'

With no response coming back, I felt the hairs on my forearms stand on end. I examined the mark on the patio again — the small patch of damp really looked like it was made by a shoe, like someone had come to the back window to look into our home. Watching me and Sophie have breakfast. It wasn't, of course, and the more I looked at it, the more I stopped seeing a shoe print. I knew what I was doing: I was projecting a quiet part of me that hoped Em would come back. My brain was tricking me into seeing something that wasn't there, that would never be there. Today was a big day for us, but Em didn't care, Em went to France with her lover. I needed to not forget that — not now, not ever. Inwardly cursing myself, I stepped back in, closed the door and locked it. I took a few deep breaths, reassured myself everything was as it should be, and finished tidying up.

CHAPTER THIRTEEN

Fifteen minutes later the doorbell rang and Frances and John came in. Straightaway they beelined for Sophie and made a fuss of her, picking her up and singing to her. At first she was annoyed — she'd been content playing on her mat and they were interrupting. But soon she was smiling and cooing. And then, as I made a cuppa for the pair, the gifts started coming in. John took three trips to and from his boot, bringing in wrapped-up box after box after box. The first trip alone put my attempt to shame. Once it was all in and the door was shut, the mountainous pile of gifts I'd imagined giving to my daughter was in the middle of my living room, and none of those gifts were from me.

'Frances, John. This is way too much,' I protested weakly, conflicted in my statement.

'No such thing.' Frances waved me away as she sat on the floor, putting Sophie on her knee.

'But it's not even her birthday.'

'And? Robbie, dear, she deserves this.'

'You're right, thank you. Sorry, that sounded really ungrateful.'

'Rob, not at all, we get it,' John said, putting his wide hand on my shoulder.

'I just wish I could do more; you know?'

'That's why we're here,' Frances said. It was well-meaning, but I heard a 'you cannot cope without us' in her voice and felt a pang of inadequacy. As Frances fussed with Sophie, opening her presents, the gifts lavish and beautiful, I smiled, thanked, expressed countless times that they had done too much. By the time they were all open, wrapping paper covered most of the floor space and Sophie was entirely overwhelmed. The small gifts I had bought were nowhere to be seen, buried under the mass of more lovely presents. Ashamed I couldn't provide for my daughter like her grandparents had, I was also grateful: because of them, Sophie wouldn't go without. Some things are more important than pride.

'Robbie, dear. We were thinking,' Frances said from the floor as she helped Sophie push wooden farmyard animal pieces into a board, her first jigsaw. My heart skipped: last time she'd said 'we were thinking', it was about Sophie going and staying at theirs. It was bad enough I had to ask if Sophie could sleep over at theirs tomorrow so I could go back to work. My leave time had run out, days ago, and we needed the money.

'About what?' I replied, trying to sound as relaxed as possible.

'We'd like to take you and Sophie for a half-birthday lunch. How does that sound?'

I hesitated. After my announcement that Em had simply left, I'd been ridiculed online by some, and pitied by others. Some created elaborate conspiracy theories about how I was still responsible for doing something terrible. And the attention didn't sit well with the Murphy's.

'Frances, are you sure? People might talk.'

'If they talk, they talk.'

Her comment shocked me. 'But—'

'What happened isn't your fault, nor is it this precious little girl's,' she said, nuzzling Sophie and making her giggle.

'I'd love to. Thank you.'

'Great, I'll book a table at my favourite place,' Frances said, getting to her feet, Sophie in her arms. 'I'll get her ready, if you want to sort yourself out, Robbie.'

'Sure, I'll be two ticks.'

I dashed upstairs and showered quickly, and as I dried I could hear Frances with Sophie in her room, changing her. Poking my head out of the bedroom door, I wanted to call across that I'd bought her a special outfit for the day, but when I looked across the landing into Sophie's room, she was already dressed in one of the new outfits Frances had bought her. My fault: I should have washed and dressed her before they came. But, again, pride didn't matter, right?

After throwing on some jeans and the least creased shirt in the wardrobe, I made my way into the bathroom to brush my teeth. Not wanting to miss out on anything, I did so quickly, and joined the others downstairs. I took Sophie from Frances and she went back up to use the bathroom, leaving me and John, both on the floor playing with Sophie. When Frances re-joined, she called out my name mid-way down the stairs, and the way she said it, a question mark raising the final syllable, I knew what she was about to ask. My stomach dropped. I hadn't been careful.

'Robbie?' she called again as she hit the bottom step. 'Is there anything you want to tell us?' She held up a box of fluoxetine, a grave and serious expression on her face. 'Aren't these antidepressants?'

I took a deep breath, tried to find the right words to stop this becoming yet another thing Frances could quote as an example of me not coping.

'They are mood stabilisers.'

'Mood stabilisers? What for?' John asked.

'The doctor insisted,' I lied; I was the one who had approached the doctor for help a few days ago. 'They're a really low dose, just to take the edge off, well, you know.'

'Why didn't you tell us?'

'Because it's not a big deal.'

'Not a big deal? Surely you being the sole parent and depressed is . . .'

'I'm not depressed, Frances, I'm just having a hard time, that's all. Surely you can understand that? This just mellows it a little, makes what we're going through a little easier.'

'Yes, but, I mean, Robbie? You have a baby in the house.'

'And that's exactly why I take them, Frances. I'm so sad Em left. I'm angry, too. I don't want Sophie experiencing any of it.'

'But . . .'

'Our job is to protect this little girl, right?'

'Of course.'

'And love her and give her all she needs. These tablets, they're helping me do that.'

'But what about side effects? You read stories about—'

'You don't need to worry, OK? Do some reading, you'll quickly see that my dosage is really low — almost non-existent — it just helps me stay level, OK? There are no side effects. I'm not sleeping more; I wake when she needs her night-time feed. I'm present, they don't take that away from me.'

'Rob, I think you need to re-evaluate this.'

'Why is it so important?'

'We've seen first-hand the long-term effect from taking . . .'

'From who? You, John? Frances? Please. I know what I'm do—'

'From Em,' Frances said, trying to hold my eye, but having to avert.

'What?'

'Em was on them for years,' John followed up quietly.

'When?'

'Most of her teens, on and off.'

'Oh,' I said, sinking against the sofa. Another thing I didn't know.

'We're just trying to—'

'Frances, please,' I said, begging her to stop. 'I can't hear any more.'

100

'We just worry—'

'Can we not, not today. Let's just celebrate, like we said we would?'

'Yes, of course.' Frances smiled, placing the box on the sill of the small window beside the front door, before quietly sliding on her shoes, making it clear to me and John that we were about to leave.

By the time we were waiting to be seated at the Fox and Hounds, a country pub outside town that was well known for its carvery, we'd moved on from my tablets and were fussing my little girl, and as the restaurant was air-conditioned and cool, we all relaxed. Frances made a comment about the heat, how it's too much, and I think it was her way of apologising. I agreed, my way of accepting her apology.

After a lovely lunch, one where I went unnoticed by curious eyes and gossip-mongers, Frances insisted we went back to theirs for the afternoon. I wanted to be at home, but really, it would be more fun for Sophie if we went. Misery loved company, but it didn't mean it should get it. As we left the restaurant, Frances pushing Sophie in her buggy, I accidently bumped into an older man walking in.

'Sorry,' I said.

'You should be.'

'Pardon?'

'Don't think we're all fooled by your desperate attempt to make it look like your wife left you.'

I know I should have left it, walked away, but I couldn't. After the few weeks we'd had, the shocks, fear, embarrassment, I just wanted some decency in this godforsaken place.

'What did you say?'

'Well, we all know you did something to her, you tried to hide it by making it look like she was struggling, and when that didn't work you made it look like she ran away. Clever, but not that clever. People still know.'

'Is that right? Where's the proof?' I said, realising how suspicious it made me sound, but my temper was boiling over. I didn't care anymore.

'Yeah, you did something to her all right.'

'My wife left me. Why don't you fuck off too.'

He sneered as he stepped towards me, his bony finger pointing at me. 'We look after our own here. You'll see.'

My instinct was to back down but I couldn't, I would never back down again, and as he took another step, I shoved him. I didn't mean to shove him hard, just enough to get him out of my space, but I misjudged it and the man staggered backwards and fell over a step at the restaurant doorway. He tried to grab hold of something but only clutched at thin air as he crashed to the floor. I should have helped him up, but I didn't. I wanted him to hurt and, for a moment, I imagined kicking him while he struggled to get to his feet, the image violent and hateful. Staff rushed to his aid, leaving me to walk away.

'Robbie!' Frances said.

'I know, I shouldn't have, I'm sorry. I'm just tired of people judging me.'

'Well, that isn't going to help is it? People talk to each other you know.'

'That's all they do, they talk and make comments and assume. Why can't people just leave us alone.' I realised I was shouting and stopped myself. 'I'm sorry, Frances, today, it's a bit much. Sophie and I, we're going to go home.' I waited for Frances to say something to stop me, but she didn't. She nodded, kissed Sophie, and walked back towards her car, leaving me and John stood opposite each other, Sophie in between.

'I'm sorry, John.'

'I would have pushed him too.'

'Thank you.'

'If you need anything, my boy,' he said.

'Thanks John, you and Frances do much more than you should.'

John nodded but offered no more. He leant over and kissed Sophie on the head.

'Ring us if you need anything?'

'I will.'

'Frances will only worry, so ring anyway, even just to say everything's all right.'

'OK. Sorry again John, I didn't mean to—'

'It's OK. See you tomorrow, yes? I'm assuming we're still on for tomorrow. Sophie staying with us?'

'Yeah. Needs must.'

'We're here for you, in all ways.'

'Thank you, John.'

I watched as John got into his car and drove away, and from across the street I could see people outside the pub entrance, watching.

CHAPTER FOURTEEN

Once home, I was calm again. Having wrestled my keys from the change bag I unlocked the door and stepped inside. Something felt off. I couldn't put my finger on what it was, but my instincts made me close the door quietly, then pick Sophie up.

'Hello?' I called out, unsure why, until I realised my instincts were telling me that what I could feel in the house was another person. Could it be?

'Em?'

I moved into the living room. The room was tidy, nothing moved from when John cleared up the carnage of presents earlier as we all got ready to leave the house. The kitchen was the same, besides one dripping tap. Sophie started to wriggle, wanting to be put down. I kept her in my arms, bouncing her as I moved through to the stairs. The feeling hadn't shifted — if anything, as I ascended it intensified, and as I reached the top I was sure I'd see Em stood in the bedroom doorway, hands clamped together in front of her, tears streaking mascara down her cheeks. I was so sure I could smell her perfume lingering in the hallway.

Hi Rob.

Em!

Rob, I'm so sorry, there's no excuse, I . . .

Shhh, its OK Em, you're home now, you're home.

And I'll always be home. I'm never going to leave again.

I pictured her running to me, wrapping her arms around me and Sophie, both of us crying with joy. Our family complete.

But of course, the doorway was clear. I checked Sophie's room, the bathroom and finally back to mine. As I stepped inside, the feeling was at its strongest. But nothing was out of place. My wardrobe door was ajar, but that was it. It didn't worry me; I'd dressed in haste and often left it open. I closed it and walked back into Sophie's room, the feeling fading quickly until it was gone. I wondered if it was wishful thinking on my part — the intensity of it making me feel and smell something that wasn't there. The day acted like a trigger of hope that Em would come home. That and the footstep outside, it was all in my head, and I had to wonder if there could be a side effect to the tablets I was on. Could they be a little more potent than I thought?

Sophie fell asleep quickly, content and peaceful, and I couldn't take my eyes off her. Sitting on the floor beside the cot bed I held onto the rail and rested my head on my arm. Watching her breathe, her tiny tummy rising and falling inside the Babygro. I wanted to stay there, fall asleep, but from somewhere downstairs, my phone rang. I assumed it was Frances, making sure we were OK.

'Hello?'

No one replied, but the line was connected; I could hear someone on the other end breathing quietly.

'Hello, sorry, I can't hear you?'

They didn't speak, but they didn't hang up either.

'Em? Is that you?'

The line went dead.

* * *

105

October 7th 2018

Emma

Having a life inside me, it's changed me, not just physically (obviously I now feel/look like a beached whale), but psychologically too. For the first time in my life, I can see things from other people's perspectives. I understand now that I was a difficult child. And wondering what kind of mother I'll be has made me reconnect with my own. We haven't seen eye to eye in forever, since I was a little girl, but now I have a little girl growing in me we have a common denominator, a reason to talk, a reason to try. She hasn't apologised for the way she treated me in my difficult teenage years, and I've not apologised for being so difficult. But we're moving past it anyway. For now. I have no doubt once my baby is here, and the euphoria has passed, Mum and Dad will be judging me again, this time less about my life choices and more about my parenting style. And the cycle will begin once more. In their eyes, I'll not be good enough. I'll never be good enough.

Despite telling myself I'd never come back to the Fens, their endless flatness and 'quirky' ways, I now live in a small, run-down three bedroom semi-detached house that looks like it should be on *DIY SOS*, but before the makeover and tears. And this 'dream home' is a staggering five miles from my parents.

Five fucking miles. That's less than fifteen minutes away. Younger me would have thrown a hissy fit and run away from the idea, and I guess a part of me still wants to. I mean, five miles? Who would want to be that close? But then I think of my baby, of the life I want her to have.

When I broached the subject of leaving London for cleaner air and a quieter life, Rob seemed unsure, and I understand that. London is all he knew, and the Fens – they're unlike anywhere else in England. The area is mostly forgotten small towns hidden among the country's intensive crop farming industry. It is aged, it is rusty. But I didn't tell Rob

106

all that. I spoke of the space, the garden we could have, the house we could afford. He started to come around. He said he needed to think about it, and later we spent the evening looking on Rightmove, just to get an idea of the cost of living. We were shocked to see how far the pound goes in a place like this. Our three-bed was dilapidated, but it was spacious, with a huge garden and an endless view. All for a lot less than we were paying in London. He really struggled with the idea of leaving, I could see it in his eyes, and I feared he would say no. Staying in London was easier, less upheaval, and I was sure our baby would be fine growing up there. But I wasn't sure *I* would be fine. I'd spent my life outrunning my mistakes. Steve was proving hard to leave behind. By the time we went to bed, Rob said yes, and I cried with relief. We were leaving; I was leaving things behind. I promised myself I wouldn't tell Steve where we were going, I would simply disappear. I felt he was beginning to obsess. The messages, the surprise visits at work. It was time to have a clean break.

Less than four weeks later, we were handing in our keys to Rob's landlord — who kindly waived the final month's rent as a gift for the growing family — and heading to our new home, five fucking miles away from my parents.

Home. I still can't quite get over that we came home.

Our house isn't ideal: it's tired, run down, and in the arsehole of the arse-end of nowhere. But we have space; a fresh start. We could have got a new build in the town centre, with its thin walls and restricted parking, but I wanted somewhere with some space to breathe, away from people, from tempta- tion. I need to heal, with Rob, with our baby, when she comes.

I feel terrible that Rob's struggling with the transition, borne out of my own failing. But he is trying, and he's the type of man who will get there and be happy. It's just his way. I see him sometimes looking out over the endless flat land behind our house, and I'm not sure if he's reflecting, or looking out to the future. Either way, he looks at it with a grace I really don't deserve.

I think, one day, I will tell him everything. I don't want to be a wife who hides things from her spouse; I don't want to carry this weight forever. I want to leave it behind, in London, and I want to look to the horizon with him, rather than over my shoulder, waiting for someone to work out what a bitch I really am.

Waiting for *him* to work out what I am.

CHAPTER FIFTEEN

July 4th 2019
Sixteen days missing

Rob

Waking with a start, it took me a moment to work out where I was, and why I was alarmed. I had fallen asleep on the sofa, fully clothed, but it didn't explain my panic. Then I heard her, Sophie, wailing in her bedroom. I looked at the time on the wall clock as I ran upstairs towards her room. It was just after seven. Sophie would have been awake for hours. I ran into her room and scooped her up: her face was bright red from crying, her nappy so heavy the tape had come undone, and her clothes were soaked in wee.

'Oh God, darling, I'm so sorry. I'm so sorry.'

I held her close until she calmed. God, what must have been running through her head? She cries, and no one comes. She cries and she is left alone. I hope her young mind didn't feel abandoned all over again. Once she settled, and to push down my guilt for being a bad parent, I told her about our coming day, even though she probably didn't understand most of what I said. Nor cared. But I did it anyway because, when she was awake, I had to be enough for two parents in every way. If Em was here we would share our plans, talking about our work days, discuss things we could do around the house or garden, and Sophie would listen to the words and learn the language. I couldn't take that away from her.

'Today, Sophie, after we have had some Weetabix, we'll head into town and we'll find a park to play in, before it gets too hot, and then, then you are having a sleepover at Nana's and Granddad's because Daddy is going back to work. How does that sound? Hmmmm? How does that sound, little lady?'

I nuzzled into her neck, her tickle spot, and she exploded into a giggle that was so infectious I couldn't help but laugh too. It was my job to protect my daughter, keep her safe, but I couldn't help but wonder if she was actually saving me.

Once she'd had some breakfast and I'd had a coffee (I couldn't bring myself to eat yet, the image of Sophie wailing unanswered for so long made me feel sick to my stomach) we readied ourselves and headed out. The walk into town did what it always did for me, and I was able to regain an element of control over how I was feeling. Despite it being so hot, I felt my heart rate come down and my head clear. I had messed up; I'd proven to myself that I'm struggling to parent — perhaps I'm even a bad one — but Sophie seemed happy, like she'd forgiven me. Life would continue, and we would limp on. As we walked, I really believed it too. Things had been rough, too rough for two people, and if I was honest with myself, I thought several times I was going to crumble, but I hadn't. Yes, I did something unforgivable this morning, but we were still moving forwards, and I was sure I'd never make the same mistake again. We were going to be OK.

Then my phone rang.

Pulling it out of my shorts pocket I looked at the caller ID. It said unknown. A flash came to me of the call I'd had in the night, and I stopped walking to answer it.

'Hello?'

'Hi, Rob, it's Harry.'

'Who?' I asked, not hearing properly as the blood was thumping in my ears.

'Harry, from work.'

'Hi, sorry Harry, bad line. If you're calling about tonight, don't worry, I'll be—'

'Rob, about tonight. We feel its best you don't come back just yet.'

'What? Why?'

'Ummm, well, I'm sure you're aware of what's been said online . . .' He trailed off, waiting for me to say I was. But I had no idea.

'What, recently?'

'Last night?' he said, uncertainty in his voice.

'Last night? No, Harry, I don't know what's been said?'

'Oh, I thought you would have seen, ummm, well, there was a video posted.'

'Of what?'

'Of some kind of altercation.'

He didn't need to say any more, I understood. Someone had filmed me pushing that man in the restaurant doorway. 'Harry, it's not what it looks like.'

'I know, I know, God knows you've been under a lot of stress. We feel you're not ready to come back yet.'

'No, Harry, I am, I'm ready, I need to come back, I need the money.'

'I understand, but until you've seen the occupational therapist, you're not cleared to come back to work.'

'Harry, I need to come back to work. What am I supposed to do?'

'I'm sorry.'

'No, no, that's not good enough, you can't stop me from coming in because of something posted online. That's not fair. It wasn't even my fault.'

'I believe you, I do, but people around here, they talk. I know Em left, but some still think . . .'

'Think what?'

'It's all nonsense, gossip—'

'Think what, Harry?'

'I don't listen to it, as your boss, I can't, as someone who knows you, I don't believe it.'

'What, Harry?'

'I'm saying this as a friend. It's not a reflection on—'

'What, Harry!'

'People still think you had something to do with her disappearing.'

'Oh, for . . .' I moved the phone away from my mouth and bit my lip to stop myself shouting, it wouldn't help, and would likely startle Sophie. Taking a breath, I continued. 'I bloody didn't do anything. She left me.'

'I know, I do, but people are nervous, and with that video.'

'That wasn't my fault.'

'Rob, this has come from above me, they were talking of your dismissal.'

'What?'

'Please, take some time. See the OT next week so we can ease you back.'

'What the hell am I supposed to do about money?'

'You'll get SSP.'

'SSP?'

'Statutory Sick Pay. It isn't a lot, I know, but it's something. A week or two, then we'll get you back on a phased return. You've been through a lot; this is for the best.'

Before I could answer, Harry hung up.

CHAPTER SIXTEEN

For a moment, I stood, dumbfounded. My legs felt weak and I had to sit down on a bench nearby. Staring out into the fields, I watched a tractor slowly rolling over the land far in the distance, and rocked Sophie back and forth, unable to think of what to do next. SSP was what? A hundred quid, maybe a little less? The bills were due out soon. I had enough to cover this month, but next? Even with the few quid I had in savings, it wouldn't be enough. Sophie needed food in her tummy, a roof over her head. I couldn't help feeling I'd lose her as well as Em.

And I couldn't let that happen, I wouldn't let that happen. Getting up, I continued into town, Sophie and I would still go to the park. She shouldn't miss out because of this. My not being able to return to work was none of her doing. I pushed that man, not her. But, I also needed to make some money. Fast. As we walked, I started to make a list of things I could sell to raise a little capital. My camera, for a start. I bought it on a whim three years ago, thinking if I owned a professional-looking SLR, I'd be a better photographer. I think I may have used it a handful of times. Sophie also had some toys and clothes she'd never played with or worn. Far too many Babygro's and rattles for one baby. I felt like I shouldn't sell her things — and I wouldn't, if I could make enough from my own items. It wasn't ideal, but it would keep us moving.

By the time we reached town I felt — not good, that's the wrong word — charged. Riled. Ready to roll up my sleeves and dig deep. Perhaps Harry was right, perhaps going back to work and burying myself in it wasn't the answer. The financial hit was going to be tough, but this was an opportunity to cull, rearrange, start again. And then, from nowhere, an image of Em came into my head. Her sat on a balcony with Steve, the sun on her face, eating a lazy lunch, laughing, drinking, and then, after, slipping into the bedroom.

Fuck you, Emma.

As I approached the same coffee shop I was photographed outside, I looked in. It was quiet, and as Sophie was asleep I thought I could pop in, grab a flat white, stay in the cool, air-conditioned room and plan.

Sitting in the far corner, Sophie positioned in the shade, I ordered from the kind owner, insisting I paid this time, and I typed everything I could think of to sell into my phone's notes. If I got the asking price on everything, I could raise around £200. I'd be prepared to take less. It wasn't a lot, but it would help.

A few people came in and out and I didn't look at them, I didn't want to catch anyone's eye and have them either pity, mock, or — as Harry had suggested — fear me. When I did dare to look up, I saw a woman sat at a table at the front of the café, basking in the sunlight with her back to me. I don't know when she came in, but I felt myself take a sharp breath, as her hair was a similar colour, similar length, to Em's. I felt my muscles begin to move, wanting to get up and go to her, and I was powerless to stop myself. My heart started to gallop up from behind my ribs into my throat; I had to swallow several times to stop it falling out of my mouth. The way the woman was sat, her left shoulder slightly higher as she leant on her elbow, the colour and length and shape of her hair, the T-shirt showing her fair and flawless skin. It was her. It was my wife.

I drew to within a few feet; she turned and looked at me. Our eyes locked, and my heart dropped back into my chest. It wasn't Em. Of course it wasn't her, and I was bloody stupid for thinking that of all the places she would show herself, it would be a local coffee shop. No, Em was in France, living a new, carefree life. Not here. I smiled awkwardly at the woman, and made it look like I was reading the chalkboard menu above her and had forgotten my glasses. I think she bought it. Sitting back next to Sophie's buggy, hands shaking, I tried to regulate my breathing once again. I was so sure, so sure. Finishing my coffee, I thanked the owner and stepped out into the heat.

The walk from the café to the park was just under ten minutes, and in that time Sophie woke. After feeding her, her change mat becoming a makeshift picnic blanket, we played on the swings before setting off home, and the rest of the afternoon felt like just another day. Food, play, stories. I tried to be in the moment, but money worries, and worries for my own sanity, lingered.

Frances and John arrived after six, to have dinner and collect Sophie, as we'd arranged. I'd forgotten to tell them I wasn't going to work. When I told them, I could see the disappointment on Frances' face.

'I'm sorry, I totally forgot. Since the call came in, I've been a bit all over the place.'

'You should have called us,' Frances said.

'I know, I'm sorry.'

'She is still coming back to ours tonight?'

I should have said yes; it was agreed and arranged. But being away from Sophie when I didn't need to felt wrong. Like I was asking someone to shoulder the responsibility for her because I couldn't. So I said no, but agreed that Sophie could go over the next night or the night after instead, even though there was no reason for her to now. It seemed to do the trick in keeping them sweet, even if it made me feel terrible.

We ate, and chatted lightly. I didn't speak of my money worries, or of Em, and I almost tricked myself into thinking that life consisting of just me and Sophie was normal. One day, maybe?

As I cleared up from dinner, the Murphy's played with Sophie, so I was alone in the kitchen when my phone rang. The caller was unknown, and I assumed it would be Harry, making sure I was OK.

'Hello.'

There was no reply.

'Harry?'

I waited for something, but all that came back was quiet breathing. 'Em, is that you?'

John walked into the kitchen. He said something, but I couldn't place what.

'Em?' I said again, louder, and the line went dead.

'Robbie? Are you OK? What was that?'

'I think Em is calling me.'

'What?'

'I think she's trying to reach me. I've had a few calls now, someone is on the other end, but they don't speak. I think it's Em.'

'I don't understand.'

'John, what if she needs me?'

'Rob—'

'She's calling me, and she can't bring herself to say she's made a mistake. What if she regrets leaving us.'

'Rob—'

'What if—'

'Robbie, stop. It's not her.'

'You don't know that.'

'I'm afraid I do. This is hard for me to say, but Emma is gone, she isn't coming back.'

'How can you know that?'

John looked at me and sighed. 'Sit down, lad.'

I sat, and I'm glad I did — after what John said next, I would surely have fallen.

'This isn't the first time Em has left suddenly.'

'What?'

'You met Em in London, right?'

'You know this — what's it got to do with—'

'Where was she before?'

'I don't understand?'

'Where do you think Em lived before?'

'Here, with you, before uni.'

'Rob, Em has never been to uni. Before London, she lived in Nottingham.'

'What?'

'Em left home at seventeen. One morning, I went to wake her for college, and she was gone. We didn't hear from her for months. And then, years later, she left there for London.'

'I don't . . .' I tried to speak but my mouth felt dry, and I needed to lower my head for fear I would pass out. Lies. Everything I knew about Em before we met, all of it, lies.

'It's a lot to take in.' He said, trying to comfort me. But I didn't need comfort, I needed the truth.

'Why didn't you tell me before? Why did she go to Nottingham?'

'Em was . . . challenging as a teen. Rebellious. She didn't like to play by our rules.'

'But why Nottingham?'

'Rob, it's ancient history.'

'Why, John. I need to know who my wife was.'

'She had a boyfriend there. She went to live with him.'

'Was his name Steve Burton?'

'No, no, I promise, we don't know who that is either. He was called Jamie.'

'Jamie who?'

'Rob, it doesn't matter.'

'Jamie who?'

'Hardman, Jamie Hardman. Rob, I know I should have said something, but I didn't want to upset you, and I thought she'd changed, she seemed different with you. I'm telling you now, because it's time to move—'

'Why didn't you tell me when she left that she had a history of doing that?'

'I was—'

'I need you to leave,' I said, getting up.

John didn't move, but stood staring at me, his mouth open, trying to find something to say.

'Please, I need some time.' I said, quietly.

'Rob, I'm sorry.'

'Please.'

'OK, we'll go. Please Rob, we didn't know how to tell you.'

'And let me live with false hope. Let me live like my wife isn't a compulsive liar. You stood by my side as we walked through that field out there, looking for any sign that she was depressed, needing our help. You could have saved me from that heartache, that embarrassment when I stood in front of the whole town and told them Em left me.'

'I'm sorry.'

Defeated, John headed into the living room and I followed, my arms crossed.

'Fran, it's time to go,' he said quietly.

'What, no, I want to stay and do bath time.'

'I'm afraid we have to.'

Frances looked at me. I didn't budge.

'What's happened?'

'Fran, I'll explain on the way home. Rob needs some time away from us right now.'

'What happened?' she asked again.

'You should have told me Em has a history of leaving, Frances. You should have said,' I whispered, tears filming my eyes, blurring her reaction.

'Oh, Robbie I—'

'Please, leave.'

Frances didn't argue. She kissed Sophie and put on her shoes. As she opened the door she took a breath to say something, but thought better of it, and once they were gone, I did what I could to not have my feelings rub off on my daughter as I bathed her and got her ready for bed.

Once I was confident Sophie was asleep, I sat on the edge of my bed and thought about what John had told me. Em had a history of running away. She'd lied to me about when and how she moved to London. She was not the woman I thought she was. And, foolishly, I searched for Jamie Hardman on Facebook. He was about my age, our age. Now married, with kids. I shouldn't have, but I messaged.

> *Hi. You don't know me, but I am married to Emma Murphy.*
> *I understand you once dated. This message might seem weird,*
> *but something has happened, and I need to know about Em,*
> *from the time before I met her. I know this sounds desperate*
> *but if you could spare a minute, I'd be grateful.*
>   *Rob*

CHAPTER SEVENTEEN

Sending the message and forcing down my shame, I got proactive by rounding up the things I knew I would try and sell, adding other things as I saw them — and as I did, I felt better for it. A spring clean of sorts. I took photographs of everything, making sure the lighting was right. In my pile were several Babygro's, a few sleeping suits, my camera and my old iPod. A rucksack. I didn't think it would sell, but it was a Berghaus and, although I loved it, I only ever used the change bag now. I also posted Em's change bag, one that was more feminine than mine, and there was something final about it. I added several of her dresses and shoes. They weren't mine to sell, but my and Sophie's hearts weren't hers to break.

Once I'd written a selling caption for each of the items, offering a brief description of each, I uploaded them onto Facebook marketplace and, with nothing else to do, I found myself in the garden, sat on the doorstep with a cup of tea, watching bats flap overhead. To my shock, only thirty minutes after posting, a message popped into my inbox from someone called Angie Walsh.

Hi, are the Babygro's and sleep suits still for sale?

Hello. Yes, they are still available.

She replied almost instantly.

Great, do you live close to Ramsey?

A few miles.

Can I come a collect them now?

Wow! Of course. I wasn't expecting anyone to show interest for days. My first time selling anything on here.

Baby things sell quick.

I can see. Which ones would you like?

All of them, if that's possible?

I couldn't believe my luck — she wanted all of them, without even trying to haggle on the price. All of them equated to just under £50. If I could sell the other things in a similar way, we might just be OK.

Fuck you, Em. Fuck you.

I messaged Angie Walsh my address, and twenty minutes later, a car pulled up outside. I wanted to greet her before she rang the bell, so as not to disturb Sophie, and as she walked up my footpath, I opened the front door, almost recoiling in shock. Somehow, I'd managed to put together that the woman smiling at me was none other than the same woman I'd thought was Em in the coffee shop. She looked at me like she knew my face but couldn't place me. I should have kept quiet, swapped the items of clothing for the cash and closed the door, and yet, perhaps because I knew she'd work it out, and would likely think I was a weirdo, or perhaps because of how similar to Em she was, I spoke.

'The café, today.'

Her face changed from quizzical to understanding in a beat.

'Of course. How funny is that?'

'I was just thinking the same. So, here are the bits. I've put them all in a bag, feel free to check them if you . . .'

'No, no, I trust they're all there. Here's the money.'

She handed me two twenty pound notes, and a ten, and I felt my cheeks flush that I didn't have any money on me to give the two pound I owed. When I asked if she, by any chance, had the right money she waved it off.

'It's only two pounds, its fine.'

'No, really, I can't.'

'Please, I'm saving a fortune, a sleeping suit alone is around twenty pounds. You're doing me a favour.'

'Thank you,' I said, my embarrassment elevated. 'How old is yours?'

'She's three months. Yours?'

'Just six.'

'They're great, aren't they?'

'Yes, she's my world.' I smiled, and for a moment there was an awkward silence between us.

'Right I should leave you to your evening,' she said eventually.

'Yes, of course.'

'Listen,' she started, tucking a lock of her hair behind her ear, just like Em used to. 'It's kind of embarrassing, but it's just me and my little girl and, well, it's not easy, you know, ummm.'

'I do, it's just me and mine here too. It's tough.'

'Yes it is,' she said, relieved. 'When, or if, you have more things to sell, once your baby has outgrown them, perhaps, could you message me before putting them on Facebook? Like I said, baby stuff goes quickly.'

'It sure does, I only posted these things less than an hour ago.'

'Sorry.'

'No, don't be, it's great. I've no doubt I'll be posting more, and before I do, I'll message you first. One single parent to another.'

'Thank you.'

'Don't mention it.'

'No really, thank you. I'm Angie by the way.'

I knew her name, as she knew mine, but the formal introduction felt right. 'Rob.'

'Rob, I better go, mine's sound asleep in the car.'

'Of course.'

'Bye, Rob.'

'Bye, Angie.'

Angie turned on her heels and, with the bag of clothes in her hand, walked back to her car. Through the tinted glass, I could make out a baby seat. As she pulled off, I waved and closed the door. Tucking the fifty pounds in my pocket, I walked into the kitchen, my gait light, hopeful and, opening the back door, I stepped into the garden. The sun was all but gone, the last of its colours were thrown from behind where I faced, the sky holding onto pinks, purples, oranges, defying the night. I couldn't help but smile. Angie had, without knowing, given me the gift of hope at a time when all hope seemed dead.

* * *

January 3rd 2019

Emma

You did it, Em, you fucking well did it. She is perfect. My little Sophie. My perfect little family.

I hope I don't fuck it up.

CHAPTER EIGHTEEN

July 5th 2019
Seventeen days missing

Rob

Frances had tried to call me on a few occasions throughout the day, no doubt wanting to make peace after I'd learnt they had kept things from me, but I wasn't ready. So I messaged and told her I would call tomorrow; Sophie and I were having a quiet day. It seemed to work. Em's ex, Jamie Hardman had also been in touch. He left his number, said I could call, but I'd not responded yet. I'd been busy with Sophie. Trying my very best to function. The day had been unbearably hot, so Sophie and I stayed in. She spent the day in just a nappy, me in a pair of loose-fitting shorts. The energy-sapping heat lasted until the sun dipped, and even then it was still too hot to function.

The items I posted online gained some traction and more of the things, mostly Sophie's things, had been provisionally sold. Pending them actually turning up with the cash in hand. I couldn't believe how easy it was to sell second-hand goods.

I kept wanting to call Jamie, but as much as I blamed the heat and Sophie's restlessness, really I was just putting it off. The courage I felt, the need to know that had driven me the night before, had vanished. Now I was just scared. But if I was ever going to heal the wounds Em had caused, I needed to know. When I was confident Sophie wouldn't wake, I took the baby monitor and a cold beer into the back garden and stood beside the peach tree. I copied his number from the Facebook message, and dialled. He picked up on the fourth ring.

'Hello?'

My voice snagged; the words wouldn't form.

'Hello?' he said again.

Shit Rob, this was a stupid idea!

'I can't hear you; I'm hanging up now.'

'Hi, umm, sorry. Is this Jamie? Can you hear me?'

'Yes, it's Jamie, who is this?'

'It's Rob.'

'Who?'

'Rob Clarke, I messaged you, about Em, Emma Murphy.'

There was a pause on the other end, and for a moment I thought he'd hung up. I was about to ask if he was still there when he spoke.

'I didn't think you would call.'

'To be honest, neither did I.'

'So, you're married to Emma?'

'Yes, well. Yes, I am.'

'I see.'

Another awkward pause.

'What do you know? About Em and me, about back then?' Jamie said.

'Not a lot — you and Em were a thing, in Nottingham, then she left for London where I met her.'

'We were more than a thing. We were together for several years.'

'Oh.'

'Engaged to be married.'

'Oh,' I said again.

'I take it you didn't know. I'm sorry.'

'No, it's OK, just a lot to take in. Dare I ask what happened?'

'Nothing.'

'Nothing?'

'Nope. Nothing. I thought we were doing well. We'd set a date, picked a venue, she'd even had her dress fitting. Then one night, I'm out with a few friends for a drink, nothing wild, home by midnight, and she was gone.'

I didn't reply; what he was saying was so eerily similar to what I'd been through.

'No note,' he continued, 'no phone call. Nothing. She just packed a few things and left.'

'When was the last time you spoke to her?'

'The night she left me.'

'You've not heard from her or seen her since?'

'Nope, not until two weeks ago when her picture was on the news saying she'd gone missing, and I thought to myself, same old Em.'

'I see.'

'I'm sorry mate, truly, I am.'

'Why did she leave you?'

'I didn't know it at the time, although looking back, I don't know how I was so blind. Em was having an affair.'

'When did she leave you?'

'Four years ago.'

Four years. The same amount of time I'd known her. Em ran away from her fiancé, and her lover, and right into my arms. Was anything I knew about my wife the truth?

'Rob, are you still there?'

'Yes, sorry, yes.'

'I know it's hard, believe me, I do. I waited two years for her to come back. But she didn't. Don't let her steal two years from you, like she did me. Get on, because she is.'

'Yeah. Thank you.'

'And it will be OK. I've got a wife now, two beautiful kids. It won't always be this bad.'

'Uh-huh.'

'I wish I could say more. I'm sorry. Take care, mate.'

Hanging up the phone, I stared out into the endless fields behind my house. Unsure of what to think. Unsure of what to do next.

My phone rang again, and assuming it was Jamie calling back to tell me something else, I answered it without thinking.

'Hello?' I said, my voice numb. There was no reply.

'Hello? Jamie, you there?'

I moved the phone away from my ear, looked at the caller ID. It was withheld.

'Em?' I said quietly, and again the line went dead.

CHAPTER NINETEEN

I went back into the house, locked up. It was only just 10 p.m., yet it felt later; a lot later. I tried to sleep in my bed but, despite being exhausted, I couldn't switch off. What Em's ex-fiancé told me, about her leaving with no explanation, no apology, it confirmed she wouldn't come back, for me or our daughter. I knew that already, deep down, but now it was the unequivocal truth, I wasn't sure I was ready to face it. Which was stupid really, as I had already faced it every day since she left.

Grabbing my pillow and quilt I made my way into Sophie's room and settled on her floor. I went onto Facebook and saw I'd received several messages. Opening them, I responded to those interested in buying some of my listed items. And then I saw one from Angie Walsh.

> *Rob, hi, I hope you don't mind the message, I just wanted to thank you for those things you sold me yesterday. They are perfect.*

I replied, telling her it was my pleasure, not expecting her to message again. To my surprise, a few minutes later, she did.

I hate to say this, but I meant what I asked yes-
terday — if you have any more things you want
to sell, could you let me know? I just don't want to
miss the opportunity.

Of course.

Thank you, being a single parent is tough some-
times, isn't it?

I wanted to respond, agreeing, but I couldn't. Locking my phone I lay back, staring out of Sophie's bedroom window to the clear night sky and, as much as I knew I shouldn't, I thought of Em. I wondered where she was in France. What she was doing. I pictured her laying naked in a bed of thin satin sheets, a thick arm of her lover draped over her. I stopped myself picturing them, it wouldn't help.

Sleep wasn't coming, not tonight so I got off of Sophies floor and went back outside, hoping the clear night and calm breeze would settle me. As I walked towards the far edge of my garden, the place where Em stepped over the fence and out of our lives, I drew level with the peach tree, my eye drawn to a carving that I'd intentionally not looked at in the days since.

Em and Rob and Sophie. Forever.

Reading those words once meant something clear to me; now, it was anything but. Em carved it a few days after we moved here, Sophie not yet born. The chaos of move day and meeting Em's parents and unpacking boxes had lulled. Exhausted, Em and I found ourselves out in the garden at night. It was crisp, cold, cloudless, and we looked at the stars. I'd not seen so many in my life. Living in London, with all its light pollution, meant that the odd twinkling was all I ever saw. But here the night was so dark, so clean, and we stood, a blanket over Em, my arm around her, keeping her warm. Looking at the heavens.

'We're gonna be happy here, aren't we?' I asked.

'Yeah, I think so. Thank you, Rob, for doing this. I know leaving London is hard for you.'

'It's all I've ever known. But you and our baby, mean so much more.'

'And we have our little dream home.'

'With our own garden.'

'And our little peach tree.' She smiled.

'Yes, our little peach tree.'

We both turned our gaze back to the heavens, and Em gasped.

'Em, are you OK?'

'I saw a shooting star!'

'Did you? Where?'

'Out there.' She pointed to the horizon, above the thin veil of mist that hung over the reservoir.

'Oh, wow. I've never seen one.'

'You will. I always used to see them when I was young.'

'So, make a wish.'

I watched as Em screwed up her face, like she did when she was concentrating, and after a moment, she looked back to me. 'You know, I don't need to wish. I've got everything I could want right here.'

Then Em took a stone from the rockery and carved our names in the tree. What happened next was one of the good memories of us, one that was personal and intimate — one of the best, in fact.

I didn't let myself remember what we did after she carved our names. It hurt too much.

A flash of light drew my attention, snapping me away from my memories, and at first I thought it was my tired eyes playing tricks on me. But when it happened again my eye was drawn out towards the reservoir. The dog walker was out again, their torch-light helping them keep their footing in the twilight. I was tempted to wave, but I suspected they often saw me in the garden, alone, and would probably think I was a weirdo. Although they were likely not watching me, I felt as if their eyes were boring into my chest, so I quickly walked back into the house and closed the door.

* * *

March 23rd 2019

Emma

I am crazy stupid happy right now. Crazy stupid fucking happy. And crazy stupid proud too. Sophie is everything I could have wished for, and more. My little bundle. My little treasure. And despite moving up here to hide, I can't help but want to show her off. Look what I made, look what I've achieved.

Screw you, haters.

I want to parade her perfect little head for everyone to see. And sometimes, even though I have no need to, I get myself and Sophie dressed into our finest clothes and go out, just so passers-by can look into her buggy and tell me how precious she is. How wonderful I look after having a baby not long ago. And I know that needing this makes me look a certain way, I know this, and I don't care. I just don't care. So, look at my daughter — look at me, her amazing, together mother. And envy the life we have.

Of course, it hasn't been as easy as I make it look. Don't gloss over that, Em. You're tired, the night-time feeds are really hard and your boobs hurt from breastfeeding — the first few weeks it felt like Sophie was drawing lava from your nipples. You cry. Don't forget that you cry. Mostly out of love, shock; trauma, perhaps. But sometimes you cry for other reasons too. You know these reasons; you don't have to write them down.

Rob has been amazing throughout these early few months. He is, for the most part, patient, supportive. He loves Sophie fiercely. Everyone can see it. He's a good dad. He has his wobbles, like me, and he has less time for me now. But then, I have less for him. Welcome to parenthood. One thing I have noticed is that now, he has the occasional outburst. He snaps — at me — sometimes has to take himself away because he's angry. But I forgive him: we're both tired, both learning how to live our new lives as parents. I'd forgive him anything. People in glass houses and all that, Em.

But, saying that, three mornings ago, while Sophie slept in her buggy after one of my walks, we had a 'discussion'. He doesn't like to use the word argument. Our 'discussion' was about something so meaningless, I couldn't tell you what it was. I had done something, or forgotten to do something, I can't remember. But I do remember he lost his temper with me. And if I'm honest — which, again, is the point of this — I was a little scared. I don't think he was going to hit me. He wouldn't. He's not that type, I don't think. But I could see in his eyes he thought about it. It was there for a moment, and then gone. A flash, a beat. But it was there. Our 'discussion' fizzled out and he went outside in the rain to calm down. Twenty minutes later, all was forgotten. Almost.

I needed to talk to someone about it; a friend I could lean on and share what happened. If only to say it out loud and hear that I'd made a mountain out of a molehill. I couldn't talk to my parents; they still struggled to see eye to eye with Rob, and if I said to them that we'd had a row and I was a little scared, they'd wade in and make things worse. It was just a moment; just one of those things. It's passed now. So we keep moving forward, because moving forward means I'm not looking back. Moving forward I am happy.

CHAPTER TWENTY

July 6th 2019
Eighteen days missing

Rob

I slept.

I slept in my bed for the first time since Em left us. There were no dreams. There was no panic deep in my chest that something had happened to Sophie. I slept, woke to tend to my daughter, and slept again. I was a normal parent.

And more. The promises people had made on Facebook to buy my things had come to fruition. The first person arrived at just after ten, bought my rucksack, a tenner. The second came half an hour later for my camera. I took a hit on that, but still, money in the bank. Four more people came, cash in hand, items out of my home. And by the time Sophie went for her morning nap, including the fifty quid from Angie, I was a hundred and sixty-five to the good.

As she slept, I got to work on gathering more things I could sell. If I could make about four hundred and fifty to five hundred in the next week or so, I could afford all of my bills, without needing to ask for help. Despite falling out with Frances and John over their lies about Em, I knew that if I asked for support, they'd jump at the chance. They had money, they loved their granddaughter, and thought I was all right. But I couldn't. Pride, maybe. Stubbornness. No — dignity. That's what I wanted to protect. Em robbed me of it. I needed it back.

In Sophie's room, I looked through her things. The Murphy's had bought her lots of new clothes and toys, and that meant some of the clothes Em had bought for her could go. Dresses, playsuits, cute cardigans that she'd outgrow by the time the weather cooled enough for her to wear them. I added up what I would sell them for as I went along. And came in just under sixty. Going onto Facebook, I opened Messenger, and typed.

> *Hi Angie, It's Rob. I have some more things I'm selling; you know how it is, they grow out of things so fast and I don't have the space for them all. I'll attach a few pictures. You have first refusal on the lot. I'll post what you don't want (if you want anything at all) on Facebook once I hear from you. No rush. I hope you are well.*

I hovered over the 'x'. I didn't want to overstep the line, but did want something to show it wasn't just a generic message. But a kiss felt too far, so I opted for a smiley face emoji and hit send. I followed up the message with pictures of all the things she could have first refusal on. I don't know why I was surprised when she messaged within a few minutes: everyone had Facebook linked to their smartphone and notifications pinged instantaneously. I guess I assumed she would have more important things to do than respond to a message from me.

> *Hi Rob, thank you for the message. I would like to take the lot off your hands, if that's possible.*

> *Hi Angie, really? You want it all? Are you sure? Do you want to take a look at the clothes first?*

134

I hit send, she messaged back quickly.

No, I was delighted with the last lot, and you've saved me a fortune. When would you like me to pick them up?

        Wow, well, I'm actually free today. If not, I'm in all day tomorrow?

Now is fine, if that works for you?

        Perfect.

That done, there was one more thing to do. Messaging Frances, I asked if she and John wanted to come over later and chat.

CHAPTER TWENTY-ONE

True to her word, Angie knocked on my front door thirty minutes after we spoke on Messenger. Sophie was in my arms, just waking from her nap.

'Angie, hi, how are you?'

'I'm good, how are you?'

'Yeah, good, thank you. I wasn't expecting you to be able to come over today.'

'Steph, my daughter, is with her dad.'

'Oh, I see.'

There was an awkward pause between us. Over Angie's shoulder, I saw the old lady across the road step out to see whose car it was and why they were outside my house. She made eye contact and shook her head at me, like I was doing something wrong.

'Sorry, Angie, come in. The clothes are in the lounge.'

'It's OK, I'll wait here.'

'Yes, of course. I'll be right back.'

What the hell was I thinking, inviting her in? For all she knows, I could be a lunatic. You read about these things: Tinder dates that end in murder and suchlike. And some people still thought I'd done something to Em. She must have known who I was and what was going on; the whole town did. As I walked into the lounge I caught my reflection in the mirror above the fireplace. My beard was thick and dark, and my eyes were heavy. Looking at the state of me, even I would have declined entering my house. Putting Sophie down on her play mat, I collected the clothes and went back to the door. Angie was looking at her phone, her expression pained.

'Is everything all right?'

She put her phone quickly in her pocket and smiled, although it wasn't kidding anyone.

'Yes, sorry, my ex.'

'Is your little one OK?'

'Oh, she's fine. He's being difficult about money stuff. You know how it is.'

'Yeah, I do,' I lied. I didn't have the faintest idea how she felt. I'd give anything for a message from Em, however bad it was. 'If you have to go, we can do this another time?'

'No, not at all. Sorry.'

'Don't be. Do you want to check the clothes?'

'No, it's fine, I trust they're perfect. I totalled it all up, my maths says it should be fifty-seven pounds. Is that right?'

'It is.'

'Thank you for messaging me first,' she said, handing over the money.

'I said I would.'

Angie smiled, then her phone rang and as she looked at the screen the smile faded.

'OK, I better go. See you soon?'

'Sure. Bye, Angie.'

Angie made her way back to the car, the phone going up to her ear before she climbed behind the driver's seat. I watched from the door as she drove away. Across the road, the older man had joined his wife in staring at my house, a bag of rubbish in his hands. I nodded towards them both — part polite, part making sure they knew I'd seen them staring. And again she shook her head, ever so slightly, as he threw the rubbish in the black bin.

'Can I help you?' I shouted across the road towards them. They didn't reply, but mumbled to each other as they backed away towards their house.

'Is there something you want to say?' I said, my temperature rising. I knew I should have backed down but, again, I couldn't. I was sick of being judged. So I stepped out onto the footpath. 'Is there something you want to fucking say?'

I must have been shouting, as a few net curtains along the road began to twitch. The old man opened his mouth to speak but his wife put a hand on his arm, silencing him.

'Well?' I said again. I knew I was an outsider here, but I was tired of people being so rude.

'We find it interesting you have people coming over all the time, is all,' the woman said, her voice shaking.

My blood boiled over, and before I could stop myself I crossed the road and stood close to their front gate.

'I get I'm an outsider here, I get that. But I'm on my own, raising my daughter, and you want to judge me for things I'm doing for her. How dare you.'

Turning, I marched back towards my house and closed the door behind me. Standing with my back to it, I took some deep breaths to calm myself down. I couldn't let one judgemental old couple ruin what was starting to look like the best day since Em left. Looking into the living room at Sophie happily playing with her activity mat, I felt like a hypocrite. The thing I hated most about Em leaving wasn't her lies, or her lover, it was that she'd left Sophie alone. And here I was doing exactly the same, to have a row with a neighbour.

Never again.

Pushing down my anger, I sat on the floor and played with my daughter, singing songs, clapping, tickling her, and I let myself be entirely wrapped up in it. Mid-afternoon, after a successful lunch, there was a knock at the door. I opened it and saw Frances on the doorstep.

'Hi, Robbie.'

'Frances. Where's John?'

'He's in the car.'

'Why?'

'Robbie, John wanted to tell you about Em's past. I stopped him. It's my fault. I'm sorry.'

'You should have told me.'

'I know that now.'

'Why didn't you?'

'I guess I was hopeful she wouldn't repeat her mistakes, because now she had a daughter.'

'You thought she would come home?'

'I did, believe me, I really did.'

'But you let me search the fields for her; you could have saved me from that heartache.'

'I know. I'm so sorry. John wanted to say the moment you called us to tell us she'd gone, but I didn't want to believe it. I thought she'd changed, I thought being a mother . . .'

'I spoke with her ex, Jamie Hardman. Did you know him?'

'We met a few times.'

'He told me to move on, get on with life. Do you think I should?'

'Honestly, yes,' she said quietly, a tear escaping. 'Rob, I'm so sorry.'

'No more lies, OK?'

'OK.'

'Promise. Because Em lied to me for our whole relationship.'

'I understand.'

'Do you want to come and see your granddaughter?'

'Yes, please.'

'And stay for dinner?'

Frances looked up at me, her eyes filming with fresh tears. And she did something unexpected. She stepped in and hugged me. Over her shoulder, I saw John walking up the drive. Behind, a few net curtains twitched once more. Frances let me go and walked into the living room. John stepped up, nodded, I nodded back. Our small gesture of apology.

Thankfully, Sophie's great mood made being with the Murphy's again much easier. We spoke of things she did that made us smile. John warned me that life would change once she started to crawl.

'You'll need eyes in your arse.'

'John, not in front of my granddaughter.'

I laughed, we all did, and somehow we stopped ourselves thinking of Em. She was there, just behind our thoughts, hanging in the gaps between sentences as we spoke, but we didn't address her. We didn't allow her in, which was hard for us all.

The Murphy's stayed all afternoon and for dinner. John insisted on a takeaway, their treat, and as he ordered from the local Indian, Frances played with Sophie and I made drinks in the kitchen. Out back the heat lingered; the shimmer over the dry fields reflected mirages like water. Oh for some rain.

My phone vibrated in my pocket and, pulling it out, I saw there was no caller ID. And my heart galloped. Stepping outside into the garden to make sure John and Frances couldn't hear me, I answered.

'Hello?'

Nothing.

'Hello, Em?' I whispered, straining to hear anything from the other end.

'Hello, can I speak to a Mr or Mrs Clarke please,' a voice said, making me jump.

'This — this is Mr Clarke?'

'Mr Clarke, its Lindsey here from Capital One credit cards. Before we continue, could I ask you a few questions to verify you're the named person on the account?'

'Ummm, sure.' I said, closing the back door behind me.

Lindsey asked my date of birth, post code, second and fourth numbers on my security code, which I guessed was Sophie's date of birth.

'That's everything, thank you Mr Clarke. I am calling today about the activity on your credit card recently.'

'What activity?' I hadn't used the card in weeks, months maybe.

'There has recently been a transaction of just over two thousand pounds on the account.'

'I'm sorry?'

My legs felt like they were going to go out from under me, so to keep the blood flowing I walked towards the back of the garden. Towards that patch of land where Em's footprints disappeared. I hadn't used the card — I had barely used my wallet — but Em had a card too. We both carried one, for emergencies. Em had not only left, but rinsed me out as well.

'Mr Clarke? Can you confirm this withdrawal?'

'Yes, sorry, yes. I can,' I said, needing to get off the phone. My head was starting to spin.

'I wanted to call to talk through other products that might be of interest to you, which would be more beneficial in the long term.'

'I'm sorry, can I call you back?'

'This won't take up much of your time.'

'I'm right in the middle of dinner.'

Before Lindsey could protest, I hung up and went online to look at my balance. It took me three attempts to log in and, when I did, I wanted to be sick. The balance, as far as I was aware, should have been around forty-eight pounds. Clearable on my next statement. The current balance was two thousand, two hundred and thirty-four. Two thousand transferred out to an account I didn't recognise, the rest interest and charges against it.

'Rob,' John said, opening the door. 'Everything OK?'

'Yes, everything's fine,' I said, trying to smile.

'Where are your wet wipes? Frances says Sophie needs changing.'

'I'll be in in a minute.'

John went back into the house, and I turned and looked out. The corn gently moved in the warm breeze. Effortless. I wished all things were the same. I blinked and a tear fell. And unbeknown to me, Frances was approaching, and saw.

'Robbie, what's happened?'

'It's nothing.'

'Robbie, talk to us. We want to help.'

'Nothing, it's OK.'

'Did Em call you just now?'

'No.'

'Something's upset you on that call. We want to help.'

'I, ummm, she . . . I'm just having some money issues is all.'

'I see.'

'Em, she — she's taken quite a lot out of the credit card, and . . .'

'Rob. Don't worry,' Frances said. 'We can help with that.'

I wanted to say thank you, but I couldn't. Instead I nodded, lowered my head and cried.

'I'm sorry,' I eventually managed to say, wiping my eyes with the balls of my hands.

'You have nothing to be sorry for. You haven't done anything wrong here, Rob. My daughter has.'

'I'm just tired. It's snuck up on me.'

'Rob, let us take Sophie tonight. You need a night off.'

'No, I'm OK.'

'Rob, we aren't saying you can't parent, we're just saying you need some time to yourself. Sophie is fine at ours. You need some sleep.'

'No. I'm Sophie's dad, and there's no reason for—'

'You are her dad, you will always be Sophie's dad, but you're also struggling. Christ, we know how you feel. Being a parent is hard. John and I, we have each other, and we still leant on my mum for the occasional sleepover when Em was young, just so we could have a break. Rob, we aren't trying to take Sophie away from you, we aren't saying you can't cope with her. We just know you need a night off,' she said. 'When was the last time you had a night for you? To have a drink, or a bath. Or watch a movie.'

I didn't know what to say because the answer was conclusive. I hadn't had a night for me since months before Em had gone.

'Let's eat together and bath Sophie here, and then let us take her to ours for the night. And don't worry about the credit card, we'll help you.'

'I don't want you to have to help me.'

'We want to. None of this is your fault. None of it. And if it means so much, you can pay us back.'

I nodded. Owing them money felt wrong, but Em had left me no choice. She'd been gone for eighteen days, and still she was making my life harder.

'And let us give you a break. Let Sophie come home with us. What do you say?'

I nodded, feeling like I had failed my daughter.

143

CHAPTER TWENTY-TWO

Kissing Sophie on the head, I double-checked her car seat was secured correctly into the Iso-fix, and closed the car door. Frances reassured me all would be fine, and I watched helplessly as they drove away with my daughter. I felt like a failure. Not knowing what to do, I grabbed a beer from the fridge, as John had suggested — he'd said he didn't know anyone more deserving of a hangover than me — and stepped into the garden. Out back, far across the horizon, the sky had darkened to a deep shade of purple. A column of thunderous clouds seemed to stretch all the way into space, blotting out the summer evening, sucking in the light like a black hole. Whoever was under that would be in for one hell of a ride. I wished it was me. A torrential, frightening downpour was exactly what I needed. A moment of terror, awe, like watching a storm-surging sea. Like something biblical. I would allow it to wrap around me, pull me in, push me away again, just for a moment.

Much closer than the storm clouds, near to the reservoir, I saw the regular dog walker with their torch. And again, I felt like they were looking at me. I should have ignored them, or stood my ground — after all, I was in my own garden for crying out loud, but I retreated to the house anyway. The house felt too empty without my little girl, and I regretted letting the Murphy's take her. I didn't want to think about what Em had done; what I discovered eighteen days ago and what I discovered today, so I cleaned things that didn't need to be cleaned. I put on music, uploaded pictures of things I wanted to sell online and drank another two beers. But without Sophie, it seemed everything I was doing was reminding me of Em. I felt trapped. I couldn't be in my bedroom; couldn't go into the garden. The living room felt sterile. I needed Sophie back. I needed her home or, at the very least, I needed to be at the Murphy's, sleeping on the floor beside her. I know it would make me appear weak, unable to cope, but I didn't know what else to do. As I pulled my phone out of my pocket, it began to ring, an unknown number. In my haste to accept the call and bring the phone to my ear, I nearly dropped it.

'Em? What have you done to me? To us?'

She hung up.

I sat on the arm of the sofa, staring at the blank screen on my mobile. It was Em, I was sure of it. I should have raged at her, forced her to speak. I should have said I knew about her fiancé and Nottingham and her lies. I should have told her not to call again. That I was too good for her, that she won't ever be able to hurt me or my baby again. Next time, I would be more prepared to tell her my thoughts. Unlocking my phone again, I went back to the call log, just in case I could dial back. I couldn't. But I saw there was a new Facebook notification. It was a message from Angie.

> *Yet again, the clothes are fab, thank you. Steph is going to look precious in them.*

I replied without giving it much thought.

> *I'm glad to hear that.*

145

I expected the conversation to end, but no sooner had I hit send, the three dots of her replying popped into the thread.

I'm not interrupting am I?

Sophie is at her grandparents'.

A child-free evening, how are you finding it?

I hear others talk about how much they love to have some independence every now and then; how it feels good to have time where they're not Mummy or Daddy. And I knew I should say something of that ilk, but I didn't want to lie. There were enough lies floating around. One more felt too much.

Honestly, I'm finding it a little tough.

Angie began to reply. The three dots pulsated for a very long time, and with each passing second, I regretted showing my vulnerability. Angie was being polite, her way of being courteous for the clothes, I guess. She didn't what to know my shit. Christ, *I* didn't want to know my shit.

I get that, I always feel a little lost when Steph is with her dad.

Lost, that was it, I was lost.

How do you cope?

I waited with bated breath. From what I understood, which wasn't a lot, Angie's arrangement wasn't a new one. Maybe she would tell me something to get me through tonight.

I stay busy. Go out, walk, see friends. Be an adult
again.

I didn't know how to respond to that. See friends, go out. Where would I go? Who would I see? Before, it was me and Em, and Sophie. That was enough. Maybe I should have tried more to be the old Rob, with people to see, things to do. Maybe Em would have stayed?

Rob, say no if you want, I wouldn't be offended.
But it sounds like you could use a pint, and to be
honest, I could too. I know it's weird, we don't even
know each other, but do you fancy meeting for a
drink? I also need to get out, and all of my friends
are busy. The Swan in town? What do you say?

I looked at the clock, it was nearly 9 p.m. It wouldn't hurt to pop out for one, give me something to do, and when I fed that back to the Murphy's — that I'd been out, had a beer in a pub — I knew they'd see it as me being OK, even if it was only a coping strategy for not being OK. I'd not been in a single pub since moving here. Not one. The idea made me feel nervous.

What would the Rob from a year ago say to me now?

Sounds good. I can be there in half an hour?

Perfect.

I caught myself smiling. *See you soon. X*

147

CHAPTER TWENTY-THREE

I hurriedly got ready, threw on a jacket, grabbed my keys and stepped out my front door. As I'd not had a drink in so long, and I'd already had a few beers this evening, I knew that after one — or at most two — more, I'd be drunk.

The air felt charged; the electricity particles bouncing inside the clouds on the horizon made my skin tingle. The clouds themselves seemed to have grown in size and deepened in colour, a black-purple beast, its chest rising and falling as it moved on the wind. There was a flash, a light escaping momentarily from the beast's mouth, and I began to count, as I did when I was young. I got to eight and from somewhere deep within it, a grumble sounded, quiet at first. The beast drawing breath. But then it opened its mouth, and thunder roared across the Fens.

A memory of Em came to me: a night in my old flat, a few summers back. We were both at the window, watching a storm rage. Her arms around my waist, my kisses landing on her head. I pushed it down. Buried it deep, kept walking.

As I reached the edge of town, the thunderclouds had crawled closer, a line drawn from them to the ground where the rain was falling. Another flash, this time a fork shooting westwards. Six seconds, and then another roar. The storm was big, the sky, dark, and it was coming my way.

By the time I could see the pub, its battered old sign showing the faded and cracked image of a swan, the clouds had pushed in front of the waning summer light and the myriad soft colours of the sky had a dark undertone, one that felt foreboding. With my hand on the pub's door, I took a breath and shook my head at myself. Rob Clarke, nervous to step in a pub — what would my old friends in my old life think of me now? Bracing myself, I opened the door and looked around to find Angie. The pub was busy — not heaving, but not the quiet working-class pub I thought it would be from the outside. There were several old men perched on stools at the bar, chatting like locals do to the bartender. A few tables had couples, some groups of three or four. As I moved into the pub the guy behind the bar smiled, his braces catching the overhead lighting. He looked far too young to be pulling pints — or maybe I was now getting old. I ordered a pint of lager, thanked the kid and turned, clutching my pint to my chest like it was some sort of security blanket. Gone were the days of me being an elbows-out drinker. Marking my space, holding onto it firmly. Opposite, a table of three looked my way — not the curious glance people sometimes exchanged in public places, but one that felt like I was a subject to be considered. I nodded towards them, a polite notice to say I knew they were watching, expecting them to return the nod and go back to their conversation. They didn't, they just kept watching. Looking away, I caught the eye of an old, weather-beaten face of a man who looked like he smoked sixty a day but would still live to be 103. I smiled towards him, but he shook his head and looked back at his pint. I began to feel like it was a mistake coming — this was clearly a locals' pub, and I wasn't welcome. Walking around the bar, which doglegged to the right, I saw a person on their own, and for a minute I thought it was Em. Did Angie really look similar, or was I just projecting that? I began to approach, wanting to get a better look before calling out Angie's name, just in case it wasn't her. Looking around, I couldn't see any other people sat on their own and, quickly checking my Facebook, I didn't see a message saying she would be late.

'Angie?'

'Rob, hi.' She smiled and stood up, giving me an awkward hug.

'Hi, did you want another drink or . . .' I shifted, unsure how to proceed. It dawned on me that this meeting was utterly bizarre and incredibly needy.

'No, it's fine, I've got one. Grab a seat.' She gestured opposite her, and I moved to sit down, thankful she did. I probably would have just stood on the spot.

'Thanks. So, is this your local?' I started, an ice-breaker.

'God, no.'

'Oh, I thought . . .'

'It's the pub that's equidistant for us. I thought it would be best.'

'I see, makes sense.' I took a sip of my pint, wracking my brain for something to say, and watched Angie do the same. The silence was uncomfortable. I needed to say something — anything — but what? Should I talk about Sophie, or Em. Should I ask about her baby? Maybe I needed to lead in with a question about her ex. I opened my mouth to say something but nothing came, and I retreated back to another sip of my pint. Thankfully, just as the silence became unbearable, the rain began to hit the window beside us. The storm didn't ease over us but hammered in a full deluge, pummelling the windows and old slate roof above.

'Jesus, that's come down quick.' Angie said, looking out of the window.

I noticed a slight slur to her words, like she'd had a few drinks.

'Yeah, wow. Hopefully it'll blow over as fast as it's come.' I noticed my words slurred too.

'Usually the way,' she said, still not looking at me. 'I love the rain.'

'Me too. God knows we've needed it.'

Angie turned her attention to me, and held my gaze for a moment. I wanted to hold her eye, show her I was at ease being in a pub with her. But I faltered and again took a mouthful from my pint. I needed to slow down — if I carried on at this rate, I'd finish the pint, have to order another to give me something for my hands to do, and then I'd end up drunk.

'Rob, thank you for meeting me here. I know it's a little weird for someone you met on Facebook to ask you out for a drink. Not that this is me asking you out, I mean . . .'

'Angie, I get it, and it's totally fine. To be honest, I'm glad. I still don't know many people up here and with Sophie being at her grandparents' . . . well, you know.'

'Yeah, I do. It's hard isn't it?'

'Harder than I thought it could be.'

'So, you're not from around here?'

'No, lived in South London all my life.'

'It must have been a huge shock moving up to the Fens?'

'Oh, yeah.' I smiled and Angie laughed. 'Em, Sophie's mum, is from around here. It was the right decision for Sophie, but wow, adjusting was hard.'

'I bet.'

'What about you? Have you always lived around here?'

'Yes and no. I travelled a bit when I was younger; lived in Canterbury for a while after uni.'

'Canterbury's nice.'

'Yeah, I loved it there, but somehow I just keep finding my way back to the endlessly flat lands.'

'It is flat, isn't it?' I laughed. 'Such a shock when we moved.'

'Yeah, it's just as big a shock when you come back, trust me.'

'Think you'll stay here?'

'Maybe,' she said, taking a big mouthful of her drink. 'I always wanted to live near water, a place by the sea, or a lake. I like the water.'

'I know what you mean. I'm the same, but couldn't afford the price of a place by the sea.'

'My uncle had a run-down old house near Boston. He left it to me last year when he passed.'

'Sorry.'

'It's OK.'

'Boston as in the USA?'

She laughed. 'No, as in the arse-end of Lincolnshire.'

'There's a Boston around here?'

'Yep, about an hour away. And a smaller place called New York.'

'No way!'

'I kid you not. It's not the loveliest location for sea-gazing, it's on the Wash, so it's pretty grim. But I've always liked it there. The wildlife is amazing, if you like that sort of thing. Used to go as a kid, always wanted to go back.'

'Why don't you?'

'The house needs work. It's having the time and money.'

'Well, I hope you do. It sounds nice,' I said, enjoying the small talk.

'The wildlife, yes. The town, it's a dump — but a fresh start, you know?'

'Yeah, I do,' I said, understanding that Angie was having a tough time of it all, just like me. Outside the rain intensified, and we both looked out.

'Well, now I wish I'd brought a brolly,' I said, and again Angie smiled. I started to feel myself relax. I could still be fun Rob, Rob who can chat to people and be engaging on an adult level. That part of me had been dormant for a while, and I'd thought it was gone. Angie finished her drink and got up to get another, insisting she bought me another pint. I agreed, but I'd not let myself have any more after. When she returned and sat opposite, the conversation felt easier. The ice successfully broken, thanks to the rain, which gave us both the nudge to start. She told me about her uni days, her life after. She spoke of Stephanie and I told her about Sophie. She was as doting as a mother should be. As Em should have been. I didn't ask, but she offered details about her ex, her reasons for her leaving him, and why it was still a daily battle now. I didn't interrupt but listened as she, perhaps, told me more than a stranger should, and I wondered if this was why she asked me to meet her — not to form a friendship, but because she needed a release with someone who didn't know who her ex was. Not that I minded. It was nice to listen, to help someone else. It removed me from my own self-pity. Gave me a new focus. As she started to talk about the battles over child maintenance payments, she had to pause before she got upset.

'God, I'm sorry, I've been ranting for about ten minutes,' she said, embarrassed.

'No, don't be sorry.'

'I'm dumping my shit on a stranger. I promise, I was once cool.'

'I think you're pretty cool — and don't worry, I get it, it's hard. I don't know about you, but mostly life is just me and Sophie. When I'm fed up or annoyed it's not like I can talk to her about it, and you can't with Stephanie. I'm glad I could listen.'

'Me too.'

Angie drained her drink and excused herself to go to the bar. When she returned she had another pint for me, another something and Coke for her and, not wanting to look stupid for having two on the go, I drained my current pint and accepted the new one. The beer would start to move around me soon, washing over me with its warm giddy glaze; already my head felt lighter.

'So, Rob, where's Sophie's mum?'

'I'm sure you know already; it seems everyone knows.'

'I've heard a few things, mostly gossip. You can tell me to shut up if you want?'

'It's fine. Sophie's mum . . .' I couldn't bring myself to say her name, 'she left us.'

'Oh, I'm so sorry.'

'No, no, it's OK.'

'Is it?'

I took a breath. It would have been totally acceptable for me to say yes, it's OK, but I didn't want to lie. There was something about Angie that made me want to be real. Perhaps it was that she was a stranger, or perhaps I saw a little of my struggle in her eyes. The bags under them heavy, just like mine. We were two people who had the weight of the world pressing down.

'No, it's not OK. But I'm working hard to make it so.'

Angie nodded, raised her glass and I clinked it. A toast to the survivors of life, and we both drank.

'It must have been hard, when she went. When I left my ex, it was my choice to, but even so it crushed me. I can't imagine being on the receiving end.'

'I wasn't there when she went.'

'Sorry?'

I told Angie about how I discovered Em was gone — the empty bed, no note, Sophie crying alone.

'Oh God, how long was Sophie on her own for?'

'I don't know, I hope only a short while. Even now, I can't bear to think of Sophie being alone all night.'

'And she didn't even leave a note?'

'Nothing.'

'That's so shit. I mean—'

'No, you're right, it is shit. I didn't even see it coming, I thought everything was fine.'

'And you've not seen her since?'

'Nope, the police looked for her, said they found evidence she went to France with another man.'

'She went to France?'

'Yes.'

'Christ, I thought I had it bad,' she said, then covered her mouth, embarrassed. 'Oh God, I'm sorry, I've had a few.'

'No, it's fine.' I smiled. 'I like that you say it as it is. It's refreshing.'

'Well, it sounds like what you've been through has been really rough. Healing takes time — you have to give yourself that time, you know?'

I nodded. 'Thanks, Angie. I just wish I understood, that's all.'

'And she left nothing?'

'I mean, she left *most* things. Most of her clothes, shoes, personal items.'

'Sounds like she left in a hurry.'

'Yeah, she did.'

Sensing it was still raw, Angie moved the conversation on. We spoke more about the Fens, the endless flatness, the odd local ways. The accent, and common mispronunciations. And we laughed, the alcohol helping us along, an old friend. Before we knew it, the barman was calling for last orders and, deciding not to have another, we upped to leave. As we stepped outside, the rain that was still lashing down had stirred up the dry soil and released the smell from the Tarmac. There was a word for it, but I couldn't remember.

'Petrichor,' Angie commented when I mentioned it.

'That's it, petrichor.' I smiled.

Angie popped her umbrella and smiled sympathetically when she saw I didn't even have a hood on the light jacket I wore.

'Thanks for this evening, Rob, I had a nice time.'

'Me too.'

I wasn't sure if I should give a hug, or a friendly kiss on the cheek, or a good, firm handshake, so I kind of amalgamated the three into a peculiar and uncomfortable exchange.

'See you, Angie.'

'Yeah, see you, Rob.'

I turned and began to walk, trying my best to keep the back of my neck covered from the relentless rain. Just before I turned the corner to walk the straight and exposing footpath back home, I looked over my shoulder. Angie was gone.

* * *

May 28th 2019

Emma

Just when you think you have it all worked out, just when you let down your guard and assume life will look after you, it throws you into a spin all over again. Steve won't let me go. He asked to meet and I said no, that it wasn't a good idea, that I had a tiny baby now who needed me. But he's threatened to tell Rob everything, and I had no choice but to agree. We settled on Cambridge as our meeting place. It's open, public, close enough to home to travel, far enough away not to be seen.

I don't need to tell myself it was a mistake, that I should have just been firm, and then told the truth to my poor husband. I should have stayed, parented, done the right thing. But I'm afraid, so I lied, and told Rob I wanted to have a few hours to myself, do some shopping. Rob said it was a good idea, he would be fine with Sophie and I should take my time.

He really is too good for me.

I've barely thought of Steve since Sophie was born, but now I had to. I wanted to show how much I've changed, to show him the woman I've become. And I'm glad I went. I told Steve I wouldn't go back to him, ever. I told him I would rather face the truth with my husband, and I would do so in the hope he would forgive me my failings. I told him I wouldn't be held by my mistakes anymore. And Steve listened; he listened and accepted.

I don't feel guilty anymore for what I've done, I just feel tired. The truth will find its way out; Rob will discover who I am. I owe him as much.

But if I tell the truth, I'm terrified what will happen. He will be heartbroken, and he has a temper on him, if I tell the truth, I really don't know how he will react.

CHAPTER TWENTY-FOUR

Rob

The walk home took me the best part of an hour, the booze and lashing rain playing their part in trying to rob me of my ability to both walk in a straight line and see where I was going. The storm had taken the heat out of the night, and as the torrent collided with the ground, it washed up smells: hot wet Tarmac and something earthy from the fields. The Fens' petrichor is different to the city's. Several cars sped by, flicking muddy puddles up onto the hem and calf of my jeans, one of them intentionally trying to soak me because they thought it would be funny. By the time I opened my front door and stepped inside I was wet to the bone. Closing the door behind me I took out my phone, wiped it on one of Em's scarves that still hung on the coat peg by the door, and checked to see if Frances had messaged. Nothing. At first I worried, but calmed myself: if something was the matter, they would have called. The silence said that Sophie was fine, and everything was OK. Noticing I was dripping water all over the floor, I stepped back onto the doormat and peeled off my clothes and, just in my underwear, carried them into the kitchen and loaded them straight into the washing machine. Wobbling upstairs I put my phone on the cistern of the toilet, just in case, and flicked on the shower. Despite it being a warm day, the rain was cold, and my muscles ached from shivering. Drunk and warmed, I got out of the shower, put on some underwear and, grabbing my phone, collapsed onto the bed. The room spun — not the kind where I thought I'd throw up, but the kind that would allow me to slip into unconsciousness. I checked again for a message from Frances. Nothing. I wanted to worry for Sophie, but she must have been OK; if she wasn't I'd know. I almost called, just in case, but stopped myself. It was nearly midnight and I wanted to show I was coping, even if I wasn't. Tomorrow, when I told them I went out, had a few beers, met a friend, they'd be happy for me, they'd think I'd turned a corner. Perhaps I had, but I doubted it. Dropping my phone on my chest, I closed my eyes; sleep would come soon. The room continued to spin, and I let myself succumb to it, let myself be washed to and fro, like I was in a boat as the storm outside raged.

Then I heard something — a faint knock coming from downstairs. I sat up, listened. All seemed quiet, all felt still; it was probably just the house moving. Old houses creaked and groaned, trying to make their old walls comfortable in their foundations. The hard ground was now saturated. It was that, it had to be. Sighing, I lay down again, but there was another noise. It sounded like a footstep. Just one, on the laminated floor in the kitchen. Getting to my feet, I staggered to the top of the stairs and peered over the banister.

'Hello?'

There was no response. As I moved towards the top step, I heard two more distinct footsteps, followed by the sound of the back door opening. Someone was in my house. Running down the stairs I began to shout, a series of expletives that didn't form anything coherent. I should have been scared, but all I felt was rage, drunken rage. How dare they be in my house, where my daughter slept? I could kill them.

Losing my footing halfway down, I fell, and rolled the final six or seven steps. Lying on the floor, looking through to the garden, I saw the outline of someone jumping over the small fence. The same spot Em did. I got up, ran through the house and crashed through the back door. The intruder was ahead somewhere, running through the fields. I gave chase, slipping in the mud that was once a lawn and skidding into the peach tree, knocking the wind out of myself. Staggering to my feet, I watched the figure disappear, but I wasn't going to give up. It might be Em, coming back for something; it might be her lover doing it for her. Climbing the fence, I ran into the tall corn, the rain and darkness engulfing me. It seemed hopeless, but I kept running anyway. I needed answers. I ran as hard as I could, turning left and right along the narrow channels in the crop, the corn whipping against my face. I didn't know what way my house was, but I kept moving until the corn broke as I climbed the slight bank by the reservoir. Pausing to get my breath, I listened for movement, but the rain was coming down hard, sounding like TV static with the volume turned up. It masked all other sounds. I saw a flash, like a phone screen, a hundred yards away, and ran towards it. Just as I was starting to think they'd given me the slip, I saw the light again, up ahead, and I pushed my drunk legs as hard as I could to catch them. The light disappeared, and I stopped. My breathing was hard; I thought I was going to be sick. Placing my hands on my knees I forced myself to take deep, measured breaths. I heard a noise, like someone slipping in the mud. I ran towards the sound and, as I rounded from one narrow channel to another, I could see the corn bending as someone moved through it.

'Hey!' I called out, cutting through the thick crop to catch them up. I cleared the dense vegetation and found myself on a new narrow path. In front there was nothing. I turned, and behind looked undisturbed too. Spinning again, I thought I saw something to my right, and began to run. Then, from my left, I was struck in the head by something hard. It took my legs out from under me and I crashed to the ground. I tried to roll onto my front and get up, but I slipped in the mud, and as blood ran across my face from the wound on my head, I saw two boots in front of me. I tried to look up, to see who it was, but they hit me again, knocking me out cold.

PART 3:
HIM

CHAPTER TWENTY-FIVE

July 7th 2019
Nineteen days missing

An angry rumble snapped me awake. I expected to see my ceiling and cheap IKEA lampshade. Above me was only sky, dark and foreboding. Rain pouring, my underwear soaked through, my body cold and covered in mud. The sky rumbled again, telling me to get up. As I rolled onto my side my head throbbed, and touching it I felt a large lump above my eye. My hand came away tacky, fingertips covered in blood. Then it all came back to me: Sophie at her grandparents', the evening drinks with Angie, coming home and hearing — no, seeing — someone in my house. The chase, being hit.

Sitting up, I groaned; my muscles ached with cold and my head hurt. Gingerly, I got to my feet, then vomited on them. I began to move as fast as I could, because despite knowing Sophie was at her grandparents', despite knowing she wasn't in the house when the person broke in, I needed to make sure. As I stumbled and slipped, my vision unable to focus on far-away objects, I thanked God Sophie wasn't at home and shuddered at how easily she could have been. What if I'd said no to Frances and John when they offered to take her? What if she'd stayed with them the night before instead? Like she was supposed to? She would have been alone all night, for a second time, or the person who broke in might have taken her.

The thought made me retch again.

On my hands and knees, I heard a noise coming from somewhere behind, and spun around to look, holding my breath. The silence that ensued made my heart gallop. They could still be there; watching, waiting. Slowly, I got back on my feet and moved towards where I'd heard the noise. Jumping as a pheasant took flight and clattered away. I forced myself to calm. Of course they weren't here, they were long gone, and my daughter was safe; my daughter was asleep, in her cot at her grandparents', who loved her. I repeated it until it became my mantra, and it worked: I felt my stomach settle and my mind begin to clear. I looked towards my home and could see, even as far away as I was, the back door was still open. But there was no sign of anyone. Whoever it was who had attacked me, whoever it was who was in my home, was gone.

As I walked, the once dry, cracked earth was saturated and boggy, and several times I lost my footing and fell. The rain hadn't stopped since the heavens opened the previous night, and the ground that had been trustworthy now tried to suck me down into it. If I were wearing shoes, it would have pulled them clean off my feet. After what felt like forever, walking and slipping, I could see the fence to my home. I prayed it wasn't late in the day; that the Murphy's weren't there, or trying to get hold of me. The dark clouds stretching as far as I could see robbed my ability to guess the time: it could be 6 a.m. or noon, I had no idea. The closer I was to home, the closer I also was to nosey neighbours and, keeping low, I tried to run the final hundred yards or so. Failing after only ten. As I hit the ground, my face slapping on the wet, sticky earth, there was a flash of lightning and I noticed something in the mud, a shimmer of light reflecting the heavens

163

above. Something metallic. I reached out under a row of corn for it. Where it lay out of sight — you'd only see it if you had your face in the dirt. At first I didn't want to believe what I was seeing, but as I half-crawled, half-scurried towards it, there was no mistaking what it was. I just didn't know what it meant.

Discarded in the mud was a necklace. Em's necklace. Em's necklace that was given to her when her beloved nana passed away; the one she always wore. Always. Picking it up, I hoped I was mistaken, as I couldn't process what it would mean if I wasn't. But there was no mistake; it was her necklace. Em had thrown away her family, but this necklace meant so much to her. The locket was intact, but the chain had been snapped. Wiping my dirty hands on my wet underwear, I opened the clasp. The picture of Em and her nana was still there. She wouldn't throw it away — she loved that necklace, and as hard as I tried to see another reason, all that came was the image of her struggling and the necklace being snapped from her neck. I had no doubt she was planning to leave with Steve Burton, but maybe she had second thoughts, and maybe he left her no choice? And maybe he came back, to find something of hers, to remove something he'd left behind so he wouldn't be caught.

Holding it tight, I slowly made my way home and over the fence, the lashing rain and sore head making the small climb more difficult than it should have been. The neighbours from two doors down saw me from their bedroom window, the same window I had to assume I was photographed from when I was climbing over the fence with Sophie in the night. But I didn't care, not now. I walked towards my house — the back door was wide open, and the cooker clock showed 6.31 a.m. Grabbing a tea towel, I dried myself as best I could, then ran upstairs to my phone and found PC Cahill's number. As it dialled I took deep breaths and tried to remain calm. There must be a reasonable explanation for it being there. But still, all I could see was that she struggled.

'PC Cahill?' she said.

'It's Rob Clarke.' My words were shaking as I spoke.

'Mr Clarke, everything OK?'

'I need you here. Please.'

'Rob, calm down. Tell me what's happened. Are you OK? Is your daughter OK?'

'I have proof someone took her, she didn't leave by her own free will, someone took my wife.'

CHAPTER TWENTY-SIX

'Here you are, Rob,' PC Cahill said, handing me a tea. She came only twenty minutes after I'd called, with someone from forensics and Sinclair, who I wasn't in the mood for.

'Thank you,' I said, my hands shaking. I was wrapped in my dressing gown after quickly showering, wet soil and blood swirling down the plughole. The blood, it turned my stomach.

'We should get your head looked at, might need a stitch,' Cahill said.

'I'm fine, thank you.' I couldn't look at her, I was so focused on the rainwater running down the living room window.

'Rob, start from the beginning. You said someone was in your house?'

'Yes, yes, someone was in my house.' Behind me, a woman in white was dusting the back door for prints. Sinclair was with them, but he wasn't watching or helping with what they were doing, he was watching me. I thought about our altercation and could see another question on his lips. I couldn't help thinking he wanted to hit me, but didn't know why. The forensic officer stopped, looked at Cahill and shook her head. No prints.

'I'm telling the truth — I am. Someone broke into my house,' I said desperately, aware that I hadn't brushed my teeth and my breath reeked of stale beer.

'Rob, please, we are trying to help. OK? You chased them?'

'Yes, over the back fence and into the field, then they did this.' I gestured to the lump and cut above my eye. 'I came to just before I called you.'

'I thought you found the necklace?' Sinclair said, unblinking.

'Yes, yes, I found the necklace in the mud.'

'So, which was it? Did you call, or did you find the necklace?'

'I've said all this. I woke up, slipped in the mud, found the necklace half-buried and then rang you.'

'Rob, we're just trying—'

'They opened that back door; I saw them do it. They had to use the handle. There should be prints. They were in my house, and I saw them open the door,' I said, staring at Sinclair. He stared back, and I wasn't going to back down.

'PC Sinclair.' Cahill stepped in. 'Do you want to have a look outside for anything?'

'Outside?'

'Yes, outside,' she said again, sternly.

Sinclair stepped out into the rain, muttering to himself.

'He really doesn't like me,' I said, once he was out of sight.

'It's just his way. Don't read into it.'

'Is it his way to shove people in the street?'

'I'm sorry?'

'The day I found out Em was having an affair.'

'He shoved you?'

'Yeah.'

Cahill didn't say anything but looked around me to the garden where Sinclair was walking along the fence. I could tell by her look that shoving people wasn't his way at all.

'Rob, are you sure nothing was taken?'

'No.'

'And you're sure someone was in your house?'

'What's that supposed to mean?'

'You've been under a lot of pressure recently.'

'Someone was in my house. How else do you think I got this cut?'

'Rob, calm down.'

'And I think it's connected to Em's disappearance.'

'What makes you think that?'

'I just know it. And Em's necklace, the way it's snapped. I think she didn't leave with Steve Burton; I think he took her.'

'Let's not get ahead of ourselves. There still isn't anything to suggest she was taken by force.'

'Or if not him, this has something to do with Melanie Timpson.'

'Who?'

'She was a childhood friend of Emma's. The day Sinclair shoved me in the street I'd been to find her, spoke with her dad. He hates Emma. He wanted to see her come to harm.'

'He said that?'

'No, but I could see it in his eyes.'

'I'll look into it,' she said, but I could see she was looking at me like I was losing my mind. Perhaps I was. Perhaps I just stopped a burglary attempt, and the rest was in my head? Fabricated to cover the fact that my wife didn't love me anymore?

But the necklace; I couldn't get past the necklace.

Sinclair came back into the house, cursed the rain and looked into the living room.

'I didn't get his name,' I continued, hoping persistence would make them take me seriously.

'Who are we talking about?' Sinclair asked.

'Melanie Timpson's father.'

'What's that got to do . . .'

'It's OK, PC Sinclair. I've got the details,' Cahill said, giving him a look.

'He was so angry,' I continued. 'He threatened to set his dog on me. He didn't like Em. He hated her, in fact. He needs to be looked at as well.'

'Interesting use of past tense, Mr Clarke,' Sinclair said, and I wanted to tell him to fuck off.

'Rob—' Cahill said, taking my attention.

'Because I just know it, Em was taken. She was.'

'Rob, the break-in is something we take seriously — there's been a spate of them recently in the town, and this is likely connected. But I don't think it has anything to do with your wife.'

'It does, I can feel it.'

'Let me give you a number; it's for a grief counsellor I know. They're really good with this sort of thing.'

'What, they have a good track record with people who know something has happened to their wife?'

'No, Rob. She specialises in marriage breakdowns.'

'My marriage was fine.'

'Past tense again, Mr Clarke,' Sinclair said quietly.

'Rob, I'm referring you to her because that is what this is. Em left you for someone else. It's tragic, unfair — cruel, even. But it is what it is.'

'But what about the necklace? What about the Timpson man? Surely you can see this doesn't add up anymore?'

'The necklace likely broke off when she was leaving. It was dark, she'd never have been able to find it. It was pure chance you slipped when you did, or you wouldn't have found it either. As for the Timpson man, it seems Emma was wild in her youth, often got others into trouble. We'll speak to him. He shouldn't make threats, but this is a small town; people don't forget.'

'But surely—'

'I'm sorry Rob, truly.'

Cahill reached into her pocket and pulled out a business card. I didn't look at it.

'Give her a ring, let her help.'

Smiling, Cahill stood and, as the forensic officer wrapped up, she said her goodbyes. Sinclair didn't, and Cahill noticed. As they dashed back to their car, their coat collars up, Frances and John arrived, their car lights on, despite it being the middle of the day. They saw the police car and, as they ran into the house to escape the elements, I could see they were worried.

'Rob? Is everything OK? Oh God, your head!' Frances said.

'I had a fall,' I replied, and I didn't know why I lied.

'God, are you OK? Is everything OK?'

I took Sophie, who was all smiles, and kissed her on the head. 'Yeah, they were just checking up on me, everything is fine.'

But everything wasn't fine. I knew in my gut Em was taken. I needed to do something. I trusted Cahill would look at Melanie Timpson and her father, which meant I could look elsewhere. And I knew exactly where I would start.

I needed to find him. I needed to find Steve Burton.

CHAPTER TWENTY-SEVEN

Thankfully, the Murphy's didn't stay long. I needed to work out my next steps, without alarming anyone. I suspected Frances and John would see it the same way as Cahill did, because of Em's past. She was a runner, but not this time, I could feel it. Not this time.

Back on Facebook, I tried to track him down again, but it was no use. Too many Steve Burtons. None of them on Em's friends list. If I was going to find out who he was, I needed another plan.

Sophie was ratty all morning, refusing her nap and, despite the weather, I knew a walk would calm her. So, after making sure she wouldn't get wet or cold, we headed out. The walk into town was tough: even with my rain mac on and hood up, I felt water on my skin; a droplet running down my neck. My feet were wet through my shoes and even though it was still summer, still warm, I felt numbed. But the walk did me good: fresh air, clean air. And Sophie was asleep within ten minutes. As I walked, I realised how to get to Steve. I needed to get access to Em's Facebook. Cahill told me they discovered a conversation on there. If I could get in, I would know exactly which Steve Burton was *the* Steve Burton.

By the time I stepped into the usual coffee shop, my jeans were soaked from the knee down. Sophie was sound asleep, and as I peeled off the buggy cover and shook it to try and remove the excess water, people gave me funny looks. Some pity, some annoyance. Taking a table in the far corner I ordered a flat white. As the coffee arrived and I took my first sip, Sophie began to stir. She stretched, screwed up her face and before I could lift her out, she began to cry. She hadn't napped for long enough.

It was going to be a tough day.

I tried to comfort her. I tried cuddling, bobbing, I tried to give her a bottle, something to eat, I checked her nappy, which was dry, and nothing seemed to work. She wasn't a happy little girl, and there was nothing I could do. On the table nearest, two older ladies looked at me — concerned expressions on their faces — like I was doing something wrong. I almost said something; a word on how she was teething, or something whimsical, to try make them see I had it under control, that I was a good daddy, but stopped myself. The only thing to do was leave, and as I fought to get her in the buggy, trying my very best to calm her, feeling like I was going to burst into tears at any moment, I felt a hand on my shoulder.

'Rob?'

Looking up I was taken aback to see Angie stood there, a takeaway cup in her hands.

'Angie!'

'You OK?' she said, looking down to Sophie, who continued to scream.

'No, Sophie's really upset, and I can't calm her.'

'Oh no, little lady, what's wrong?' Angie said, lowering herself down to Sophie's level. Sophie continued to cry.

'Oh dear, do you mind if I pick her up?'

'No, not at all.'

Angie scooped up Sophie and gently bobbed her, talking to her quietly, and within a minute Sophie began to settle. Her wail became a cry that became a whimper.

'Pass me her bottle,' Angie asked and, shocked, I did so without questioning it. The bottle went in and Sophie, who only moments before was inconsolable, settled and drank her milk. Angie sat in my chair, and I perched on the one opposite, gutted I couldn't calm her like Angie just did.

'Sometimes a baby will play up for a parent. Trust me, I know. Don't overthink it.'

'Thank you for helping,' I said, meaning it.

'Rob, what happened to your head?'

'I bumped it this morning on a cupboard.' I replied quickly.

'Looks sore.'

'Masked my hangover well.' I smiled.

Between us, Sophie babbled and started to chat happily. On the table nearest us, one of the ladies who had looked at me like I was doing something wrong leant in and spoke to Sophie.

'There, you're so much happier now aren't you, little one. All you needed was your mummy, wasn't it? She really is a beautiful little girl.' She said, looking at Angie, who I could see was stunned at the comment.

'Yes, she is,' I said, jumping to her aid. I didn't correct the lady, as I knew she would be embarrassed, or perhaps even look at me judgmentally. Besides, none of it was really her business. The old lady smiled tightly towards me and turned back to chat with her friend. Only then did Angie react to the assumption she was Sophie's mother.

'God, thank you, I froze.'

'No, it's OK. No harm.'

'Yes, but . . .'

'Honestly, Angie, its fine. Just an honest mistake.'

Sophie knocked her drink onto the floor, and I leant down to pick it up, making my cut and bruise throb. When I sat upright, Angie was looking at me with deep concern.

'Rob, are you OK?'

I smiled, tried to make it look like I was great, but I knew she could see straight through it. I remembered how easy it was to talk to her before. How light I felt after, and almost told her what happened there and then. But it wasn't the time.

'Yeah, I'm OK. You know.'

'You sure?'

'Yeah, honestly, I'm all right.'

'I know we barely know each other, but you can talk to me. If you want to, of course.'

I nodded, lifted my cup and drained a mouthful of luke-warm coffee.

'Sorry, I shouldn't . . .'

'No, don't be sorry, Angie, I'm grateful really. Just, I can't talk, not here. Not in front of Sophie.'

'Rob?'

I wanted to blurt out that my house was broken into, I was attacked, I found Em's necklace, and ask what she thought about it all. I didn't want to assume anything; I knew I couldn't trust my own thoughts.

'Can I message later, though, once Sophie's down for the night? I need someone to . . .'

'To what?'

I paused, desperate to say what had happened, desperate for her to see it from my side; to believe me. But Sophie was watching, and although she might not comprehend what was being said, she would understand something was wrong.

'Can I message you later, maybe?'

'Yeah, of course.'

'Great. Thank you, Angie. I better get this one home.'

I stood, took Sophie from Angie, thankful when she went into her buggy without complaint. I fastened down the rain protector, said my goodbyes and stepped back into the rain.

CHAPTER TWENTY-EIGHT

Whereas walking into town helped tame my anxiety around the break-in, the necklace and what it all meant, the walk home was the complete opposite. The Fens wind drove the rain into my face, making it impossible to see, and Sophie wasn't happy either. She cried and protested from the second we walked through the front door to the moment, hours later, when she finally settled in her cot. I hated that I needed her to be quiet. But I had to think, to plan. I had to find my wife. And Sophie not being a happy girl consumed all my energy. But, just as I started to get ratty too, I remembered the god-awful feeling I'd had that morning, imagining Sophie at home when the break-in happened. Imagining my little girl being taken too. And I calmed. None of this was her fault, and I had to keep her safe. I knew all parents had despairing days. I knew it wasn't a sign of failing — but still, I felt like I was failing. Always failing. To keep my daughter happy, to keep my wife safe. Two things I swore I would always do.

And the relief, the happiness, when Sophie went to sleep, just made me feel worse.

Downstairs, I grabbed a notepad and pen to write down a plan to find Steve Burton, starting with writing down everything

I thought might be a password for Em's Facebook. I listed memorable dates, words, places we had visited, it could be any one of them, and none at all. A text pinged from an unknown number. I hated that I thought it could be Em. Holding my breath, I tapped the screen and the message opened.

Hey, Rob, it's Angie. I hope you don't mind. I took your number from Facebook; I was worried about you earlier, you looked like you'd not slept in a week (no offence). I know you're probably busy, but once Sophie is down, message me. I want to help.

I didn't reply straight away as I wasn't sure what to say. Angie was someone I met to sell clothes to; could I tell her my secrets, my fears? I know I had in the pub, but that was different. We both shared, we both drank. Sober, I wasn't sure I could offload. So I put my phone away and continued to work on possible passwords. A tennis match played in my head, back and forth, as to whether I should message or not. The match lasted for thirty minutes, then I decided that she had asked, so she wanted to know, and I messaged her back.

I wasn't sure where to start — I composed message after message, all of which made me look like I was losing my mind, just as Cahill had seemed to suggest. So I rang her instead.

'Angie?'

'Rob? Are you all right? I hope you don't mind me taking your number?'

'No, thank you for caring.'

'Rob, what's going on?'

'After the pub last night, I came home, and someone was in my house.'

'What? Have you called the police?'

'Yep, they came around, didn't help much.'

Above me I heard a noise. Lowering the phone, I grabbed the baby monitor — I couldn't hear anything, and panic set in. What if he was back? What if he was in my daughter's room? With the phone in my hand I ran upstairs. I was aware

176

of Angie calling my name, but I didn't respond. My sole focus was on Sophie. Running into her bedroom, I saw her window was still closed. I looked into her cot, and in the low light I couldn't immediately see her. I felt I was going to pass out, but as my eyes adjusted I could see her shape, gently breathing, sound asleep.

'Rob? Are you there?'

I stepped backwards out of Sophie's room and slid down into a sitting position on the top step. My legs felt hollow, my hands shook.

'Yeah, sorry.' I said, trying to sound composed.

Jesus, Rob, keep it together.

'Rob, what's going on?'

Taking a deep breath, I told Angie about chasing the intruder, finding the necklace in the mud, how Em wouldn't ever leave that. And for a while, Angie didn't respond. When she did, I felt my blood run cold.

'Sounds to me like she didn't just leave.'

'Thank you, Angie. Thank you for seeing it the same way I do. There's no way the break-in was a coincidence. No way.' I started to cry. I cried because of the shock of what was happening in my life. I cried for my wife. I cried through relief that someone believed me. 'I think she was taken. The police don't believe me — I don't know what to do. I'm trying to find Steve Burton on Facebook, but I don't know which one he is.

'Have you looked at her friends list?'

'He's not on there. But the police told me they found a conversation in her messages. I just can't access her account to find out who he is.' I whispered, not daring to speak any louder through fear I would openly sob.

'Rob, do you need someone? I'm free if you need me, I can be round in half an hour.'

I wanted to refuse, to say I was coping, but I wasn't. I was lonely; afraid. So, so afraid.

'I think I do, Angie.'

'I'll come right over,' she said.

177

CHAPTER TWENTY-NINE

In order to calm myself down as I waited for Angie, I went onto Em's Facebook. Somewhere in her conversations was an exchange with Steve Burton: if I could find it, I could find him. So I tried to log in. I went through my list, trying our daughter's name, her name, her date of birth, Sophie's date of birth. I tried her favourite holiday destination. None of them worked. Then I tried my name, then I tried the date we got together, May 2nd 2016, and her page loaded. It brought a tear to my eye.

In her inbox was one message exchange with Steve Burton.

I've added you from my new Facebook page.

OK.

I didn't know Em had another Facebook page.

Coming out, I searched her name, but could only find the page I knew about. Then I searched for her under her maiden name, Emma Murphy, and there she was. Thankfully, her email was the same; the password was not the date we got together, but Sophie's date of birth instead. Her new page had only a few friends, and one Facebook Messenger chat, between her and Steve. That's why I couldn't find him in her friends list — they weren't friends there, but on here. I wondered why the police didn't tell me she had a separate page; they would have known. Reading the exchange with that man was tough. They spoke of lust, of love. Of their new life together. They set a date to leave: the night Em went missing. But it still didn't make sense. If she was going to leave, like she planned, to start again in France, why wouldn't she have taken more things? A suitcase, clothes, personal possessions? If she left according to plan, why was her necklace in the mud?

Going onto my Facebook account, in case he saw Em's was active, I searched for Steve Burton again and, knowing which photo was his, I found him. His page was almost non-existent but for a few pictures. I wanted to learn more. There wasn't much to see, but I could send him a message. Without thinking, I tapped on the icon and began to type.

I know you had something to do with Em going missing. I'm going to find out what.

I hit send and locked the phone.

There was a knock at the door and I jumped, even though I knew it would be Angie. I checked over the downstairs of the house; it was clean enough. The back door still had remnants of the forensic dusting for prints, but I doubted she'd see it. Answering the door, I smiled, and she did too, waiting patiently for me to invite her in out of the rain. I eventually got wise.

'Sorry, come in.'

Angie took off her coat and I hung it up to drip dry.

'Bloody weather, wish it would make up its mind.' Small talk.

Having Angie in my house felt strange. Almost like I was doing something I shouldn't. I think she could tell; when I invited her into the living room to take a seat while I made us both a cup of tea (it didn't feel right to offer wine), I watched her rubbing the palms of her hands on her jeans, uncomfortable because of the awkward welcome. As I came back in with our hot drinks, I smiled, trying to show I was relaxed, but it didn't land, and Angie tried in earnest to start a conversation, something that was free flowing, like in the pub the night before.

'Is Sophie upstairs?'

'Yep. Sound asleep.'

Simultaneously, we both took a sip of our teas, and Angie looked around the living room. It took me a moment to consider her. She really did look a little like Em. And I couldn't help but wonder if that was part of the reason I felt closer to her than anyone else here. Even her top, a light blue blouse, was something Em would wear. In fact, I was sure something very similar was hanging in the wardrobe. Angie's eye landed on a fixed spot and she squinted to see it more clearly. I followed her eyeline. She was looking at a picture of Em on the shelf above the TV.

'I should really take it down . . .' I began, even though I had no intention of doing that, with any of her pictures. Surprisingly, Angie stood and walked over to the picture and picked it up. She examined it for a moment and, although I really wanted her to leave it alone, I didn't say anything.

'She was really pretty.' Angie said, placing it back on the shelf and turning to me. 'Rob, talk to me, are you OK?'

'I feel foolish now . . .'

'Does that mean you don't think someone took Em?'

I considered the question. 'No, I still think she was taken.'

'But the police don't?'

'Nope. She has a history of running away.'

'Why do you think she was taken?'

'I always have — she wouldn't just leave Sophie. I buried it when the evidence said otherwise — but the intruder, the necklace.'

'What do you think happened?'

'Em was having an affair. She had planned to leave with him. But I think she had second thoughts, about leaving, and he took her.'

'By he, do you mean Steve?'

'Yeah and I've messaged.' I didn't tell her I hacked my wife's Facebook and read their lusty exchange.

'Can I see it?'

'Sure?' I said, wondering why she would want to. I didn't question it — I'd asked her here for her help, a fresh set of eyes, wasn't that the point? Unlocking my phone, I handed it to her. I thought for a split second I saw the start of a smile, like she'd worked something out that I'd not seen, but it quickly turned into a shoulder shrug.

'He's read it.'

'Yeah, but no reply.'

'Because it's you. I bet you've already been blocked.'

'So now what?'

Through the baby monitor, I heard Sophie begin to stir. I thought she'd settle, but the grizzle became a full-on cry. Hearing her cry out like that made my heart drop into my stomach and, without excusing myself, I ran upstairs, two at a time. I didn't care how it looked. Sophie was on her back, tears streaming down her tiny face, and she was shaking. When I picked her up, she buried her head into my shoulder, and as soon as she did, she began to settle.

'Oh, darling, have you had a bad dream? Don't worry, Daddy's here. Everything's OK, Daddy's here.'

I stayed with Sophie for around ten minutes, until she fell asleep again, then gently lowered her back into her cot and went downstairs to join Angie who sat, brow furrowed, thinking. Only when I hit the third from bottom step, which creaked, did she look up.

'Hey, is she OK?'

'A bad dream I think, she's settled again.'

'I'm glad. Scary isn't it, when they cry like that?' Angie smiled.

'Yeah, sorry, I'm a little panicky about things.'

'Don't be sorry, I'd be exactly the same — worse if I was in your place.'

'Thanks.' I sat beside her.

'Rob, I've been thinking. What if there was a way you could talk to Steve Burton without him ever knowing?'

'I don't follow?'

'I believe you, about Em. The rest could be a coincidence, but I don't know anyone who would leave their baby alone like she did.'

'Exactly. Yes, Em, I just know Steve Burton took her against her will. She needs us to find her.'

It wasn't until I'd finished my sentence that I realised I'd called Angie by Em's name.

'So, what do we do now?' she said, not embarrassing me by noting my mistake.

'We?'

'We both know I didn't offer to come over just so you could offload. I'm here to help.'

'Why, though?'

'Because if I was in your situation, I'd want someone to help me.'

'Thank you,' I said, having to get up and move as her kindness was overwhelming. The relief in having someone believe me was palpable. 'But I don't even know where to start. How would I talk to him without him knowing it's me? I could go through Em's Facebook, perhaps?

'Try that.'

Grabbing my phone, I went into Em's secret account. But the conversation thread had been deleted, and when I tried to connect to Steve Burton's page, I couldn't. It had been blocked. I went back to Em's main page, and it was more of the same. He too had access to her accounts, and made it look like he didn't exist.

'I can't get in,' I said. 'He's blocked her accounts.'

'Then create a fake profile. Maybe he'll accept a stranger, assuming he must know them.'

'I doubt that would work.'

'It might. Think about how many friends you have on your Facebook, and how many of them you actually know?'

Angie had a point. I had only a handful of real friends, most in London that I hadn't taken the time to stay in touch with, maybe Harry from work, and her, if I could call her that, yet around eight hundred on Facebook. Why didn't I think of that before? A fake profile might mean I could worm my way into his world.

'That's a great idea. Thank you.'

'Rob, I better go, you look like you need some sleep, and Steph will wake up soon for her evening feed, her dad Facetimes me . . .'

'Yes, of course.'

Taking her mug, I set it down on the coffee table and walked her to the door. She put on her coat, and as I opened the door she leant in and kissed me on the cheek. 'Speak soon?'

I didn't reply, taken back by her kindness, support, and — if I was honest — the closeness. I hadn't had someone, other than my daughter, as close to me as Angie was just then in weeks. Angie ran to her car, and once she was pulling away, her window wipers battling the rain, I closed the door and locked it.

CHAPTER THIRTY

I tried to settle in bed, but I couldn't. I kept having flashbacks of someone being in my house, and being so far away from Sophie made me feel unsettled, so I dragged my duvet into her room and tried again. My eyes stung through tiredness, but I couldn't sleep, not yet. Angie's idea of a fake profile was good and, feeling bold, drawing that energy from her, I sat up against Sophie's cot bed and set to work on creating a fake Facebook account that might lure Steve Burton into accepting me. I thought about creating a woman, but, if he was anything like me, he'd assume it was a bot account and block it. So, I'd be male. Steve's profile picture showed him stood with a mountain bike, his legs covered in mud. Sunglasses and smiles. I thought he was around forty. So I went with that. I created a profile for a man of a similar age. Thinking back to the Eighties, I recalled the names that were popular at the time. I wanted my profile to be someone Steve might think he went to school with. I settled on Dan — everyone knew a Dan from school, didn't they? The surname wasn't so easy. Again, I wanted it to be something that might sound familiar. After several attempts, sounding out the full name, I went for Murray. Daniel Murray. It was as good as any other name. The profile picture was just as hard. I scanned Google for a man's face. Most of them were model-quality pictures, or celebrities. Dan Murray wasn't either. Scrolling through endless perfect smiles and hair, I found one of a man stood at the top of a mountain. He was wearing sunglasses and a beanie; two thumbs up. He looked about the right age and, with Steve Burton being a mountain biker, it was perfect. If he didn't think he knew Dan from school, he would assume it was through recreation. I hoped, once the profile was set, linked to a fake Hotmail account I made in a similar name, Steve would recognise him enough to accept his friendship. I added a few details on his bio, and uploaded pictures of mountains, climbing, scenic shots. Some with the back of a man in them, so he'd assume they were all taken by, or with, Dan Murray. I added his interests; that he was in a relationship. I added a university degree, made him appear successful and settled. Disarming. And in the bio, I added NEW ACCOUNT, hoping he'd assume they were already friends. People did it all the time: one account would be full of shit, and instead of cleaning, people just dumped it and started again. These days it was easier to bin something than do the work to make it right.

By the time Dan's page was ready to load, share, and add friends, it was nearly midnight. All I could do now was hope that the random two hundred or so people I'd added would accept my fake account, including Steve. I hoped by morning I could find out more about the man who took my wife. Closing my Facebook app, I lay down, listening to my daughter's gentle breathing.

And I let myself visualise finding Em after all this time.

CHAPTER THIRTY-ONE

July 8th 2019
Twenty days missing

Rob

I woke to the sound of Sophie jabbering in her cot, and as I rolled onto my back, I looked at the time. Just after 5 a.m. I lay and listened to her for a while. It wasn't often she was content to be in her own space, doing her own little thing. And I enjoyed every second of it. I had no idea what she was saying, or what she was doing, but the fact she was entertaining herself felt like a huge milestone that was both liberating and terrifying. Sophie was showing signs of independence. She was becoming her own little person, one that wouldn't always need me. After a few minutes, she began to call out. Stretching, I sat up, and she beamed a smile. As I lifted her out, I was aware that my muscles ached. The lack of sleep, even more than usual, was beginning to show as fatigue. I'd get an early night tonight and try to catch up before I made myself unwell.

'Good morning, darling. You slept well, didn't you?'

I drew Sophie closer to give her a kiss, and she returned it by sucking on the end of my nose and grabbing my eyebrow, tugging it. It hurt a little, but it was her affection, so I didn't care. Taking Sophie downstairs I switched on the kitchen light, then the kettle and, knowing she would be hungry, popped her in her highchair before turning on the CD player. The only disc inside was one of her nursery rhymes, which I sang along to as I made her breakfast.

Outside, the rain continued to fall. Somehow, it seemed heavier than ever; the sky still an impenetrable dark mass. The relentless rain had completely flooded the back garden: overnight, the large, lawn-destroying puddles had merged to make a small lake. Even the peach tree looked beaten, its limbs bent under the weight of sodden foliage. I hoped the ground beneath it would stay firm enough to keep it upright. I loved that tree.

'Well, looks like we might be in for the day,' I said to Sophie as I put her Weetabix in front of her and made a coffee. Just as I got comfortable sitting opposite her, singing along to 'Hickory Dickory Dock' as I fed her, I felt my phone vibrate in my pyjama trouser pocket. I pulled it out; the caller ID said it was an unknown number. My heart galloping, I moved away towards the sink and answered.

'Hello?'

There was no reply.

'Hello, is someone there?' I asked again, my voice shaking, hoping it would be Frances and the line was poor because of the weather. Again, there was no reply, but breathing, as before, and I felt my pulse begin to thump in my temples. Sophie began to grizzle, frustrated that I had stopped feeding her. I spooned in some Weetabix, and as she mulched it in her mouth, I turned my back, I didn't want Sophie hearing me.

'Whoever this is, I know you have something to do with Em going missing,' I hissed. 'I will find out where you are. I will find out where Em is.'

'Highly debatable,' the voice said — one that sounded like it had been filtered through some sort of voice-altering

187

software — and then the line went dead. It took all my effort not to fall over. My head swam. Even though Angie saw it from my perspective, a part of me had still thought I was losing my mind. But Em didn't leave. I had proof, the voice, they didn't deny it, didn't try to plead innocence. He was daring me, taunting me. I was right about Em, I'd felt it all along, but this was proof — undeniable proof. Em had been taken. She didn't leave me, she didn't abandon Sophie. She was removed from our lives unwillingly. Em loved our family. Em loved me, she loved me.

My mind raced — where was she? What had he done to her? I wanted to do something — fight or run or shout. I wanted to reach inside the phone and throttle him until he told me where she was and gave her back. Sophie called out — she wanted feeding — and it snapped my thoughts of violence away. So, instead of reacting, I sat opposite her, smiled, and fed her. My heart raced, my muscles twitched, wanting me to act. But I couldn't. It took Sophie an impossibly long time to eat her breakfast and, if I was honest, I was getting frustrated with her for it. But once she was done, I cleaned her up and we both went into the living room. I left Sophie watching *Peppa Pig* and stepped into the doorway, anxiety spilling out of my pores. I went to the call log, tried to ring back, but it wouldn't connect. I didn't know whether to tell the police or message Angie. She wouldn't be able to do anything, and I doubted the police would care. But I had to do something; I had to respond. Then I remembered my late-night Facebook session and, tapping the app, I logged into Dan Murray's profile. There were dozens of notifications. All of them acceptance of friend requests. It seemed my time-consuming work had paid off. I looked on my — or rather Dan's — friends list. One hundred and twenty-six strangers had accepted. I scrolled to see if the only person I cared about had done the same, and my heart skipped a beat when I saw he had. Tapping his profile, the page sprang to life. And there he was. I could see photos, information, posts on his timeline. Popping my head into the living room, I saw Sophie mesmerised as George and Peppa played hide and seek with their dad. Satisfied she was OK for a moment longer, I tapped on his information section. I wanted to look at pictures but dared not. Because of who he was, I was fearful of him. I knew if I looked at him too much I'd cripple myself to act. He didn't have much information on his profile, but what was there was telling. His school was listed (I'd edit my profile to say the same). It didn't say where he lived, but it did offer his place of work. Or at least, where he used to work before he took off for France. If in fact they did take off for France. I couldn't see how a woman under duress wouldn't be noticed leaving the country. 'Highly debatable', that's what he'd said. Not 'Leave her alone, she's happy', not 'She doesn't love you anymore', but 'highly debatable'. He'd done something to her, and he knew I'd never know what. But I would find her. I could feel it. I tapped on the name of the place where he worked and it showed me a pub in London, not far from where Em and I used to live. Even if he wasn't there anymore, I had to go. I might discover something about him. I had finally pulled on a thread, I was finally acting. Copying the address of his place of work into Google Maps. I saw where to go.

I was going to find him and find my wife.

I sent two messages. The first was to Frances, asking if she would be able to have Sophie that night. The second was to Angie. I said her idea had worked, and I told her I was going to London to get my wife back.

189

Being back in London felt conflicting. It was strange to smell the lifelong-familiar smells, and even stranger to be in close proximity to people all the time. Shoulder to shoulder on the Underground. Avoiding eye contact. No one speaking. No one caring about the other person's business. It was once so ordinary: now, I felt like a tourist. And I suspected I looked like one, too. Eight months in the land of the big skies, wide open spaces, living in a town with a small population, and I was already someone else entirely. London was fast, noisy and, until then, I hadn't realised how tense it really was, being there. But I wasn't there for long. I had a job: find Steve Burton, find my wife, and once I had, we would go home to Sophie. I didn't like that I wasn't with my daughter. I didn't like that I'd lied to Frances and John, telling them I'd been invited out by old work friends, and thought it might do me good to go. The lie worked, of course, and they were happy to see I was my old self again. I didn't like being away from my baby, but what choice did I have?

It was just after six in the evening when I got off the Underground at Clapham Common. I wanted to turn left out of the station, towards where we used to live, towards the life that was uncomplicated, safe, where I knew who I was and didn't fear my own shadow. A life where I had Em. But I couldn't. I had to find him.

According to the Maps app, the bar he worked in was a ten-minute walk and, without hesitating, I began to follow the directions. As I weaved apologetically through the thrum of people, all seeming to be going the opposite way to me, I tried to play out my next step. I imagined he was still at the bar; I imagined the moment he and I came face to face.

Shit, it's you.

Yes, it's me. I fucking know what you did.

I, ummm . . .

Where is she, you piece of shit? Where is my wife?

He would try to run, and I would shoulder-barge him into a table, sending him over it, glasses smashing, people shouting. But I wouldn't care. I'd jump over, grab the scruff of his neck and smack his head into the floor until he told me where she was. He would tell me, or I would kill him. I was so caught up in my fantasy of how it would go, I walked straight into an old man, almost sending him into the road. Thankfully, I managed to catch him by the elbow to stop him falling.

'Oh, God, I'm so sorry.'

'What the hell?' he barked, a thick East End accent instantly making him less fragile.

'I'm so sorry, I wasn't watching where . . .'

'Pull your head out of your arse then,' he said, shaking free from my grasp and walking off. I tried to call another apology, but it sounded weak and pathetic. As I turned to continue my walk to the bar, the daydream of how I would confront Steve was gone. Beaten out of me by a man who was double my age. After a few more minutes, I spotted my destination. A small, underwhelming place. As I approached the door, I tried to recapture something from the brave, strong version of events I envisaged, but the images wouldn't return.

I almost knocked on the bar door before entering, like I was invading. Cursing myself, I stepped inside. It was post-work pint time and the small, tastefully-decorated bar was heaving. The few tables were full of people, as was every available space to stand, and the long serving counter was covered with the elbows of those leaning to drink. But I wasn't here for a pint, nor to find a space to carve as my own. I was here to see if I could find the man who had something to do with my wife disappearing. Looking around, there were loads of men with the same kind of height and build I assumed he would have. Although it was hard to tell from a small photo. Moving through the crowded pub, I made eye contact with several men. Some nodded, some looked past me, like I wasn't even there, and some gave me a glare as if to say 'What the fuck do you want?' Although I didn't really know what he looked like, I knew he would know me. But no one reacted like they knew me. Feeling like I was sticking out like a sore thumb, I plucked up the courage to find a gap at the bar. I ordered myself a pint, and once it was poured, I asked the barman if Steve was in.

'Who?'

'Steve? Steve Burton, he's an old friend of mine. I was hoping to catch him.'

'Sorry, I don't know Steve. I'm new, only my fourth shift.'

'Oh, OK, who would know . . .'

Before I could finish asking who would know when Steve was last in, the barman walked away. Taking a sip of my pint, I thought about what he'd said, Steve hadn't been in for — how long was four shifts? A week, maybe? I asked a few drinkers beside me if anyone knew the Steve who worked there. No one did. No one. Feeling like I might be sick, I put my pint down and walked out of the pub, the cool rain hitting my skin helping me feel better. I'd hoped to find him, or find an answer, but all I had was more uncertainty.

Downbeat, I began to walk. My journey seemed to have been entirely wasted. It had cost over thirty-five pounds to get here. Thirty-five pounds for nothing. A food shop, a new toy for Sophie and some new clothes as she grows, my gas and electricity for a week — wasted. I was no closer to finding Em, no closer to anything other than the breadline. I'd have to sell more things just to get by. Each step I took I was more and more pissed off with myself. So pissed off I stopped caring who I bumped into, or that the rain had soaked through to my skin, making me feel clammy and cold. I stopped caring where I was — and then, before I knew it, I'd walked almost up to the front door of the building where we used to live. I stopped opposite it; looked up to the window that was once ours. I could see movement inside, and before I could hide, a woman approached and looked out. She didn't see me, and in her arms was a baby, a little younger than Sophie. She was pointing at the trees to the left of me, showing her baby them. I could almost hear her telling her baby about what trees are, and why they're so important. Then, from behind them, a man approached and hugged them both, and after a moment, they all moved away.

That could have been us. That could have been Em and Sophie and me. They looked so happy, and it hurt seeing it. It hurt deep inside, and I needed to see my little girl more than I needed anything else in the world.

Head down, I began to walk quickly towards Clapham Common, and as I drew close I noticed something different. I was so caught up in my own thoughts, I couldn't tell you when it happened, but the rain had stopped, and although the sun was still behind a dark cloud, there was a glimmer of it poking through. A glimmer of hope. I couldn't stop myself thinking it meant something. At the station I boarded the Northern Line and, several stops later, arrived at King's Cross, knowing that if I ran, I'd make the 9.30 p.m. train. Seeing my train was leaving from platform eleven, I began to move through the thick crowds. I felt my phone vibrate and pulling it out, I saw it was Frances. And she'd left a voicemail. I tapped the play button and put the phone to my ear.

'Rob, its John.'

My heart dropped into my stomach, and a sparrow began to peck at it.

'Before I carry on, Sophie is fine, she's fine.'

I could hear something in his voice, something I couldn't place. John and I didn't speak much. Frances was the one to call and message. John didn't even have a phone. But he sounded vulnerable, and I'd not heard that from him before.

'Rob, you need to come home, as soon as you can.'

CHAPTER THIRTY-THREE

I managed to make the train, a bead of sweat running down my back, and finding a seat, I tried to ring John back, to tell him I was on my way and would be at Huntingdon Station at just after 10.30 p.m. But it rang and rang, and no one picked up. I tried again, and it clicked into voicemail. At the third time of trying, I left a message.

'It's me, what's happened? Please call me back. I'm on the train now.'

My mind raced, trying to work out what was going on. Sophie was OK, John had said it twice, but still, there was real panic in his voice. Could Frances have been hurt and he needed me back so he could be with her? That would be why he wasn't picking up the phone. I hoped she was ok. I tried to push down my anxiety by busying myself with other people's nonsense on Facebook. I knew most would be doom and gloom, but maybe there would be an interesting post I could dive into, even just for five minutes. As I scrolled, I saw there was a post on the vigil page for Emma — a link to a news article. The tagline made me feel like I was going to pass out.

BODY FOUND IN FENLAND RESERVOIR

My hands shook and I felt like I was about to throw up. I didn't want to connect the dots, but what else could it be? I tried calling John over and over again, but no one was picking up. It made me spiral. I wanted to dismiss it entirely, like when you see an ambulance race past in the direction of your home, and for a split second you think they're going to your address. There must be dozens of reservoirs in the Fens; thousands of missing people. A hundred and eighty thousand of them a year, in fact. The odds that it was Em . . . and yet, I couldn't stop myself thinking it. It was in the sound of John's voice. The desperation for me to come home. As the train announcer stated that Huntingdon was the next stop, I stood, wanting to get off as fast as I could, but almost fell. Shock wreaked havoc on me. I could barely move. Somehow, using the backs of train seats to keep me upright, I managed to make my way to the doors, and when they opened, I stepped out into the cool evening. The sweat on my brow acted like a cold compress as the gentle wind blew. Fighting the ticket barrier with numb hands, I gave up trying to slide my ticket in the machine and clambered over the top. A woman shot me a disgusted look, but when I looked back, she could see I wasn't in my right mind, and looked away.

Half-walking, half-running, I went outside and found a taxi. Climbing in the back, I struggled to tell the driver my address and, still unclear as to where I wanted to go in the town, he took off. I watched the meter climb higher and higher. The little rectangle that indicated when another ten pence would be added was hypnotic. I watched the small red dash rotate clockwise. One, two, three, four, five, six, seven, eight. Then back to one. Outside, the flat lands rolled by, and I was unable to discern exactly where we were. Then, as we entered town, I got my bearings and directed him into my road. It was chaos: several police cars blocked the road; every neighbour was out. As I got out of the taxi, Sinclair was across the road; the old lady from opposite talking to him. He had his head low, pinching the bridge of his nose. He looked up and saw me, and I half expected him to come over and hit me. If looks could kill. I knew then, without a doubt, Em had been found. On hollow legs, I walked up the drive. Before I got to the front door, the sparrow in my stomach flapped its wings and I threw up into a bush, three heaves before it stilled. With watering eyes, I approached my front door. I didn't need to find my keys, as it swung open, and a uniformed officer nodded politely and let me in. I saw John sat on the sofa, his head in his hands. Sat opposite, nursing a cup of tea, was Cahill.

'John, where's Sophie, where's my daughter?' I said in a panic, my legs working once more and catapulting me into the living room.

'Rob, Rob, calm down,' Cahill interjected. 'She's upstairs, Frances is just settling her.' I didn't wait for an invitation — I ran up, three at a time, falling mid-way, and turned at the top for Sophie's bedroom. Frances was sat on the floor, her head resting on the rails of the cot bed, watching Sophie sleep. Slowing down, I stepped in and sat down beside her.

'She's sleeping like an angel,' Frances said quietly, looking at me, her eyes bloodshot. 'I could watch her all night,' she added, looking back to Sophie.

'Frances?'

'When the police told us, I thought it was best Sophie came home. John wanted me to keep her there, but I couldn't be alone.'

'Frances, what's going on?'

I knew, but I needed to hear it out loud for it to be real.

Frances opened her mouth and took a breath like she was about to speak, but before the sounds came, her chin wobbled as she fought to hold back her obvious pain.

'I'm so sorry, Rob,' she eventually said, at barely a whisper, before turning and smiling the saddest smile I'd ever seen at my daughter.

'I wish I was a better mother.'

'Rob?' A voice came from behind me and, turning, I saw Cahill stood on the top step, her knuckles white where she held the banister. 'Can we talk?'

Nodding, unable to speak, I gingerly got to my feet and followed her downstairs. As I sat beside John, he lifted his head, smiled a smile just like Frances', and gently rubbed my shoulder.

'PC Cahill?' I asked, still desperately hoping that this had nothing to do with Em.

'Rob, earlier today, a farmer made a discovery out back, by the reservoir.

'OK?'

'There's no delicate way to say this, so I'll just say it. Rob, Emma was found.'

I was vaguely aware of Cahill saying something, but her words didn't make sense — it was background noise, like someone trying to talk to me while I was underwater. I needed to breathe; needed some air. I stood up, tried to move, but three steps was all I managed. Three small steps, and the world began to spin, then it went black.

CHAPTER THIRTY-FOUR

At first I was aware of voices above me, calling my name, whispers on the wind, soulless, but as the world began to return I could place PC Cahill's and then John's.

'Rob, Rob, are you all right?'

I opened my eyes, confused as I couldn't focus on anything, the world shrouded in a thick fog. Then, as is cleared, I saw John's face looking down at me. Why was I on the floor?

'Rob, that's it son, take it easy, you're all right.'

I tried to speak but the words wouldn't come, and then I was being hauled up under my arms into a sitting position.

'I don't understand?' I eventually asked, my breath still shallow as my diaphragm fought to free itself.

'You passed out,' John stated, matter-of-factly.

'Oh.'

'It's OK, you're all right, give it a minute and you'll feel better.'

Then it came flooding back. The news report, the police, Em. Oh God, Em. I pushed down on the sofa seat, trying to drag myself up onto my feet. But I was hollowed out. I tried again, falling hard. I needed to see Em, I needed to be with her.

'Rob, take it easy.'

'I have to see her.'

'You can't right now, she . . .' Cahill started tenderly.

'I need to see her. Where is she? Where is my Em?'

My diaphragm was released, and I was able to take a deep breath before the tears started to fall. The last of my energy transferred to my grief and, sobbing, I slumped into John's shoulder. I could hear someone murmuring 'oh God, oh God', and wasn't aware straight away it was me. John consoled me, held my head in his arm, emotional too.

'Take a breath Rob, shhhh, I have you boy, I have you,' he repeated, over and over, and I let him hold me, burying my face into the fabric of his jumper. After a while I felt the tears slow, but I didn't move. I just sat there, breathing in John's outdoor smells. Feeling safe for the first time since Em left — no, since she died.

Died. My wife was dead.

Around us police were taking photographs, moving things. Searching for God knows what.

'What's going on?' I asked Cahill.

'Rob, I know this is a hard time, but we have to take a look around.'

'It might not even be her,' I said desperately. 'I mean, no one has formally identified her — have you seen her, John? Has Frances? It could be anyone, it could—'

'Rob, you're right, no one has formally identified her.'

'You see, you see—'

'Rob, it's her, it's Em. We're sure.'

'Can't you see he's grieving? Give him a minute,' John snapped, leaping to my defence as I lowered my head and tried to stop the world from spinning.

'I know, and I'm so sorry, but the sooner we move on this the sooner . . .'

'John, it's OK,' I said, sitting upright and wiping my eyes.

'We just need to look around, to see if we missed anything.'

'I've searched this house top to bottom.'

'I know, but now we need to.'

The front door opened and Sinclair stepped in, the hate still drawn on his face.

'Even after three weeks?'

'Even after three weeks,' she echoed, standing up. 'Mind if we start upstairs?'

'No.'

'PC Sinclair, would you come with me?' Cahill said, likely because of the shoving incident and the look on his face. Sinclair nodded, joined her, and they went upstairs to look around. I followed. They started in the spare room, clothes and toys all over the bed.

'You going somewhere?' Sinclair asked.

'No, just selling a few things.'

Cahill put on a glove and picked up one of Em's dresses. 'Are you selling Emma's things?'

'Ummm, yes, a few bits. Stuff she wouldn't wear.'

They exchanged a look and continued to search. Cahill went into the bathroom while Sinclair continued to look in the spare room. I couldn't help thinking he was considering Em's clothes too much. Almost as if he was imagining her in them. He saw me watching and put down the coat he was holding. Backing out, I turned to see Cahill in the bathroom, looking in the cabinet.

'Rob, you said you've searched this house, top to bottom. Did you write a list of things that were missing?'

'No.'

'No?'

'I mean, I still haven't noticed anything missing, besides her robe and trainers, the bag and some jeans. And her dress.'

Coming out of the bathroom, she walked into my bedroom. Sinclair headed for my daughter's room and I stopped him.

'Not in here, please.'

'Why not?'

'Because my daughter is asleep in there.'

201

'Uh-huh.'

Sinclair stared at me, but I wouldn't back down. Not in my own house; not when I'd done nothing wrong.

'I'll wait until we have proof you killed Em,' he hissed at me, speaking like he knew her. I've never wanted to hit someone so much. I didn't respond and, smirking, he turned to join Cahill in my room. Cahill was delicately looking at things, opening drawers, wardrobe doors. Sinclair was less delicate — he pulled the bed to one side to see under. Cahill opened her mouth to say something but stopped. Under the bed was one of Em's socks and a lot of dust. I don't know why he wanted to look under my bed, but then I don't know why he hated me so much either. Maybe he did it because the bed is a sacred, safe space and he was just trying to piss me off. He seemed annoyed when Cahill asked him to put the bed back and, as he did, the wooden floorboard he stood on beside the bedside table slipped, like it had been dislodged. Sinclair looked at Cahill, and Cahill took out her torch.

'This floorboard isn't attached.'

Sinclair shot me a look, but I didn't meet it.

'Give me a hand will you?' Cahill asked, handing Sinclair the torch and lowering herself to the floor. The floorboard came away easily, and under it was a small cavern between the bedroom floor and the living room ceiling, as deep as the width of a support beam. Cahill shone her torch into the void.

'There's something here,' she said. 'Rob, want to tell us what it is?'

'I — I have no idea.'

'Hold this,' Cahill said, handing Sinclair the torch again so she could get low and pull it out. It was a carrier bag, something wrapped inside. Opening the top, she slid out a dark brown hardback book.

'I have no idea what that is,' I said when Sinclair looked at me.

Cahill opened the book, and from the doorway I could see it was page after page of handwritten notes. She skimmed some of the pages, then skipped to the last page of written words, about halfway through the notebook. She read it slowly, her brow furrowed in concentration.

'What is it?' I asked. She didn't respond but handed the book over to Sinclair, who read it too.

'What does it say, let me see?'

Cahill didn't respond, but whatever was written down, it made her harden. Sinclair looked ready to kill.

'What is it?' I begged.

'Mr Clarke,' Cahill said. Not Rob anymore. Mr Clarke. 'Did you know she kept a journal?'

'No, no, I had no idea. Does it say anything about him? About Steve Burton?'

Cahill didn't answer me, instead she took out her phone and made a call. I tried to listen to what she was saying, but Sinclair spoke, blocking out her quieter tones.

'Mr Clarke,' Sinclair said, a hint of a smile on his smug face. 'Why would your wife keep a journal and hide it from you?'

'I don't know, what does it say?'

'Is there any reason you should be angry with your wife?'

'What? I don't understand what you're saying. What has she written?'

Sinclair didn't answer me, but watched me intensely, Cahill did too, and I couldn't help but feel I was being interrogated. I wanted to leave the room, go and see my daughter, but as I took a step, I was asked to stay, as DI Keats was on his way. After a few minutes, I heard someone coming up the stairs, and Keats walked into the room.

'Mr Clarke,' he said, as he brushed passed me and gestured for the notebook. Cahill handed it over, still open on the last page of writing. He read for a moment. Then he closed it and told Cahill to bag it for evidence. He looked at me, and when he spoke he was calmer than perhaps he should have been.

'Mr Clarke, do you know who might have wanted to hurt Em?' he asked.

'I think it was him.'

'Steve Burton?'

'Yes, him.'

'Mr Clarke—'

'That's why I was in London, I was trying to find him. I made a fake profile and befriended him and went down. He works in a bar in—'

'Mr Clarke. I've heard enough,' Keats said, standing up. Cahill stepped forward, a sad acceptance written all over her face. 'You can try to send us down the garden path with this.'

'What? I don't understand?'

'Robert Clarke, I'm arresting you on suspicion of the murder of Emma Clarke . . .'

Cahill told me to put my hands behind my back. She placed cold handcuffs around my wrists, tightening them until they pinched my skin and hurt. DI Keats continued to speak but his words were lost, and before I could protest, call for help, beg to see Sophie, plead my innocence, I was escorted out of the house. Frances and John watched in disbelief as I was loaded into the back of a waiting police van.

PART 4:
YOU

CHAPTER THIRTY-FIVE

June 17th 2019
The day before

'Steve'

My darling Emma,

In order to complete the perfect crime, you have to make a list. You have to be patient, bide your time. You have to stay diligent to the task and tick things off in the order they need to be completed in. You cannot jump the gun, you cannot get ahead of yourself, not if you don't want to be caught. To commit a perfect crime you have to slow down, even when your mind and body are telling you to hurry. You need to take one step at a time, focus on the one task at hand. Nothing more. It's that simple. The perfect crime is no different to a successful supermarket shop.

Only, I wasn't going to kill time wandering up and down aisles. I was going to kill you, Emma.

I will kill you and no one will ever know.

It isn't an ideal solution, you know that. And even as I kill you, I think you will know that I was supposed to be with you,

Em, you and I against the world, forever. That was what you promised, remember? When you were engaged to that man in Nottingham, when we found each other again in London. You promised a life different to the one I've ended up with, you promised me your love. You promised a family. But you didn't live up to your promises, you didn't focus on one thing at a time. Instead, you ran away, you ignored my calls, you avoided me when I came to see you at work. You moved to the arse-end of nowhere, just to avoid me. And you married him, had a baby with him, and I've had to watch you fake being happy, laughing at shit jokes, pretending to be a devoted wife and mother. And that day in Cambridge when we agreed to meet, I saw in your eyes you meant it this time. You were leaving me behind. You were becoming someone else. I hoped it wasn't true. I hoped, but when I knew it was, I needed to change my plan. If I couldn't have you, as I deserved, no one could. So, I calmed, I listened and I let you tell me about your new life. We spoke of everything, another catharsis for you. You told me about your nana, your wedding, your life as a mum. You did it to make me see you weren't coming back to me — to us — and it did. But it also gave me what I needed to kill you and get away with it.

I begged you one more time to think about what you were saying, think about the life we could still have.

But you wouldn't do it.

And again, if I couldn't have you, the one person who deserved you, no one could. So, as you told me about your new, better life, I listened and planned. And when we said goodbye, I knew what I must do, what you forced me to do, and I made my list.

The first step was to create your affair. In order to make you disappear, I needed to have you disappear with someone. I called him Steve. I made him seem superior to your husband; it wasn't hard. Steve became me, our stories spoken through him, our love existing because he now existed. He would steal you away from your husband, and you would flee with him forever, or so they would think.

The second step was to write a diary. Just in case. I went all the way back, layered in Steve, the on-off lover that is really me. I made sure I spoke of truths, as hard as they were to recall without longing for you. Our meet-ups and flings and sordid encounters under your husband's nose. I also spoke of truths about your new life with him, things you've told me about Rob and the baby, all of the sticky, bitter things you told me as we said goodbye to each other in Cambridge. I had to make them sound as real as they could possibly be. That bit was really important because, if it is needed and found, I need your husband to confirm those truths, in order to make the lies truth by proxy. It took time, research, patience. The diary had to appear real, just in case you are ever found. It would have to be somewhere the police would find it. Somewhere hidden from him in the house. They needed to believe it's really yours, the details too personal for anyone else to know.

You really shouldn't have told me everything, Emma. You shouldn't have sat with me, talking in depth about your new man, your new love, because I remembered every word. Every single word. And I knew, deep down I knew, I might have to use them against you.

Then, once the truth was down and undeniable, how you and he met, the small details of your love affair with him, things that would be easy to confirm as truth, I added lies about your husband having a temper, about you feeling afraid. About him hitting you and shouting at your daughter, and then I mixed it all together, the truth and the make believe, into one delicious book of entrapment. If you are ever found, they would discover the book, and no one would be able to tell the truths and lies apart. I made you fearful of him. I would make him look like a monster, you a poor battered wife. I've given probable cause.

Step three: Create your new Facebook page, as near to your real one as I could get it. And then create a conversation between the new you and the fictional Steve Burton. Keep the page hidden from public view. They will find it, and they will think you've left for France, just like you promised me time and time again. I will tell the story that should have been ours. The story your husband robbed us of.

Step four: Follow your husband. Learn his routine, so when the time is right, he won't be there, and you and I can have our final time together.

Step five: Lure you out of your house. I doubt it will be hard. After our last conversation, I know the mere idea of me stepping into your little home and sharing your dirty secret about us will be enough to make you leave to meet me. I will tell you to leave your baby in the house, we would only speak for a few minutes. I will say I only wanted to say goodbye, and that I would not bother you again. You'll buy it; you always do.

Step six: Hide you. After you're gone, after you're dead, I am going to drop you in the reservoir. Far enough out of the way to not be found, close enough that if you are, it points at him.

Step seven: Take a few things. Not a lot: your passport, a few toiletries. A scattering of clothes. Enough to fill a rucksack. Take a credit card, and if I have time, hide the diary. If not, I'll come back.

Keep your house keys.

Try not to look at that baby.

Step eight: Change how I look. Dye my hair to look like yours. Make sure some of the clothes taken are ones the husband would be able to identify. There's a red dress I've seen you in a few times with him, take that one.

Step nine: When the time is right, drive to the coast, buy two tickets to Dieppe in your and Steve Burton's names. Pay on your card, I made a note of the PIN when you paid for lunch the last time we met. Take out the maximum from an ATM with a CCTV camera, then, when the time is right, transfer as much as possible from your credit card to an off-shore account. Make it look like you've fucked over your husband. So he hates you when he finds out.

And then sit back, watch the results of my hard work and see the man who kept you from me suffer because of it.

In order to complete the perfect crime, you have to make a list.

CHAPTER THIRTY-SIX

July 9th 2019
One day dead

Rob

Still in a daze, I was unceremoniously escorted from the back of the police van and processed. They took my photo — a broken man looking back at the camera — they collected my fingerprints and took a swab from inside my cheek. My rights were explained to me. I had the right to counsel, which I declined, as I was worried it would make me look guilty of something I didn't do, and I had the right to tell someone where I was. Frances and John knew exactly where I was, and the look on John's face as I was walked from my house was the look of a man who didn't know what to think or believe. So I asked to call Angie. I know I shouldn't have, but she'd believed me before; I hoped she would again. I knew she wouldn't be able to do anything, but just having someone in my corner would help on the worst day of my life.

Her phone clicked to voicemail.

'Hi, its Angie. I can't get to the phone right now so leave a message.'

After the beep I didn't know what to say, my voice froze in my throat, so I hung up. The custody officer behind the counter looked at me quizzically, but I didn't offer a comment. I was then escorted into a small, windowless room, consisting of a table with recording equipment on it and four chairs tucked under. I was told to sit and that someone would be along soon. And, terrified, I did so without questioning. The door closed, and I was alone. Looking around the room, I saw a small camera mounted high on the wall, almost at the point where it met the ceiling, its lens pointing down on me. Somewhere, I was being watched. And I sat for what felt like forever: silent, alone, thoughts of Em's body being found flashing in my mind. Each time it did, she had died a different way. One flash she was strangled; another flash, drowned. Flash. Stabbed. Flash. Set on fire, flash. On an endless loop. I started to count, to push it back, but there was no escaping it. Em was dead, Em had been murdered. Steve Burton had killed my wife, and something in that book they found said otherwise. He had killed her, and he had set me up. I picked my nails, counted out loud each flick. One, two, three. I didn't stop, and in that small task, the horrifying images my head wanted to play out faded in the background.

One hundred and fifty-four.

I was startled by the door opening. Sitting upright, I rubbed my sweaty palms on my jeans. DI Keats, the one who arrested me, saw me do it, and I knew it must have looked like the action of a guilty man. A man trying to rid the blood from his hands. Beside him, a woman in a dark grey suit I hadn't met.

'Mr Clarke. This is DS Wainwright.'

I tried to nod towards them both, but only just managed to meet their eyes. Just. I hoped Cahill would come in. Even Sinclair. I knew them — well, her, at least. I could appease her, make her see I didn't kill my wife. But these two, they looked hardened. They looked convinced without me needing to say anything.

'Have you been offered a drink?' Keats said.

'No.'

'I see, would you like one?'

'A water, perhaps?'

'Of course.' Keats stepped out of the room and Wainwright took a seat opposite me. She didn't speak, but considered me, her hands neatly folded on her lap. I wanted to hold her unblinking gaze, show her I had nothing to hide, that I was innocent of what happened to my poor Em. But I couldn't. Fear crippled me — I knew it made me look more culpable, but I was powerless to change it. Keats was gone for no longer than a minute, and when he opened the door, I jumped. Nodding, as if giving permission for me to drink, he took a seat next to Wainwright. They exchanged a look, like they'd discussed options before stepping in. They were agreeing non-verbally what one they would take, and then Keats spoke.

'Interview with Robert Clarke commences, the time is 12.34 a.m. In the room are DI Keats, DS Wainwright and Robert Clarke. Mr Clarke has refused legal counsel.'

Keats paused, waiting for me to add something, perhaps? I didn't, but took a sip of the cool water. I focused on the sensation as it washed down my throat. Forcing down the bile that wanted to spill.

'At 1.51 p.m. on the 8th of July, officers, myself included, arrived at the location, a reservoir three hundred metres behind your house, and discovered a person's body.'

'Dead a long time,' Wainwright said, her eyes burning into me.

'Weeks,' said Keats.

Again, a pause. Waiting for me to comment. Again, I took a sip of water. Keats took a deep breath and asked the question I expected him to ask. 'Mr Clarke, is there anything you want to tell us?'

'I have been trying to find my wife,' I said quietly, tears filming my eyes. 'I didn't hurt her.'

'We followed your search for her. It was all quite public.'

'What's that supposed to mean?'

'Have you seen her diary?'

'You know I haven't.'

'It makes for some interesting reading.'

Keats turned and produced a book. Em's diary; the one discovered under the floorboards in my bedroom.

'For the tape, DI Keats has placed Emma Clarke's journal on the desk.' Wainwright said, still staring at me, unblinking.

'Mr Clarke, what can you tell us about this book?' Keats continued.

'Nothing. I didn't know it existed until today, when PC Cahill found it.'

'OK, can you tell us what you think it is?'

'You just said it was a diary.'

'A diary, yes. Mr Clarke, do you know what this diary contains?'

'I've already said, I don't know. I didn't know Em kept a diary.'

'She says some interesting things.' Keats cleared his throat and, opening the book on the first of several tabs I could see, he read.

'I made the first move, not drawn by lust, more curiosity. I bought him a drink, he thanked me, and we talked.'

'Is this true, Mr Clarke? Did she buy you that first drink?'

'Yes, she did.'

Keats nodded, skipped to the next tab and read.

'Rob and I picked the wrong day to move me into his flat: the first autumn storms had blown in, the rain was relentless . . .'

'Yes, that's true too, the weather was terrible on the day she moved in with me.'

'I see. What about this?' He said, skipping again.

'I wanted to be his wife before we announced our pregnancy.'

I felt a pang of sadness, but pushed it down; now was not the time to fall apart.

'Mr Clarke, is this true?'

'Yes.' I began to cry. 'We went to Gretna Green and married in secret.'

213

I saw the officers give each other a look, before Keats continued.

'What about this, Mr Clarke?'

'Rob sometimes gets angry. I don't blame him, I'd be angry too, I'd also want to hit me from time to time . . .'

I recoiled, his words like a sucker punch. I felt I'd made the wrong choice in refusing counsel.

'I–I've never touched my wife.'

'You would say that, wouldn't you. I mean, isn't that what everyone who hits their partner says?'

'Yes. But I'm telling the truth.'

'Mr Clarke, Emma writes about domestic violence four more times in this book, all happening within the last year.'

'I never touched my wife!' I said, raising my voice. Regretting it straightaway.

'Mr Clarke, she also writes about you not coping as a parent.'

The room started to spin. 'What?'

Keats flipped the page over and read from the next tab.

'Sophie was crying, terrible colic. I wanted Rob to understand, to help, but he said to me, "I wish that fucking baby would shut up." I understand, Sophie cries a lot, and he can't do anything to help her. But I wish he wouldn't shout at my baby; I wish he wouldn't call her such horrible names.'

I tried to open my mouth to reply, but the words wouldn't come.

'Mr Clarke?'

'That's not true,' I said eventually, the words barely audible. 'I would never, never say anything bad about my baby. I love her. I love her more than life.'

'But you could hurt Em?' Wainwright asked, her stare making me feel pins and needles in my hands.

'No, never.'

'And yet, here we are,' she replied coolly.

'What about Steve Burton, her going to France. What about that?'

214

'I'm glad you brought up Steve Burton. But before we do, can we talk about Daniel Murray?'

'Who?'

'Who? Now, Mr Clarke, surely you can remember the names of your fake profiles?' Keats said, a small smile creeping onto his face.

'Oh, yes. Him.'

'Why did you create it?' Wainwright asked.

'I did it so I could find him.'

'Who?'

'Steve Burton. I added him as a friend. Knowing he wouldn't accept it if it was from me.'

'And why would he not accept your request?'

'Because he was having an affair with Em. He's the one who killed her.'

'Mr Clarke. Steve Burton wasn't having an affair.'

'Emma has another account, a secret one. You know this, you're the ones who found it. There's a thread where he and she talk about leaving with each other.'

'That's not possible.'

'You're the ones who told me!' I shouted, slamming my hand on the table. Wainwright and Keats didn't flinch.

'Mr Clarke,' Wainwright said quietly, 'it's impossible because Steve Burton does not exist. It's a fake account, like your Daniel Murray. Designed to make people think Em went to France.'

'No.'

'You created that profile, in the same way you created Dan Murray.'

'No.'

'And Emma's other profile. We think you created that one too. I have to say, it's clever: create two fake accounts, build an affair, then when the police investigate her disappearance, they'd assume she left you for another man.'

'But the ferry tickets?'

'Booked online.'

'No,' I said again, my pulse pounding in my head. I couldn't make sense of what I was being told. Steve Burton wasn't real? 'But what about Em being seen down in Newhaven, on the CCTV at the ATM?'

'A red dress, a distorted image, it could be anyone.'

'What?'

'You could have, say, paid someone to take the money out.'

'No.'

'You planned it all, didn't you, Mr Clarke?'

'What about the necklace? I called you when I found the necklace. Why would I do that if I hurt my wife?'

'It's not confirmed to be hers, Mr Clarke.'

'I called you, when I found out she was missing. I called you!'

'Yes, you did.'

'Why would I do that if I hurt her?' I said, gasping for air, my diaphragm crushing my lungs.

'Perhaps you wanted to be caught?' Keats said, shrugging.

'No, I don't think it's that at all,' Wainwright continued. 'You rang in about the necklace because you'd got away with it, and it was too easy. You rang in because you think you're smarter than us. You called to tell us you had proof she didn't leave you, knowing we wouldn't act. You presented as a man unhinged to hide what you did to her in plain sight.'

I slammed my hand on the table again, knocking the glass of water onto the floor. 'I didn't kill my wife!'

'We believe differently,' said Keats.

'Where is the proof? Where is the proof I did anything to her? I'm innocent, and you're treating me like a killer.'

'And yet you say it's someone called Steve Burton, who doesn't exist.'

I didn't respond but pinched the bridge of my nose, struggling to process what was happening. Then I remembered something.

'What about Melanie Timpson? I mentioned her father, how he hated her.'

216

'Yes. We spoke to Mr Timpson.'

'He wanted her to come to harm. What if it's him behind all this?'

'An ageing, disabled man?'

'Yes. It could be him.'

'It's true, Mr Timpson did not care for Emma. His daughter and Emma were close as children and teenagers, they both dabbled in recreational drugs. Melanie was caught in possession of some ecstasy tablets. He claimed they were Emma's drugs she was holding. Emma got away with a warning, Melanie took the rap, expelled from school. He indicates she has struggled since.'

'Then he has reason to hate her, to want to hurt my wife.'

'Mr Timpson has COPD. He can't walk up a flight of stairs without oxygen. No, Mr Clarke, it wasn't him who killed your wife. Just a convenient misdirection.'

'Reeks of desperation to me.' Wainwright added.

The tears started to fall, clouding my vision. I blinked them away just in time to see Keats and Wainwright exchange a smirk.

'Mr Clarke. Can you tell me about this picture?' said Keats.

He slid a print-off towards me, and looking at it was confusing. It was the image of me and Em, the night of our engagement, where I had to wear that T-shirt saying I was hers. The arrow pointing to Em. I told them exactly that, but as the words fell from my mouth, something felt wrong. I wanted to look at the picture again, but before I could it was pulled away from me.

'You posted that image on Facebook. Is that right?'

'Yes, that's right.'

'The caption underneath stating that you hated slogan T-shirts.'

'I do.'

'Did you ever wear it after your engagement party?'

'Once or twice, as a sleep T-shirt. Em did too. I don't understand?'

217

'Mr Clarke. I want you to now look at this picture.'

Obliging, as I didn't know what else to do, I took the picture from Wainwright, handed to me face down. When I turned it over, I dropped it on the floor and looked away, a strange noise coming from my mouth; a moan, a cry, I wasn't sure which. I only saw the content of the image for a split second, but I would never be able to un-see it. It was of Em. Or what I thought was Em. She was unrecognisable. Her face was bloated, covered in greenish-black blisters. Her skin like wax. Her cheeks were missing, like they'd been feasted on, as were her eyes. In the void where her cheeks should have been, clamped in her teeth, was fabric of some kind. It barely looked like her, but her hair . . . I knew it was her.

'Why did you show me this?' I sobbed.

'Mr Clarke. Tell us about how she died?' Keats said, ignoring my question.

'I don't know.'

'She was strangled. Evidence is hard to find, as you can imagine — she's been in the water for what? Three weeks now? But we've found definite bruising on her windpipe, suggesting she was choked. And if that didn't kill her, the T-shirt stuffed down her throat would have.'

'What?'

'Your T-shirt. The one that says you're Em's. You were always gonna be Em's, weren't you Mr Clarke, and she was always going to be yours. One way or the other.'

'I didn't kill my wife,' I said, trying and failing to do so with authority. 'I didn't kill my wife,' I echoed, and lowered my head onto the table.

'Mr Clarke, here's what we think. You and Em had grown distant. You discover she wants to leave you. She's had enough of you controlling her.'

'No.'

'You know you want to kill her — after all, if you can't have her, right? So you create Steve Burton, to take the blame when she goes missing. You planned it all for months.'

I could feel my pulse thumping behind my eyes, my lips started to tingle. 'No.'

'You planned her disappearance by creating Steve Burton and buying cheap ferry tickets to France. And once you were set, you confronted her. Knowing the outcome,' Keats said, his tone neutral.

'She was pleading with you,' Wainwright continued, her words striking like venom. 'Begging you to forgive her, but you needed her to be quiet, you needed her to stop talking. So you strangled her.'

I couldn't reply. I kept my head on the table, my eyes closed tight.

Keats took over. 'And she knew it, too. She knew what you were capable of. Here's her last diary entry.' Keats picked up the diary and opened it.

'*I hope he understands it from where I am; I hope he lets me go, I hope he realises I'd be happier with someone else. I deserve to be happier with someone else. But I've seen what he can do, I know the darkness he has inside. When he knows the truth, all of it, I know, if I am not careful, if I don't keep my wits about me, he'll likely kill me.*'

Keats closed the book and let the silence hang for a full minute. Then Wainwright leant in and spoke quietly.

'And once she was dead, it couldn't be undone. But you were still angry. Unsatisfied that your rage hadn't diminished. You weren't thinking straight. So, you took that T-shirt. The one you hated so much. The one that said you were Em's and Em was yours, and you stuffed it down her throat. You made her eat her words. Didn't you? You were always going to be Em's, and she was always going to be yours. But you had to hide the evidence. So you dragged her out back and dumped her in the reservoir. Then you came home, tidied and called the police to report her missing.'

Opening my eyes, I looked into the soulless face of my dead wife in the photograph on the floor, and the sob turned into a wail. I wanted to tell them they were wrong. I wanted them to understand I loved her, would have forgiven her for her affair. That I couldn't hurt a hair on her head.

'I think I'd like to have a solicitor,' I said quietly, knowing how guilty it made me sound. From the corner of my eye I saw Keats stand; Wainwright kept staring at me.

'Interview terminated at 12.52 a.m.' Keats said, before they both left the room.

* * *

June 19th 2019
One day after

'Steve'

My darling Emma,

I expected more from last night. What sort of more, I don't know. But something. After I called, and you agreed — or rather, when you realised I would tell Rob everything about us — I waited patiently for you. I was as excited as I was scared. I read somewhere that humans think up to sixty thousand thoughts a day. Most are subconscious, and only push their way forward in difficult times. Like when you've been forced to wait for something you've wanted for so long. Then each and every thought is there, bouncing around your head. You were late meeting me, Em. I waited over seven minutes for you to arrive. Seven agonising minutes, 292 thoughts, shouting over one another to be heard. Thoughts of you not coming, thoughts of you ringing the police and throwing wild accusations because of your cowardice; your inability to do what is true to your heart. Thoughts of my life after you were gone. Each and every one of them could, and should have been avoided, if you'd just turned up when I asked. But you were worth the wait, frustrating as it was. When I saw you close your back door and run across your garden, I couldn't help but smile.

The last time you tried to forget me I told you you'd one day run back.

I hoped to see a baby in your arms, even though I said to leave her behind. Even knowing you wouldn't leave with me and have the life we both dreamed of, I still hoped you'd had a change of heart. Seen the mistake you were making.

Em, I loved you so much, I was willing to raise that baby as my own. But as you climbed the fence from your back garden, you were empty-handed. I knew then that what I feared — the nightmare that woke me most nights — was going to come true. I had planned for this, but until that moment, a part of me still hoped I wouldn't need to do it. That whole 'plan for the worst, hope for the best' thing. But there would be no best, not for us. As I watched you run towards me, stumbling in the dark, I desperately hoped you were running because you were dying to see me. Really, you were running so you could get home faster, be there with your baby, wait for your fucking useless husband who kept you from me to finish his night shift and come home. You were not running towards me, you were running away from us. You coward, you fucking, fucking coward. By the time you reached me, you were panting. You looked so weak, so feeble. You needed me, Em, you always had.

I kept you safe from harm, I cared for you in a way no one else could.

You took a breath, ready to speak. But I already knew what would fall from your vile, lying little mouth.

'What do you want?'

'Emma, I need you to think about what you're doing.'

'You can't just come to my house in the middle of the night, demand I come and see you. We're over, I can't go back, I won't. I have a family, don't you get that?'

'A family. Something you promised me, Emma, don't you remember?'

'Yes, of course I do. And at the time, I meant it. But I grew up. Life changes. You have to accept that.'

'No, Emma, no. You promised me a life together. I changed everything for you. I left Nottingham when you ran away, to find you, to be with you in London. And I left there to come to this shithole to make you understand.'

'I didn't ask you to.'

'No, but I know deep down you need me, you need to understand.'

'Understand what? Understand what?'

'That you and I, we're supposed to be together.'

I hoped you would see, Emma. I hoped you would see we were meant to be together, even then. But you didn't, did you? You reiterated we were over, we were done. And you turned to walk away.

'I'll tell your husband. I'll tell him everything,' I said, hoping you would stop — because, despite planning to end your life, I still wished I didn't need to. You stopped and turned back to me, and I almost felt hope, Emma. Almost.

'If you come near me or my family ever again, I'll call the police. Understand that!'

You turned to leave again, and I knew that whatever hope I had was false. I grabbed your arm and pulled you towards me.

'Let me go! Get off my arm. You're a sicko, a freak. You are the biggest mistake of my life. I have a family now, I have love, real love. Why on earth would I leave that for you and our fucked-up relationship?'

'Our relationship wasn't fucked up.'

'Yes, it was, it was a train wreck. Always hiding, always in secret. Who wants to live like that?'

'I'll tell him!' I screamed. 'I'll tell him everything. How you slept with me just after getting engaged. How you and I are sworn to each other.'

'We are not sworn to each other, you need to get that, you need to move on. And you can't threaten me about my past anymore. I love my husband. I'm going to tell him everything.'

'He'll leave you.'

222

'And if he does, I deserve it. But I'm not lying to him anymore. If you ever come near me again—'

I needed you to stop talking, I couldn't hear what you were saying because it would stay with me forever. I asked you to stop, but you wouldn't, you kept talking, kept throwing your threats.

I had no choice, Em, you did this to yourself. You did this to us.

After, I went into your home, and I did something I shouldn't; something that was on my list of things to not do. I watched your daughter sleep. Her breathing deep and calm. She looks like you Emma, same nose, same chin. She's perfect, just like you used to be. She deserved us as her parents, me and you. Together, we could have taken on the world; together, we could have raised her to be perfect. And now, she's stuck with your husband. Who wasn't good enough for you and isn't for her. I held her, Emma, and she slept on, comfortable and safe and warm. I breathed in her scent and knew that, even with you gone, I would be better for her than he could be. The sound of him coming home early from work snapped me away from a daydream that was forming, and I left before he got to the house. And from the field behind your house, I watched him discover you were gone.

Back at my car, tears streaming down my face, I knew, even as I grieved for you, I needed to focus on the next step in the plan.

CHAPTER THIRTY-SEVEN

July 10th 2019
Two days dead

Rob

I was escorted from the interview room to a holding cell where I spent the day pacing, worrying about Sophie. I wanted nothing more than to see my daughter. I hoped she was OK, that she was happy. I had no way of knowing either way, and the powerlessness crushed me. But I had to push the feeling deep down, into the circling pit with everything else I was feeling. I tried to force down the image of Em too, bloated and blue, but it was impossible; that picture would haunt me for the rest of my life, in the space where my eyelids close as I blink. Somehow, I managed to fall asleep — exhaustion, grief and fear leaving me no choice. I slept deep and dreamless until my cell door opened and I was greeted by a large, balding man who introduced himself as Brian Mayer, my solicitor. A man who didn't make eye contact and had the body language of someone being overworked. I could tell from our introduction that he was only vaguely aware of why he was there, and he looked more sleep-deprived than I was. I introduced myself. Shook his hand, took in his smell of stale cigarettes.

'What time is it?' I asked and he looked at his watch, sighing like I'd asked too much of him.

'Seven twenty-eight.'

'A.m. or p.m.?'

'P.m.'

I tried to add up the number of hours I had been in the cell, but I couldn't. My brain felt foggy.

'About nineteen,' he said, reading my thoughts.

'Shit. I need to ring my in-laws.'

'Given the circumstances, I don't think that's a good idea.'

'They have my daughter, I need to know she's OK.'

'I'll get them to send a police officer over.'

'No, I need to see my daughter.'

'Mr Clarke. Perhaps you don't fully understand. Right now, you're in a holding cell, and they want to charge you with murder. Your daughter is fine.'

'How do you know?'

'Because you would know if she wasn't.'

'I didn't kill my wife.'

'Then sit tight, let me do my job. I understand you've been interviewed already?'

'Yes.'

'You shouldn't have done that without a solicitor.'

'I did nothing wrong.'

'Well, what's done is done,' he said, wiping his hand over his thinning hair. 'Now I'm here, they'll want to interview again. Don't say anything. Let me do my job. I want to know what they know; it's likely they're just speculating. Digging for you to slip up.'

'I didn't kill my wife,' I said again, staring at him.

'Just don't speak, that clear, Ron?' he asked, breathing heavy. I could see sweat on his brow.

'Rob,' I corrected, expecting an apology, but it didn't come. I started to think that appointing help was a bad idea,

225

but that feeling left as soon as an officer escorted us back to an interview room. Keats and Wainwright came in shortly after. As the overweight, exhausted monster of a man beside me came to life, he cooled a lot of the heat Keats and Wainwright had thrown my way. The questions fired in, some of which had been asked before Mr Mayer was by my side. Although they were asked in a different way; a softer way. He reminded me that I didn't need to say anything, before reminding them they had twenty-four hours to either charge me or get an extension. But if the grounds of either were dodgy, he would come for them with both barrels. The interview was paused when an officer came in, and Keats left the room. Wainwright sat still with her arms crossed for a moment longer than she should have, before she too left, and I was alone with my solicitor.

'You're doing a good job,' he said quietly. 'They don't have enough to charge, or they would have by now. Let's hope DI Keats hasn't just left because they have something.'

'They won't.'

'I have to say, their argument is compelling.'

'You don't believe me?'

'That's not my job. The diary doesn't help show your innocence.'

'It's all a lie.'

'Maybe, but—'

The door to the interview room swung open, and to my surprise, Sinclair came in. Before I could say anything, he leapt over the table and hit me in the face, knocking me backwards in the chair. As I hit the ground, the back of my head took the brunt of the fall.

'I'll kill you!' he screamed, as two other officers, one of them Cahill, ran in and dragged him back before he could climb over and hit me again.

'You killed her you bastard, you killed her!'

Sinclair was dragged out of the room. Getting to my feet, I touched my lip; it was swollen and cut. Not badly, but enough to hurt like hell. The chaos of his attack quickly died down, and as Cahill came back in, a cold compress in her hand for my lip, I saw Mayer smiling beside me. Once she left, I was escorted to a holding cell.

'You'll be home tonight,' Mayer said, as the door closed.

Thirty or so minutes later the lock snapped, the door opened and, as my eyes adjusted to the light pouring in, I saw the shape of Keats, arms crossed. Extremely pissed off.

'Come on, time to go.'

'What?' I said, still squinting.

'Get your shit, we're done.'

'I can go home?'

Keats didn't respond but turned and walked away. Behind him, the custody officer who'd booked me waited. Still confused, I got up from the bed, put on my trainers and walked out of the room. The custody officer asked me to come to the desk, where he explained that I was released pending investigation, and I wasn't to go anywhere but home. He advised I would be checked up on, and I was to wait to hear otherwise. I signed to say I agreed, and he gave me back my personal belongings. My wallet, keys and, most important of all, my phone. As I went to leave, Keats reminded me that I was still under investigation. I had to be close to home, available at the drop of a hat, and I wasn't in the clear yet. That last part was really emphasised. They were still investigating me. They were building a case against me. I think they were hoping I'd crumble and confess, making their life easier. It would explain why they laid it on so heavy before I had Mr Mayer in the room. They wanted a quick close. And Keats was pissed off I didn't oblige. I had no doubt they were releasing me to see what I would do next. As I turned to leave, Mayer approached. Smiling.

'I bet you're glad to be going home?'

'I am — I just don't know how?'

'Well, they were running out of time, and I've no doubt they were going to file for an extension, but it turns out that

Sinclair fella, the one who hit you, hasn't been totally honest in this case.'

'How do you mean?'

'Turns out he grew up around here, and he had a thing with your Emma when they were young.'

'What?'

'Yep, and as he was one of the arresting officers, there's no way anything he discovered can be submitted as evidence. Not without contention at least.'

'So I'm no longer being investigated?'

'I'd not go that far but, for now, they can't do anything. They fucked up; you were lucky.'

'Thank you.'

'Don't thank me, thank him for coming into the room and smacking you in the face.'

With my belongings in my hand, the custody officer came around from behind the counter and asked me to follow him. I did as I was told and was let out into the warm, wet night. He didn't say anything, just closed the door behind him and returned towards his desk. I didn't mind. I wanted to breathe in the fresh air, take a moment, let the rain wash away the feel of the holding cell, but I needed to know if Sophie was all right. I'd only been kept for a short time, but it felt like weeks. I missed my daughter. My phone took ages to come to life and once it did, I saw it was nearly 10 p.m. I rang Frances. It rang eight times; she picked up a beat into the ninth. But it wasn't her, it was John.

'Rob?' John's sleepy voice said.

'I'm sorry it's so late, did I wake you?'

'No, no, I'm not asleep,' he said, the heaviness in his voice telling me he wouldn't sleep properly ever again.

'Is Sophie OK?'

'She's fine.'

'They released me.'

'Good, that's good,' he said, before we fell into an uncomfortable silence.

'John? Are you still there?'

'They said they have evidence,' he said quietly, the weight in his words suggesting he wasn't sure what side of the fence he was on.

'No, John, they don't. I can't explain it. But I didn't do anything to Em. I wouldn't. I loved her, John.'

'They said they have evidence, Rob, what am I to believe?'

'I don't know how, or why, but someone is trying to set me up for . . .' I couldn't finish my sentence. Until I had proof, I would just look more guilty. 'John, I need to see Sophie.'

'Rob, we don't think that's a good idea.'

'But . . .'

'They've threatened social services.'

'They can't do that!'

'You're probably right, but still.'

'John, I need you to know, I had nothing to do with . . .'

'I want to believe you. But the police—'

'—are wrong.'

'Rob, Sophie's fine here. Don't come over, it won't help.'

I hated the fact that I had to stay away from my own daughter, but John was right. She was safe, oblivious and I shouldn't jeopardise that because of my own needs.

'You OK getting home?' John asked.

'Yeah,' I lied.

'OK, well, want me to send a picture of Sophie asleep?'

'Please. I miss my girl.'

'OK, and I'll do the same in the morning. The social services thing, it will blow over.'

'I hope so.'

'Rob, I'm going to ask this once and only once. Did you hurt my daughter?'

'No. God, no.'

'OK.'

'John, I promise, I didn't hurt her.'

'I'll send a picture now.'

The line went dead and I opened my messages as there was a new one from Angie.

Hey, sorry I missed your call, is everything all right?

          It's been a rough night. They found Em.

I saw the news; I've been hoping to God it wasn't her.

          They think I did it.

What? Are you with someone?

          Nope, they've just released me. They said something about a T-shirt, they said . . .

I couldn't finish my message, I couldn't re-see the image of Em, her skin, her missing eyes, that T-shirt visible through the hole in her cheek. So I deleted it. Angie sensed my hesitation and messaged again, telling me her address, telling me to come over.

***

June 21st 2019
Three days after

'Steve'

My darling Emma,

Even though I know you are not coming back, even though I know you are gone, and the afterlife is just a thing to help us feel like there's meaning to our existence, I still see you in the shadows of coffee shops; I still smell you in the air. Three times since our last night together, I've thought I've seen you in the face of another. Three times in three days. I wonder if your husband has done the same. I suspect he has. After all, it's you. You're hard to forget, Emma.

I remembered something about you, the necklace you loved — when I choked the life out of you, when I watched the light in your eye flicker and die, you weren't wearing it. You always wear it. I know it must have fallen off somewhere. I've been back, at night, with a torch, hoping to find it in the field where we last were. Hoping, and failing. I even saw him, Em — your husband, in the garden. He saw me too, my torch shining at the ground, searching. I lifted my torch towards him and he hid behind a tree before running back into the house. You deserved better than that coward. He turned you into the weak woman you became. I blame him as much as I do you.

I went to your house today, to see if I could get in and search, but I couldn't, it was like a circus — news cameras everywhere, as well as nosy neighbours and town folk. I liked blending in, watching it all unfold.

I still dream about you, Em — the life we could have had, me and you, and your baby too. We could have been perfect.

We should have been.

We should have been.

231

CHAPTER THIRTY-EIGHT

Sitting in the back of a taxi, staring out of the window, I watched the rain thrum on the glass, trying to count the rain drops to keep my control. Now there was a moment to reflect, a moment of stillness, I felt my lungs crush from inside. Em was dead, my wife was gone. I had wished a thousand times she hadn't left me, but now, I begged she had. I begged she was having an affair, I pleaded to God or Allah or whoever, that this was all just a dream, and my wife was in France with her new lover. As the cab rattled along the Fens, the driver tried on three occasions to pluck up a conversation. I answered, but, with a gun to my head, I couldn't tell you what I said. When we entered town he slowed and turned into a cul-de-sac, and pulling up beside a small new build, the driver indicated that we had arrived. Paying him with some of the cash from the things I had sold, I stepped out into the rain. He drove away and I took a moment to allow the rain to wash over me, hoping it would calm me as it did only an hour ago. No such luck. I also hesitated as I wasn't sure I should go in. Angie was nice, kind, but I felt like I was abusing that. She and I only knew each other because of Facebook. Should I be confiding in her the day I discover my wife was murdered and I was a suspect? I hadn't even stopped to consider that being here right now might make her complicit. Deciding against it, I turned to walk back into town and home. After a few steps, the front door opened and Angie, wrapped in a dressing gown, called me.

'Rob.'

'Oh, hi Angie.'

'Come in, it's raining cats and dogs.'

As I reached her doorstep, she leant in and hugged me. I expected her to offer her condolences, but she didn't. She just held me tightly and I felt myself sag in her embrace. After a moment she pulled back, her dressing gown and hair wet because of me.

'You OK?'

'No.'

'Come on, let's get a sweet tea in you.' Angie whispered in the way a parent did when their baby was upstairs asleep.

'Thank you.' I managed to say as I stepped over the threshold of her house. Angie told me to take a seat in the living room while she went into the kitchen. I heard the kettle being filled and flicked on. As Angie made a well-needed tea, I took in her home. Small but very tidy. Nice furniture. A trunk in the corner of the room, which was no doubt full of baby toys. On the walls, dozens of photos of baby Steph.

'She is beautiful.' I said when Angie returned, two steaming teas in her hand.

'She is, but I'm biased.'

'No, I totally get it. Is she?' I pointed above my head.

'Yeah, she's sound asleep. Her dad brought her back early; he had a work thing come up.'

'I bet that made you happy,' I said, grief panging as I had the realisation I might not be able to see my own daughter for a while.

'Of course, but I didn't tell him that,' she smiled as she handed me my tea. I cradled it, warming my fingers.

'Thanks.' I replied. 'I didn't do it.' I found myself continuing. 'I didn't hurt my wife.'

'Rob . . .'

'I didn't.'

'Rob, I know.'

'Do you?'

'Yes, I cannot see how you'd do anything to hurt anyone.'

'Thank you, you have no idea how much that means.' I tried to smile, but it didn't come. 'You know that Steve Burton. The man we created a profile to speak with, the man I went to London to find. He didn't do it.'

'But, it has to be him? Surely, he wanted her to leave, she wouldn't, and he . . .' she didn't finish her sentence. 'Sorry Rob.'

'It's OK.'

'How do you know it wasn't him?

'Turns out he isn't real. Turns out it's a made-up profile.'

'Why would anyone do that?'

'The police think I did it.'

'What?!'

'They said I created it to fake a trail leading to a dead end. I'm being set up.'

'Shit.'

'They found a diary in my house, said it's Em's, said she had written that she was scared, Angie. It said she was really scared, of me.'

'What?'

'She wrote it in her diary, I didn't even bloody know she kept one. She said things, horrible things; she said I wanted to hurt her, she said I resented my daughter.' It was all too much, and I began to cry. Angie sat beside me and rubbed my back, not offering any kind words, knowing I needed to let it all out.

'The police.' I continued after I calmed enough to speak. 'They grilled me, told me all the reasons why I did it to her.'

'Do you know who it could be?' Angie asked.

'Steve Burton.'

'But he's not real?'

'I know. It's whoever created that profile. But I don't know who. Em had a friend, Melanie Timpson. Her father hated Em.'

'Do you know why?'

'Something to do with drugs when Em and his daughter were young. And then there's PC Sinclair.'

'What about him?'

'He and Em were going out. He hit me tonight. I think he loved her.'

'Then surely he needs to be investigated? They both do.'

'What if I'm charged Angie? What if they take Sophie away from me?' I started to cry again. 'I can't live without my daughter. I can't.'

'They won't, you didn't do anything.' She said, taking my hand.

'Innocent people go to prison all the time.'

'Rob.' She said, taking my face in her hands and lifting my chin so I had to hold her eye. 'They'll find him.'

'I hope you're right.'

She smiled at me and, feeling exhausted, I leant in on her shoulder. I needed someone to carry the burden in my head, just for a moment. Angie wrapped her arm around me, told me it would be OK. I wanted to believe her; I almost did.

'Rob, they will find out what really happened.'

I lifted my head and looked at her. She sounded like she truly believed what she was saying, and I needed confirmation. I needed to see it on her face. Angie held my eye, and in that moment, I felt it too. She looked just like Em. Before I could stop myself, I leant in to kiss her. Angie leant away, and got to her feet.

'Shit, I'm sorry,' I said, mortified.

'Don't be,' she replied.

'No, I shouldn't have . . .'

'Rob, it's OK. Honestly. I get it, I do. But right now isn't the time.'

'Yes, you're right. No excuse.'

'It's already forgotten, OK?'

'Thank you,' I replied, struggling to hold her eye, as the guilt of what I just tried to do crushed me from within.

'Rob, you look exhausted. Do you want to grab a shower or something?'

'Yes, that's a good idea,' I replied, hating myself.

* * *

July 3rd 2019
Fifteen days after

'Steve'

My darling Emma,

Now that you're gone, I should just stay away. Watch, enjoy the spectacle, and boy, did he cause a spectacle, putting your photo up all over town, asking anyone nearby. You even made the TV. It was far more than I could have hoped. I knew when I followed through on my final few steps that I would get away with what I did to you, and you would be forever mine. Like all good things, it's about waiting for the right moment. When I got wind of the vigil in the town centre, I knew then the tickets to France needed to be bought. The final thing I needed to do to complete my list.

I made myself look like you; I wore your clothes, which still smelled of you, and I went to the coast. I took out some money from an ATM, making sure I was seen in the CCTV. Then, I bought the tickets. They would assume you had left for Dieppe with the likely-to-be infamous Steve Burton. It would make him, your husband, look stupid, and everyone would believe it too. I would do this final step before the vigil that has been planned. A crushing blow to the man who robbed you from me. And if they find you, they will find the book, and they will assume he paid someone to pose as you. They will think he planned it meticulously, that he was almost too clever. But he won't be as clever as me, no one will. As I've said, in order to plan the perfect crime . . .

People leave their partners every day, why wouldn't they assume it was as simple as that, a jilted husband, worth

236

pitying, especially as he was too blind to see his wife didn't love him anymore. A vengeful husband, twisted by jealousy, if you are ever found.

I should have backed away for good after, but I couldn't. I couldn't stop thinking about your daughter, how peaceful she was in my arms, how she is the best parts of you. I kept feeling myself being pulled back, I wanted to see her, I was beginning to feel the pull to her as I did to you. So, I found a way to stay close. It wasn't difficult; I created the perfect cover. The perfect excuse to be close to it all. And I also kept your keys. After all, it was part of step seven.

Being in your house was exciting. The ability to go in and out whenever I liked, without raising attention, had an addictive quality. He nearly caught me, on the morning when he gave her some poorly wrapped gifts. I arrived to search for your necklace, and if I was lucky, see the baby. I had to hide behind the shed, my face ended up covered in cobwebs, listening to him call out your father's name. He was only a matter of metres from me. It was a huge risk, as is every time I go into your house, but it is worth it. I've enjoyed that I have been able to see your world, touch your things, smell your perfume. Spend time in your daughter's room. But it's bittersweet enjoyment, not because I miss you, but because it's a reminder of the life we could have had. The family pictures should have been with me, the bed he snores in should have been ours, and on the nights I stood in your daughter's bedroom and watched her sleep, I realised two things. The first is something you would have been told a lot no doubt — she looked so much like you — and second, like the bed and the pictures and the mess and the joint account and the bills, she should have been ours too.

I've not been able to think of anything since.

So, maybe now one plan is complete, it's time to write another?

I wanted to be with you Emma, to have the family you promised me. And I realise Emma, I can still have that, a family, even if I can't have you.

CHAPTER THIRTY-NINE

Rob

As she led me upstairs, the bedroom doors were closed. I looked to my left and saw the name Steph proudly hung on a bespoke wooden board, and I missed Sophie even more. Angie walked into the bathroom, turned on the shower and left me to it. Thanking her, I closed the door and waited until the steam coming from the shower covered the bathroom mirror in condensation, hiding the man who looked back, one I didn't want to recognise anymore. I stepped in and the hot water rushed over me, dissolving the arrest and the smell of the holding cell. But my shame, my guilt, held firm. And then, as the water ran through my hair and over my face, I thought of an early memory of my daughter, splashing in a shallow bath, Em and I laughing as she kicked and thrashed and giggled. And then I remembered, Em was dead, my daughter wasn't with me, and I had just tried to kiss another woman.

Fuck, Rob, how could you?

I wanted to hit something — a wall, the shower screen glass — but instead I beat the side of my head with my palm. I hoped it would stop me crying, but I didn't think anything could, and the tears fell, mixing with the shame-filled water that washed off my body and circled down the drain. I thought if I cried the hitting would stop, but it didn't. I wanted to smash my own brains out. My wife was dead, my daughter was at her grandparents', and I'm trying to kiss a stranger so I can feel better about myself.

'Rob? You OK?' Angie asked quietly from the landing, and I froze. Had she heard me cry?

'Yeah, I'm fine.'

'There are some clothes outside the door.'

'Thank you.'

I waited to hear her footsteps go down the stairs before opening the door a crack to pull the clothes into the bathroom. They smelt old, like they'd been hung up for a long time. But they fit, if a little tight. It was better than being wet, or wearing the clothes that smelled of the police station.

Stepping out onto the landing, I looked towards Steph's room, desperate to see my own daughter, and tiptoed downstairs.

'Looks like Steph is a really good sleeper.' I said as I walked into the living room.

'It's a miracle, she usually doesn't sleep too well. I might just pop up and check on her. You all right to sit here for a bit?' Angie said, putting her cup down.

'Of course.'

Angie left without looking at me, and I knew that when she came back down, I'd need to leave — what almost happened between us was a mistake. I moved to grab my things and, picking up my wet jacket from the end of the sofa, I accidentally knocked over Angie's tea.

'Shit.'

I tried to find a tissue box but couldn't see one and, assuming Angie wouldn't mind, I went into the kitchen. As I grabbed the kitchen roll, I saw something stuffed down the side of the fridge. It looked familiar. Above me, I heard Angie go into the bathroom and, knowing I had a moment, I stuck my hand down the small gap, dragging out a bag. A rucksack. Holding it, I was sure I knew what it was; I just couldn't work out what it was doing there. I unzipped it, hands shaking, hoping I was just being paranoid. Once it was fully open, I reached in and pulled out a carrier bag. Inside were clothes: a pair of jeans, some underwear and socks. And a red dress.

I dropped it like it was electrified and something fell out of the front pocket of the rucksack. Before I picked it up I knew what it was, but I had to see, despite what I knew it would mean.

It was a passport. And when I opened it, I saw a picture of my wife.

I grabbed the kitchen side, fearing I'd faint if I didn't. Em's missing things were in Angie's kitchen, and at first I couldn't work out why. I looked at the passport again, hoping I was somehow wrong — Em and Angie looked similar, after all. But there was no mistaking it, the name was in black and white. Emma Louise Clarke. My wife.

Then I knew why, when I was in the police interview room, I'd wanted to see that picture of me and Em again. The picture where I was wearing the T-shirt she was choked to death with. Taking out my phone, my hands shaking so violently I struggled to unlock it, I went to my Facebook and scrolled furiously to find it. Em and I were in the foreground, her pointing to the T-shirt, me feigning my protest, despite loving that I was, in fact, Em's. But I wasn't interested in us — pinching the screen, I zoomed in behind Em's left shoulder to someone in the crowd of people at the bar. Her hair was darker, her skin tanned, but there was no mistaking it. A woman stared at the back of Em's head. Hate in her eyes. Angie. She was there, on that night, and Em and I had no idea. Angie was there. I had to wonder, how often had she watched us? How often had she been that close without us knowing? Reaching into the rucksack once more, I rooted around for anything else I could find of my wife's, still hoping I was horribly wrong. In the back pocket, I found a folded piece of paper tucked right at the bottom and, pulling it out, I unfolded it. My wife's handwriting was clear to see.

To my wonderful husband, Rob.

There is no easy way to say what I need to say, so I'm just going to lay my cards down. When you read this, I have no doubt you will be angry, but please, read to the end before you say anything. I need you to understand, or at least, be informed. I owe you that. I owe you so much more.

Rob, I am flawed, horribly, horribly flawed, and I have wronged you in the worst way. You have done nothing but love me, support me, you've shown me what life could be if I let it, you've given me a daughter who I love with everything I have. And I have repaid you by keeping the truth from you. So, here it is, the truth, finally. The truth at last.

I am not the woman you think I am.

When I was young, growing up, I wanted to be different to everyone I knew — I had a chip on my shoulder about my family and its wealth. I hated that I grew up privileged and so tried to do everything I could to fight that. I got into trouble. And then I ran away to be with my older boyfriend. Someone called Jamie, who I intended to marry. He was a kind man, a nice man — in some ways, a little like you. I'm sorry if reading this is a shock, about me being engaged before. And I'm sorry that there's more to it. As I hit eighteen, and was able to go out, I went out every weekend — there were drugs, drinking — and I met someone I didn't expect to like. Her name was Angie: she was wild, fun, exciting, everything I thought I wanted to be. I cheated on my fiancé. And after some time, I knew I couldn't do it anymore. So I left Jamie — it was unfair to stay with him — and in leaving, I said goodbye to Angie too. I wanted to start again, leave my old ways behind. And then I met you. And I need you to know, my Rob, I loved you the second I met you. I didn't feel good enough, I didn't feel I deserved you — and I wanted to tell you about my past, my engagement, my cheating ways, but the

more I got to know you, the more I realised I couldn't. Because
you might decide you didn't want someone like me in your life.
I wouldn't want someone like me in my life. And the longer
I left it, the harder it was to say. I was so sure it wouldn't
matter, as I wouldn't go back.

But, my darling husband, this is the hard truth, and the
hardest thing I have ever had to write. As we were dating, I
slipped up. Shortly after we were engaged, I slipped up again;
I committed the most horrendous of all crimes. Maybe I was
scared, maybe I'm just a disaster, I don't know, but I found
myself in Angie's bed once more, and I've hated myself ever
since.

I never meant to hurt you Rob, I never meant to betray
your trust, and instead of running away alone, as I did before,
I ran with you. Up here, close to my family, because I wanted
the normal things in life; I wanted it all with you.

Angie followed us here, she showed up, she's threatened
to tell you everything. I've seen her watching us in the park
with Sophie, I've seen her at the supermarket. She has such
power over me, protecting my lies, but I won't let her anymore.

Rob, I have failed you, I have failed our family. And
I hope that you can forgive me. I hope you can love me still.

Tonight, I'm meeting Angie, out back of our house, and
I'm telling her I won't let her ruin my life; our life.

I hope we can fix this. I hope you can see that I will
never do anything to hurt our family again.

You are my husband, my love. You and Sophie are my
life. And I hope you see, by telling you the truth about me,
that I am willing to fight for it.

Forever yours,
Em

Grabbing Em's things, I stuffed them back in the bag,
knowing I needed to get them to the police. I wanted to pass
out, but I couldn't — I needed to move, get out, get help.
Scrolling to Cahill's number in my call log I turned to leave,

ready to ring as soon as I was outside and running down the road. I made it two steps before I saw Angie at the living room doorway.

'You shouldn't have snooped, Rob,' she said, her voice low and level.

She looked different, dangerous; her small frame somehow filling the entire space that was my escape. And the way she looked at me, I knew she did it, I knew she killed Em.

I ran towards her — I was bigger than she was, I could push my way past, run out of the house, shout for help. As I charged, she sidestepped and, using my own momentum, shoved me into the doorframe face-first. I stumbled back, blood running down the bridge of my nose from a cut to my forehead, and raised my hands to defend myself. I'd not been in a fight since I was a kid. And Angie, she moved like a professional. Angie stepped towards me and I swung wildly, a punch she easily dodged before somehow striking me on the right side of my face, sending stars shooting across my eyes. As my vision returned I couldn't see her and, spinning around, assuming she was now behind me, I didn't have time to react and stop the heavy object in her hand from crashing down on the side of my head.

PART 5:
SOPHIE

CHAPTER FORTY

July 11th 2019
Three days dead

Rob

I tried to open my eyes: one seemed to work, the other didn't. Rolling onto my side, I heaved onto my elbows and violently threw up on the floor. Using what little strength I had, I managed to rock back onto my knees. Everything felt foggy, and for a moment I couldn't place where I was, or what had happened. My hand went to my face and came back crimson. My eye was swollen shut, and a few of my teeth at the back felt dislodged. But it didn't hurt — the shock, I assumed. I slowly got to my feet and recalled where I was: Angie's house. Then it came back. The picture with Angie clearly seen in the background, the bag, Em's passport. Em's letter.

I staggered into the living room. Angie wasn't there. In the hallway, I could see her shoes, which were by the front door when I arrived, had also gone. She'd left. I looked for the bag; that was gone too. I needed help, so finding my phone I called Cahill. I'd been told not to, and I knew I was the prime suspect in Em's death, but I didn't know who else to turn to. It rang and rang, going to voicemail. I didn't leave a message but hung up and dialled again. As I hung up and tried for the third time I needed to move, or my adrenaline might crash, and I'd pass out. Angie was gone, that was clear. But I needed to make sure Steph was all right. Taking the stairs slowly, I looked to make sure Angie wasn't in either of the rooms before committing to the top step. The house seemed quiet. Looking into Angie's room first, I saw clothes scattered on the bed, her drawers and wardrobe doors open. She'd packed quickly. She was flee-ing. Turning, my head swimming, I walked towards Steph's room and opened the door. What I saw didn't make sense. I was expecting to see a cot, maybe a mobile hanging over it; some toys. There was nothing. The room was empty but for a few boxes and a clear plastic crate. In it, I could see Sophie's clothes. The ones I'd sold to Angie. Why were there no baby things in the baby's room? I couldn't see how Angie could pack so quickly and also deconstruct a cot bed. The realisation of what it meant hit me so hard I thought I'd be sick again. She didn't clear the room before fleeing. The room was always clear. Running back downstairs, I grabbed pictures from the mantelpiece in the living room and looked at the baby in them. The smiles were too perfect, the lighting just right. The baby was the same in each, but there were no parents in any of them. Opening the back of one of the frames, I pulled out the image. It wasn't a photo, but a printed piece of paper. I did the same on a few more: all of them printed. Googling 'baby pictures', it didn't take long for me to find the same photo. Steph's photos were from the internet. Steph wasn't real.

My phone rang; Cahill was calling me back.

'Mr Clarke, you shouldn't be ringing me. Especially not now.'

'PC Cahill. It was Angie.'

'What was Angie, Mr Clarke?'

'Angie, my friend. It was her; I have proof she killed Em.'

'Rob, that's a serious accusation, I don't think . . .'

'I'm at her house, I found Em's missing things, she attacked me.'

I heard Cahill's tone shift, her police training kicking in.

'Is she there now?'

'No, she's gone. Looks like she packed things and ran.'

'How badly are you hurt?'

'I've been better, but I'm OK,' I said.

'Rob, are you inside her house right now?'

'Yes, PC Cahill. She faked being a mum, she doesn't have a baby. I think she made up Em's diary too. To frame me.' Cahill asked for the address, and I gave it to her.

'Sit tight, I'm on my way. Don't touch anything, OK?'

'OK.'

I hung up. Cahill didn't seem troubled by Angie faking a baby, but it scared me to death. Angie and I met because of her baby. And if her baby wasn't real . . .

Sophie.

Running out of the house, I began to head down Angie's road, hoping when I reached the edge of town I would find a cab. As I stumbled, my head throbbing, I dialled Frances' mobile number. It rang and rang — I thought she wouldn't answer, but the line connected.

'Frances it's me — someone's coming to try and get Sophie. Frances, are you there? Frances!'

'You're too late,' Angie said, and the line went dead.

***

July 11th 2019
Twenty-three days after

Angie

My darling Emma,

I've made a new list Emma, something to work towards, something set in stone. But that doesn't mean I can't adapt when needed. And adapt I shall.

The funny thing about it all is that I will get away with what I did to you, because of you. If you weren't always so secretive about us, if you'd spoken to your friends and family about me in the same way you spoke of male lovers you had, everyone would know who I am. But you didn't, did you? You couldn't, even after all these years. Even after you and I fell in love. Even after we both knew our souls were intertwined. You cared too much about what people might say.

If you could hear them talking now.

The rest was easy. I knew that, in the wake of you, your husband would be a desperate, sad man, struggling as a single parent. To get close, I had to pose as one too. My story was easy to create. It went something like this:

My ex is a bit of a dick, but tries; we argue about money. I'd make sure your husband knew. A fake phone call with him would do the trick. As for my baby, my secret weapon, I'd make her a girl, a little younger than yours, so he felt he could offer advice and support. A girl would also bring us closer; after all, we share something in common. Something other than you. I'd call her Steph, the name you and I spoke of so many times when we imagined our own little family. She would live between houses. I would miss her, and be vulnerable for it; fragile. Just like him. I would be struggling to get by. I suspected I would make my move in a coffee shop or supermarket to draw close. Buying nappies or staring lovingly at a photo of a baby for him to see. But I didn't need to. He drew me close to him, selling baby items. Your husband sold me the things you bought for your girl, who would soon be my little girl. I like that.

I wanted us, but in the wake of knowing it would never be, it became a bittersweet irony that you keeping us a secret from the world would make your death easy to hide. After all, with no one suspecting you as being bisexual, no one would look my way. And that fact has meant I've been able to stay close the whole time. Speak with your husband, sit in your house, hold your daughter. A woman mistook Sophie as my daughter. People assume. Once we were gone, no one would doubt she's mine. She's like you, Em, I will make sure she's perfect.

I've enjoyed consoling your husband for his loss, knowing I took everything from him — well, not everything. Not yet. And it was all part of my new list. Because if you want to commit the perfect crime, you have to make a list.

This one's shorter than my list for you, Em. In it, he will go to jail, and once he has, I will take your daughter, and I will go and start the life you promised me with her. She will be my baby; she will be my family. I wanted your daughter the moment I held her in my arms, but if I took her too soon, it would throw his guilt into doubt. No, before I could take her, he needed to be in jail. Otherwise it wouldn't work. I had to be patient — but after a lifetime chasing you, being patient is something I'm good at.

Ironically, for this to work, for me to take your daughter, I needed you again. I spent so long working out how to hide you, and now I needed them to find you. I needed your body to be discovered. So when he was out in London, searching for the fictitious Steve Burton, I planted the diary somewhere it would be found and dragged you out of the water, dumping you on the bank, knowing a farmer or dog walker would stumble across your body. And once he was arrested, I planned to take her, travel to Hull where I'd get a ferry to Holland with my new daughter, and disappear.

The plan was going perfectly until Rob rang after he was released without charge. I told him to come over, because I wanted to know how he got away with it. Every finger pointed to him, I'd made sure of that, and I was expecting him to go straight from the police station to prison. So when he turned up, I pulled him close, became that friend he could trust, to learn what happened. Knowing he would bare all to me, because he's weak. But then he did something I hadn't anticipated. He looked where he shouldn't have looked, and he found what he shouldn't have found. Perhaps I should have burnt it all — the clothes, the bag, your pathetic letter — but

250

then how would I recall my reasons for doing what I did? How would I be able to keep you close, to smell you on your clothes, to hear your voice in your words? He forced my hand, just like you did, Em. He forced me to take action.

He has forced me to kill again.

I can't wait for him to be charged, it's now or never. I have to take your daughter — no, my daughter now — and burn your parents' house to the ground with them inside. By the time the dust has settled and they realise there are no charred remains of a baby, I'll be gone. Rob told me an interesting fact once: a hundred and eighty thousand people per year disappear in the UK. One every ninety seconds. Your daughter will be just like you: another number, another statistic.

Start counting, Em. One, one thousand, two one thousand, three . . .

CHAPTER FORTY-ONE

Rob

I found a cab in town and, giving the address, told the driver to move as fast as he could. The rain was coming down again, and the driver had to take it steady. I called Cahill back to tell her what had happened. I could barely speak, my lungs burnt, and I couldn't fight the necessity to cry. What words did manage to scramble their way out were garbled. I kept saying Sophie, taken. Murphy's. Cahill struggled to understand, but got that she needed to be where I was heading, as quickly as she could. When I hit their street, I hoped to see Angie's car there, I hoped she'd been delayed. But it wasn't, and at the end of the road, where their house was, an orange glow lit the night sky.

'No, oh god no.'

The driver stopped and I jumped out without paying and ran the rest of the way. Some of the neighbours were out, looking in horror as Frances and John's house burned. But I didn't stop moving.

'Sophie, my baby Sophie. Where is she? Where is my girl?' I cried, pushing my way through the gathering crowds.

Frances and John's front door was wide open; thick black smoke poured out into the street. Covering my mouth as best I could, I went inside. The heat was intense and even through my wet top my lungs ached within seconds. The smoke was so thick I couldn't see anything, and tripped over John who was lying face down in the middle of the hallway, blood pooling from his head. I stepped over him, desperately trying to see or hear my daughter. Running upstairs, I called out, my throat dry and hot. Flames licked the walls and singed my arm hair, but I didn't stop pushing forward. I wouldn't. I crashed into the spare room where Sophie slept. The smoke was thick, but no fire yet. Frances was lying on the floor. She was moaning, coughing — a nasty cut on the back of her head had matted her light hair into a dark brown mass. I stepped over her as well, hoping Sophie was still in her cot. But it was empty.

'Frances, where is she? Where is Sophie?'

Frances didn't reply, so grabbing her under the arms I hauled her up and dragged her down the stairs, both of us coughing so hard we retched. In the street, one of the neighbours took her and I ran back in, searching the whole house for sign of my daughter. I knew it was in vain, but I didn't know what else to do. Angie had taken her, left, and I didn't know where she had gone. Once I'd searched the house as much as my burning eyes and broken lungs could manage, I took John by the wrists and dragged him outside, falling onto the sodden lawn, exhausted. Coughing and almost blind, I staggered from person to person, asking if they knew where my daughter had gone. My words blurred, my lips and hands tingled. By the time Cahill arrived, the house was an inferno. As Cahill stepped out of the car, her face in shock, I stumbled towards her.

'Rob, what the hell has happened?'

'She's taken Sophie, she's taken my girl. Oh God, she's taken my baby.'

'What? Is anyone in the house?'

'My baby, she took my baby.'

'Rob, is anyone in the house?'

'No. no. She's gone. My daughter is gone.'

Pain, exhaustion and fear forced me to my knees; Cahill tried to catch me on my way down, but I was a dead weight. Lowering herself, she wrapped her arms around me, begging me to tell her everything I knew. Her questions greeted by incoherence.

'Rob, get it together. We need to act now; we need to find out where they've gone. Start at the beginning.'

A paramedic arrived and placed an oxygen mask over my face as I sat on the floor, and I breathed as deep as I could. It hurt like hell, but I could feel my lungs working once more.

As I began to offload everything, right from when Angie and I met, to me discovering Em's things in her kitchen, several more police cars turned up. The house was cordoned off, paramedics made their way to treat Frances and John. Firefighters began to work on controlling the fire. Officers started to talk with neighbours. DI Keats was there too, and Wainwright. Keats came over, asked for a recent picture of Sophie, a steely determination in his eyes. I opened my wallet and gave him the only one I had of her.

'It was taken a few weeks ago,' I said.

He nodded and walked away.

'Rob,' Cahill said, snapping my attention. 'Think, did Angie ever mention anywhere else? Anywhere she might have gone?'

I wracked my brain, trying to think. She said she lived all over but grew up here. She created Steve Burton, faked going to France. Oh God, was she going to try and take my baby girl out of the country? I said it all to Cahill and she nodded, taking me seriously, before turning and getting on her radio. After a few minutes, she came back to me.

'We'll have Met police looking into London. And border police will too. Keats has already sent Sophie's image to HQ to be distributed. We act fast when kids are involved,' she added, trying to make me feel better. I managed a fragile nod.

Cahill stepped out of the way so a paramedic could tend to my cuts and bruises and check my oxygen levels. He told me I would probably need a few stitches, that my oxygen levels were low, that I had burns on my arms and likely some down my throat, but I didn't care. I needed to think — there had to be somewhere else she'd go, but where? I hit myself on the side of the head, hoping it would knock a thread, a moment, a memory of Angie I could pull on. Did Angie ever say anything, did she ever let slip her plans? My mind drifted back to a conversation we had that night in the pub. How she moved to the Fens because of family. But wanted to live near water. I felt my heart skip a beat — she'd said something. But I couldn't place what. I had drunk that night, she had too. Our guards were down.

What did she say? Think, Rob, what did she say?

I thought about the place instead of the words, hoping it would take me back. We were in the pub; the rains had begun; the clouds thick and dark overhead. She'd been drinking. We chatted, small talk. I had asked her if she'd always lived in the Fens, and then it came. Closing my eyes, blocking out the noise around me, I replayed that moment.

'. . . Have you always lived around here?'

'Yes and no. I travelled a bit when I was younger, lived in Canterbury for a while after uni.'

'Canterbury's nice.'

'Yeah, I loved it there, but somehow I just keep finding my way back to the endlessly flat lands.'

'It is flat, isn't it? It was a shock when we moved.'

'Yeah, it's just as big a shock when you come back, trust me.'

'Think you'll stay here?'

'Maybe. I always wanted to live near water, a place by the sea, or a lake. I like the water.'

'I know what you mean. I'm the same, but couldn't afford the price of a place by the sea.'

'My uncle has a run-down old house near Boston . . .'

'Cahill!' I called out, pulling myself away from the paramedic and to my feet. 'Cahill?'

PC Cahill ran towards me. 'Rob? What?'

'She said something about a small place that belonged to her uncle in Boston, by the Wash, a run-down place, over-looking the sea.'

'Boston? Are you sure?'

'Yes, she said she loved being by water. She said she wanted to go back there.'

'OK, great, well done.'

Cahill walked away and told Keats and Wainwright what I'd just said. Wainwright got on the radio. Over the noise I could hear her ask for a background check on family to Angie Walsh. She waited, and Cahill watched as Keats moved on to lead the investigation. As the paramedic began to bandage my head, John was loaded onto a stretcher, an IV line in his arm and oxygen mask over his face. Still unconscious. Shortly after, Frances came towards me, sobbing. I walked away from the paramedic to join her by the ambulance. She too had an oxygen mask on, which she removed when she saw me.

'I couldn't stop her, Rob, I'm so sorry.'

'It's OK, we'll find her,' I said, trying to believe my own words. I kissed her on the back of her hand just before they loaded her into the ambulance. We held each other's eye until the door was closed and the ambulance pulled away. As I turned, Cahill approached purposefully. 'Rob, well done. We found that Angie did indeed have an uncle who left her his place in Boston.'

'Is she there?'

'We don't know, Lincolnshire police are on their way. We're going now.' Cahill walked back towards a parked police car, as Keats and Wainwright spoke beside it. Whatever they said, they were all in agreement, and as Wainwright walked away, back towards the house, Keats opened the driver's door to the car.

'Wait!' I called out. 'Cahill, wait.'

She turned to me.

'If you're going, I'm coming too.'

'Rob, I don't think . . .'

'She has my daughter; she has my girl. I'm not asking you, I'm telling you.'

Cahill shot a glance to Keats, who looked at me with a steely gaze. I approached. Spoke quietly.

'Have you got kids?' I asked Keats. He nodded.

'How many?'

'Two.'

'Boys or girls?'

'One of each.'

'What would you do?' I asked, holding his eye, and I saw the steely demeanour drop.

'Get in,' he said, opening the back door to the police car for me to climb inside.

CHAPTER FORTY-TWO

We sped up the A16 towards Boston in silence. Cahill and Keats were focused, determined; I was something else. Sophie had become my heartbeat. She was the thing that forged my moral compass and motivated me to move. She was my teacher, my guide, helping me overcome the obstacles of life. I didn't want to wonder, but the question kept forcing itself forward: what if I was wrong? What if Angie hadn't come to Boston? What if I never saw my daughter again? Every beat of my heart belonged to her; if I never saw her again, my heart would die too.

I stopped myself thinking by asking Cahill to open the back window so I could get some air.

'Are you all right, Rob?' she asked, turning to face me.

I nodded.

'We'll find her, OK?' She tried to reassure me, but I could hear worry in her voice. I nodded again, and she turned back to the front. She caught Keats's eye; he put his foot down and the speedometer crept up to just under ninety miles an hour.

Looking out to my left, night held firm, but to my right I could see the sun begin to break on the horizon. It was a new day, and the rain had stopped. It was a new day, and I didn't know how it would end.

I thought of how I'd fallen into the trap Angie had laid out. Realising that I let myself trust her without question. I should have noticed she didn't have a child; I should have realised my mobile number wasn't listed on Facebook like she said. She had my number because Em did. When I felt someone was in my house, I should have followed it up. At the pub, when we got drinks, she bought them. I assumed she had alcohol, but now I realised she didn't get drunk at all. I did. She manipulated me in every way, and now she had my daughter. I knew all this now, I just didn't know why she had done it.

I forced myself to stop by looking out of the window and counting trees.

Two hundred and twenty-one.

I let myself think again, making sure I focused not on what I hadn't done for my girl, but what I would do. I would love her. I would be there more, not just in body, but in spirit. I would take her out, show her the world. I would teach her how wonderful her mother was, and how much she loved Sophie. But first, when we found Angie, I would pry my daughter back. She may have beaten me twice now, but I wouldn't let her do it again. If it came to it, I would kill Angie to get Sophie.

I imagined Cahill and Keats, along with local police, knocking the door in at the address, several officers running inside, grabbing Angie, forcing her to the floor, cuffing her as she fought in vain. I would be at the rear of the group, Angie and I would lock eyes, and she would see I was a father who wouldn't ever let anyone hurt my girl. And I would find Sophie in a cot. She'd be crying, and then she would see me and beam. And I would hold her in my arms, and I would never let go. I visualised that moment so much, I could almost smell my little girl.

'Rob?' Cahill said, snapping me away from my moment. 'We've just had a call. Angie's car has been captured on ANPR just outside the Boston area.'

'Does that mean she's there? She must be there? At the house.'

'Local police have checked the address, she isn't there yet, but we'll find her.'

* * *

July 11th 2019
Twenty-three days after

Angie

My darling Emma,

Taking your baby went exactly as it should. The house will burn, and only then will they know she isn't there. But why, Em, is your baby unable to hold her tongue? She has wailed for the entire drive. A pneumatic drill. I thought, as we set off, quiet music playing, she would calm. But perhaps she's as needy as you are for comfort. Unable to hold her own. I know, deep down, she deserves me, deserves a good future with someone strong. But it seems everyone is against that idea. It doesn't matter, I'll find a way. I always find a way. But the hurdles are high, and a screaming baby isn't helping. I need her calm before we continue to Hull; I need her calm so I can get her out of the country.

And yet, as I arrived in Boston, I knew something hadn't worked as it should. Three police cars were parked outside my uncle's old place. Somehow, they knew I was coming here. Then I remembered. I'd told him about this place, I'd told him like it wouldn't matter. Your husband is smarter than he looks. Never mind, I can always create a new plan. I'm smarter than him, smarter than them all, but I can't think because your child won't stop crying.

So, I've had to drive to the Wash, park somewhere quiet and leave her in the car. She will cry herself out, and then sleep. And in that time, I'll plan our next step. Because she and

I will go on, we will be a family, she will love me like she loved you. And as I can't have you, I will be you, a better version of you. I won't be a coward as you were.

Looking back in the car, I can see Sophie is finally asleep. My daughter is beautiful when she sleeps, just like you were. Just like you always will be.

CHAPTER FORTY-THREE

Rob

Keats stopped the car opposite the house where several police officers stood outside. As he got out, I saw them stand up a little straighter. One of them approached, and she and Keats began to talk fervently. I strained to listen. I couldn't hear what was being said, but Keats nodded several times. His steely gaze set.

'Rob?' Cahill caught my attention from the front seat. She looked at me expectantly, like she'd asked me a question.

'Stay here, OK? I'm going to find out what they know, so we know what to do next.'

'No, I want to come.'

'Rob, that's not a good—'

'Cahill, it's my daughter. I need to know.'

'Stay put, let us do our job. I know it feels helpless, but doing nothing actually helps. If . . .' she hesitated, looked away from me. 'I mean, when we find out where they've gone I'll be straight back to tell you, and when we find Sophie you'll be the first to see her.'

I nodded, feeling powerless. My daughter needed me; I dreaded to think if she knew exactly what was happening to her. I dreaded to think how I'd explain, when she's older, that I let her down, that I allowed Angie to take her. She was probably scared and confused, alone without me, and here I was, sat in the back of a police car doing nothing. I wouldn't be that man anymore. I did nothing when Em was taken. I sat back and accepted she'd left me and carried on. I did nothing when I realised who Angie was. I let myself be hurt when I should have fought tooth and nail to get to Sophie first.

'Cahill, I feel a bit queasy, can you open the window again for me?'

She looked at me sympathetically and opened the window on the other side of the car. I knew what she was doing; she was making sure I didn't look, that I couldn't hear what was happening on the side where I was currently sat, close to Keats and the other police officers. She wanted me to scoot over and look the other way. But that worked well for me. I scooted over and listened. I could just about hear Keats talking.

'Sit tight. I'll be back soon,' Cahill said as she climbed out of the car, closed the door and made her way over to join the conversation. I couldn't pick out much but, carried on the wind, Keats's voice found me again. I distinctly heard the words 'car' and 'found', and my heart leapt in my chest. Cahill came back, bounding towards me, slowing as she opened the door. I looked up and met her eye.

'Anything?' I asked.

'We're going out on foot, doing a door-to-door. As soon as we know anything, I'll be back. OK?'

I nodded, and she closed the door once more, making her way back to a gathering gaggle of officers. I had heard right; I was sure of it. They'd found Angie's car, and it was close by, or else they'd not go out on foot. I wasn't going to just sit there, waiting for fate to control my life anymore.

I placed my hands on the window and pushed the glass the rest of the way into the frame. Making sure no one was looking my way, I climbed out. Scurrying away, I waited for someone to call my name, but as I turned the corner onto a different road, it didn't happen. I didn't know where I was going to search. But I knew I would find my daughter, somehow.

* * *

July 11th 2019
Twenty-three days after

Angie

My darling Emma,

    I watched you with your baby before you passed, and since, I've watched your husband with her. I've seen the smiles and playing, heard the giggles and cooing. But you and he have misled me. I didn't know how impossible it is to calm a screaming baby. That day when I took Sophie from Rob, in the coffee shop, and calmed her when he couldn't, I felt like I knew exactly how to parent. But she won't stop fucking screaming, Emma, she won't be quiet. As soon as I lifted her from the car seat, as soon as she woke and saw my face, she began to wail once more. She's going to give me up to the police, she's going to fuck up everything I've planned, she's ruining the future I've let myself see. A vision planted in my head, by you. You taught me to dream, and I let myself. I dreamed of a perfect child: calm, obedient, doting. But she is rejecting me. Just. Like. You.

    Em, what will happen next is your fault. Because if it wasn't for you, I wouldn't dream. If it wasn't for you, I wouldn't try and see a new future. This is all on you. I wanted a good time, the thrill of being your bit on the side, nothing more — not until you started talking of us having something else. As far back as when we lived in Nottingham, you spoke of one day telling the world about us, regardless of whether the world was accepting or not. You spoke of us becoming a family. And when you ran away, I wanted to forget that. But in London, on our nights together, it all came back to me. And

264

I knew we deserved the future you once spoke of. Even after you were engaged, I let you convince me that dreams were perfect little bubbles that protected an image. But really, the bubble only suffocated them, digested them, and then, when the bubble popped, all that's left is the faint odour of failure.

I would have been a great parent to her, I would. But now I see she may be more like you than I thought. She won't stop fighting this, just like you wouldn't stop. I've had to leave my car and carry her on foot — I have to find somewhere to hide, to wait.

Emma, if you can hear me from wherever you are, calm your child, or she will join you. Calm your child, or I will have to create another plan.

CHAPTER FORTY-FOUR

Rob

I ran aimlessly, hoping to spot Angie walking down a street with Sophie in her arms. But I didn't know where to look. The area was vast; so many places to hide and hope the police didn't find you. I felt sick — sick with worry, sick with fear, but I couldn't let myself stop, I had to keep moving, I had to try. As I approached a row of terraces, I caught sight of the Wash behind. A vast open space of mudflats, reeds, interconnecting streams and bogs that led out to the sea beyond. The sun had forced its way over the horizon, bathing the shimmering waters in a brilliant orange glow. In any other context, I might have found it beautiful. But now the sun was blinding me, robbing me of one of my senses; one I desperately needed. I called out, shouted for Sophie to respond. It would be in vain, but I couldn't stop myself.

'Sophie! Sophie!'

I thought for a moment I heard her cry on the wind.

I expected the police to hear me, to come and escort me back to the police car and stop me interfering. But I was too far away from them. I suspected they would focus their efforts on searching close to the house and car, then sweeping out. That's what I would do, and I bet Angie knew that. Despite the assumption she was here, somewhere close by, she could have been anywhere — another car could have collected her when she realised the police were approaching. If she was here, she'd be far away from the police as possible. My eye was drawn back to the Wash. Angie wanted to be by the water, she explicitly said that when she got me drunk. And Em, she had lured Em to the water too.

I found myself running towards the blinding dawn sun, my hand over my eyes. Behind me, I was sure I heard Cahill shout my name. But I didn't look back. If Angie was here, she would be by the water. I could feel it in my bones.

Clearing the row of houses, I felt the wind buffeting my right side, carrying the smell of salt and rotting vegetation. I looked to my right, into the wind, scanning the swollen, flooded marshlands for something out of place. Then I heard it again, the faint sound of a baby crying, and there was no mistaking it; no assuming it was wishful thinking. I could hear my daughter's voice. Snapping around, the sun making it near-impossible to pick out anything in the distance, I almost didn't see them — until Angie moved. She was there, on the Wash, my daughter in her arms. I shielded my eyes and could see her bobbing my girl, trying to quieten her.

'Give me back my daughter!'

My legs propelled me, running as fast as they could until I ran out of Tarmac. I had to climb over a wall, and continued to move as quickly as I could over the uneven, sodden ground.

'Rob!' Cahill shouted behind me, 'Rob, get back here, it's not sa . . .'

She trailed off, because she'd seen her too. As I drew closer to Angie, I could hear her shouting at Sophie, shouting at her to be quiet, to stop being like her mother. To love her. Sophie cried in her arms, and I felt my legs move faster. My muscles ached; my lungs began to burn, but none of that mattered. I would push my legs until the ache ruptured my skin; I would let my lungs burn until they engulfed me in a raging inferno. Angie looked up when I was a few hundred feet away. Between us was soft, boggy ground, covered in surface water that rippled in the wind.

'Give her back to me,' I shouted, my voice full of fear, rage and love. 'Give her back to me and walk away and I promise I'll not come after you.'

'Come after me?' she shouted, following it with a maniacal laugh that shook her whole body; that shook my daughter. 'How would you come after me? You are pathetic, you're weak. You don't deserve to raise your daughter.'

'Give her to me,' I repeated.

'You know, Rob, Em loved me. She loved me — for years we loved each other. She told me how she was going to leave you and we would run away together. Get a place by the sea, start again. She wanted to be with me.'

'Angie. Give me Sophie.' I took a step towards her, and my shoe sank into the earth.

'But then she fell pregnant, and because she was a coward, she stayed with you.'

Sophie continued to cry; she was so distressed I had to fight the urge to run for her. I didn't want her to get hurt. But I did manage to take a step without Angie realising, as her attention was back on my terrified daughter.

'Why won't she be quiet for me, Rob? Why won't she be like that time in the coffee shop, remember?'

'Yes, I remember.' Another step, but it was hard to take, the bog acting like a vacuum that nearly sucked off my shoe.

'Answer me!' she shouted. 'Why won't she stop crying?'

'Because she needs her daddy, Angie. She needs me. Give her back, let me help you stop her crying.'

Angie shook her head, bobbed Sophie up and down. I saw a tear fall on her cheek.

Step.

'Angie. This has to stop; Sophie is my daughter.'

'She should have been mine. She should have been mine like Em was mine. She loved me.'

'I think you're right, Em did love you. And yes, maybe she was scared, and stayed with me because of it.'

268

'She did. She wanted me. Stop fucking crying!' she yelled at Sophie. For the first time in my life, I wanted to kill someone. 'She's just like her mother, a coward, pushing me away.'

'Angie, Sophie isn't Em.'

'Too afraid of change; too afraid of being able to see a better life.'

'Her life is with me.'

'If she wants her mummy so much, she can go to her.'

The world slowed down as, in horror, I watched Angie drop Sophie in the water and turn to run. I dragged my sinking foot out of the bog and forced it forwards, then one in front of the other. Sophie was a few hundred feet away, in the water, and I couldn't hear her cry. Not a single thought was in my head besides moving — move fast, move faster. The bog tried to hold me back, tried to drag me down, made me slip, but I fought with all of my might. I was taking too much time — Sophie had been underwater for too long. I was going to watch my baby die.

Move.

I hit the water's edge, and my feet were free. I waded through, the waterline only shin-high, but enough. Falling to my knees in front of my daughter, I scooped her up. Turned her over to see her face was blue.

'Oh God, no.'

I put my head to her chest, I couldn't feel her breathing. My baby wasn't breathing. I didn't know how to do CPR, but I placed my mouth over her mouth and her nose, and blew. Three times and Sophie still wasn't breathing. I checked her pulse, it was there, blood was still pumping. Placing my mouth over hers again, I filled my baby's lungs. Again, and again — until the most amazing sound rang out as she spluttered and began to cry. Turning her over, I tapped out the remaining water from her mouth, and began to cry too. Stripping her soaking, freezing clothes off, I placed her under my T-shirt. Her cold skin on mine. I held her tight, my body doing what it could to warm her.

'It's OK Sophie, Daddy's got you. Daddy's got you.'

CHAPTER FORTY-FIVE

November 21st 2019
Several months later

Rob

It had been a long time since I'd put on a tie, and although the knot was easy to recall — something I learnt as a schoolboy and could never forget — judging the length it should be was something else entirely. The first attempt, the wide part was far too short, and I looked like one of the cast of *The Inbetweeners*. The second attempt, I adjusted too far the other way, and it hung down between my legs. As I removed it to begin again, there were three light taps on my bedroom door.

'Everything all right?' John asked, leaning on the door-frame, his expression reflecting how nervous I was feeling.

'Yeah, I would be if I could get this bloody tie to—'

'Here,' he said as he came in and took it from me. Turning to face him, I studied his features as he put the tie around my neck and knotted it at the right length. He was visibly older than he'd looked before Em died. But somehow, he was softer, too. The weather-beaten thick-skinned man I knew had warmed. Once, John and I had kept a distance; now, as he folded down my collar, I felt an outpouring of love for him. That night, when Angie took Sophie, John had fought to stop her, and the beating he took, it nearly killed him. He was in hospital for weeks after, in a coma for seven days of that time and, when I could, I sat by his bedside with Frances and Sophie, waiting for him to wake up. And when he did, the very first word that came out of his mouth was my daughter's name.

'There, all done,' he smiled, before his expression changed to worry. 'Are you ready for today?'

'I kind of have to be, don't I?'

'You don't have to do this, Rob, they made that clear. If you don't want to go, you—'

'No, I want to. I want to make sure it ends today.'

John nodded, and then, unexpectedly, he reached in and hugged me, and I hugged him back.

'I'll be downstairs when you're ready.'

'Thank you.'

John patted my shoulder twice and turned to leave. And I looked at the scar on the back of his head, the constant reminder of the worst day of my life.

Turning my attention to the window, to stop me staring as he left, I looked outside. Last night was cold, and my car windscreen was frozen, as was the lawn. Across the road, the supermarket car park glistened in the early morning sunshine. Moving from where we lived had been a hard decision. It was obvious that house held so many bad memories — but it also held Em's memories, and leaving it meant I was losing a little bit more of her. But bringing up Sophie there, it wasn't right, and she had to come first. The new house was small, no third bedroom, but the two of us didn't need a third. And we were closer to Frances and John, who were rebuilding their home and their lives. We brought the peach tree too. John got a few friends to help dig it up and re-plant it. The carved Em etched

271

into its trunk now faced my kitchen window. I didn't ask him to do it, but he knew.

Dressed in my one and only suit, I took a moment to consider the man looking back in the mirror. His shoulders were straight, his chin up. He was still hurting, there was no doubt about that, but he looked like someone who might just be OK. In time, with patience, with kindness from others, and kindness from himself. I didn't like to think back, it was painful. But today was all about that. I would be asked to recall everything about Angie. How we met, how she came to be so important in my life. They will learn of my loneliness, my naivety. I have been warned that I'll be asked why I didn't see the signs. Angie faked having a child, to get into my and Sophie's world, and I didn't see it, and those moments, when I could feel someone in my home and thought I was losing my mind, it was her, letting herself in and out at will with Em's keys. As well as talking about that time in my life, and everything leading up to Sophie being dropped in the Wash. Something I'd never be able to forget, something that would haunt my dreams, for the rest of my life. They would, as part of the case against Angie, talk of Sophie too. How she had water in her lungs and spent a week in Boston Hospital. They said if I was a minute later . . .

They would also want to talk about Em and her. I'd been warned that they would go into details of their affair, and Angie's consequent obsession. I learnt Angie was planning to leave the country with my daughter. If I hadn't woken up in time, or if I'd got too drunk to remember her talking of Boston, I wouldn't have seen my daughter ever again. She'd planned it meticulously too, the diary being both true to life and entirely false. She knew details of me and Em; she knew details I thought only I knew. The diary was convincing. Speaking of my life with Em, speaking of Em's life before. The on-off love affair my wife tried to leave behind. There were so many details that were real. So many things that proved she was watching us for some time, things only Em and I would know. And she weaved in lies of my violence and anger so well, it was almost impossible to tell the difference. I had no doubt that if I hadn't stopped her, she would be gone with my baby, and I would be in prison. Even thinking it is too much. But I had to think about it, one last time. Today everything would be aired, today everyone would know every detail of my wife's life and the mistakes she made. They would learn of how she tried to rectify them, for her daughter. I hoped they would hang on to that, her love, her determination to be someone new. Her sacrifice in trying to leave her mistakes behind.

I hoped.

There was no question of my innocence anymore; the diary was in Angie's handwriting, and there were inconsistencies: dates wrong, events in the wrong order. She was clever, but not as clever as she'd hoped.

They would also show how Em died, and I'd have to listen as they spoke of the details around that too. I was told I didn't need to be present, for any of it. But the prosecutors said it would help. I wasn't sure how, probably so that the jury could see my suffering. I should have been offended that I was being used. But I wanted it done. I wanted to move on.

I looked at my watch, saw the time and took a deep breath. I needed to get going. Walking downstairs, I was greeted at the bottom by Frances, who tried her best to smile my way, but it didn't quite reach her sad eyes.

'You OK?' she asked.

'Yeah, I'll be glad when it's done.'

She nodded, and as I reached the bottom, she too hugged me. When she let go, her eyes were full of tears.

'It will all be over soon, Frances, and we can get on.'

She nodded, and wiped her eyes when Sophie crawled towards me, holding her arms up to be lifted.

I sat on the bottom step and picked up my girl so I could look her in the eye. 'Sophie, I have to go out for today. You and Nana and Grandad are going to have fun while I take care of something.'

Sophie didn't reply, of course; she couldn't. But the way she looked at me told me she understood, and she didn't want me to go.

'I have this one job to do, one little thing, and then Daddy is here, with you and Nana and Grandad, always.'

Sophie seemed content with my answer and struggled to be put down. I managed to get a quick kiss before she crawled back into the living room and began to play again with John.

'What time will you be back?' Frances asked as I stood.

'I don't know, it might be late?'

'Let us know if you need anything.'

'Thank you.'

Frances reached over and kissed me on the cheek.

'I do love you Rob, you know that, as a son, I love you.'

'I love you. Both of you.'

I put on my shoes, coat and scarf, and said my goodbyes. John, sat on the sofa, gave me a nod. And Sophie waved, but didn't look my way as *Paw Patrol* was on the telly. I watched her for a moment. My girl. My precious little girl. My girl who was taken, my girl I nearly lost. Taking her all in, her little head that tilted to one side when she concentrated. It was just like the way her mother used to sit when she was engrossed in a film. The more my little girl became her own person, the more I could see — we all could see — how much impact Em had on her. They say life is either nature or nurture. I think I agree. Sophie's nature was just like her mum's and, therefore, Em would live on. It was my job to nurture a relationship between my two girls. So Em would always be present, and Sophie would know who she was.

I watched my daughter, and I absorbed it all, until I could close my eyes and the image stayed. Catalogued with the thousands of others I had archived in my mind. Locked behind a vault door that no one had a key for but me. Then, with one final nervous smile to Frances, who didn't try to stop the tears falling, I stepped out of my front door, looked up the thick winter clouds above. It had started to rain, and I pushed down the feelings that wanted to stir because of it. I set off to say what I needed to say, to hear the verdict given. And then I could come home, to my girl, and we could begin again. We could begin again, and we would honour Sophie's mother, my wife Emma Clarke, for the rest of our lives.

THE END

THE JOFFE BOOKS STORY

We began in 2014 when Jasper agreed to publish his mum's much-rejected romance novel and it became a bestseller.

Since then we've grown into the largest independent publisher in the UK. We're extremely proud to publish some of the very best writers in the world, including Joy Ellis, Faith Martin, Caro Ramsay, Helen Forrester, Simon Brett and Robert Goddard. Everyone at Joffe Books loves reading and we never forget that it all begins with the magic of an author telling a story.

We are proud to publish talented first-time authors, as well as established writers whose books we love introducing to a new generation of readers.

We won Trade Publisher of the Year at the Independent Publishing Awards in 2023 and Best Publisher Award in 2024 at the People's Book Prize. We have been shortlisted for Independent Publisher of the Year at the British Book Awards for the last five years, and were shortlisted for the Diversity and Inclusivity Award at the 2022 Independent Publishing Awards. In 2023 we were shortlisted for Publisher of the Year at the RNA Industry Awards, and in 2024 we were shortlisted at the CWA Daggers for the Best Crime and Mystery Publisher.

We built this company with your help, and we love to hear from you, so please email us about absolutely anything bookish at feedback@joffebooks.com.

If you want to receive free books every Friday and hear about all our new releases, join our mailing list here: www.joffebooks.com/freebooks.

And when you tell your friends about us, just remember: it's pronounced Joffe as in coffee or toffee!

www.ingramcontent.com/pod-product-compliance
Lightning Source LLC
Chambersburg PA
CBHW011453170626
46814CB00009B/3031